BESSIE BUNTER
OF CLIFF HOUSE SCHOOL

THEY DESCENDED INTO THE SHED, WHERE FOUR PAIRS OF EYES
AND A PAIR OF SPECTACLES FASTENED ON THEM

BESSIE BUNTER OF CLIFF HOUSE SCHOOL

By
HILDA RICHARDS

Illustrated by
R. J. MACDONALD

First published 1949 by Charles Skilton Ltd.

This edition published 1991 by:
HAWK BOOKS LTD
Suite 309
Canalot Studios
222 Kensal Road
London W10 5BN

ISBN 0-948248-82-3

Printed in England by Redwood Press Ltd.

CONTENTS

CONTENTS

CHAPTER I

BAD FOR BESSIE!

" BESSIE ! "

Bessie Bunter did not reply immediately.

She couldn't.

There was an impediment in her speech. That impediment was a large bite from a large pear, which filled the largest mouth in the Fourth Form at Cliff House to capacity.

Had Miss Bellew, her form-mistress, been taking the Fourth just then, Bessie Bunter would not have been eating a pear in class. Miss Bellew had a keen eye and a determined chin. But it was Mademoiselle Lupin who was taking the form in French; and with Mamselle one could take chances.

Still, Bessie was cautious. It was a luscious and tempting pear, ever so much more attractive than French verbs: but it remained in Bessie's desk till Mamselle's attention was fixed elsewhere.

They were doing " La Poudre aux Yeux," and Marjorie Hazeldene was translating so precisely that a pleased smile had dawned on Mamselle's lean visage, and she seemed to have forgotten for the moment that the life of a French mistress at an English school was no bed of roses. It looked, to Bessie, as if Mamselle meant to keep Marjorie running on, following the line of least resistance as it were.

Obviously, it was the moment to take a bite at that pear.

As there might not be an opportunity for a second bite, Bessie naturally took the largest bite possible, and nearly half the pear disappeared from view.

For a moment, Elizabeth Bunter was completely happy. With her mouth full of luscious pear, her eyes had a dreamy look of happy contentment behind her big spectacles. Life, for that moment, seemed one grand sweet song.

But it was only for a moment.

The next, Bessie came back to earth again, as Mademoiselle Lupin rapped out her name.

Certainly, Mamselle would have preferred to keep on with Marjorie. It was quite a nerve-rest to Mamselle, to deal with a pupil who treated French as a language, and not as a tiresome infliction to be endured somehow till the forty minutes were up. Nevertheless, she turned to Bessie Bunter, who was anything but a nerve-rest in the French class or any other.

Her little black eyes fixed on a fat red face, which bulged on both sides with that tremendous mouthful.

Bessie blinked at her. She could do nothing else for the moment. That mouthful had to go on the downward path before Bessie could speak.

" Bessie! Zat you go on from ' il me plait beaucoup ce garçon '," rapped Mademoiselle Lupin.

But Bessie Bunter could not go on from that or anything else. She could not go on at all. She was making a frantic effort to bolt that too large bite. It went down, and Bessie choked. Then at last utterance came, but it came neither in French nor English.

" Urrrrrgh! Wurrrggh! Oooooogh! Oh! Ooooh! "

There was a giggle in the class. Marjorie Hazeldene smiled. Clara Trevlyn laughed. Dolly Jobling chuckled. Barbara Redfern and Mabel Lynn leaned over to pat Bessie on the back. She seemed to need it. Perhaps the pats were a little vigorous. Bessie did not seem grateful for their kind attention.

" Urrgh! Ooogh! Leave off smacking me, Babs." Bessie found her voice. " Mabs, if you smack me again, I'll scratch you! Oooogh! "

" Barbara! Mabel! Zat you keep ze place! Bessie,

is it zat you eat in ze class? Is it zat you eat one pomme—
one apple, n'est-ce-pas?''

"Oh! No!" gasped Bessie Bunter. "I wasn't
eating an apple, Mamselle——.''

"You have somezing in ze desk?"

"Oh! No! Yes! Oh, dear! Ooogh!''

"You have one apple——!''

"No!" gasped Bessie. "A—a—a pear.''

"A pair!" ejaculated Mademoiselle Lupin. "A pair!
Zat is two! You have two apples in ze desk, n'est-ce-pas?
Bessie, you are ze greediest girl in ze school. It is alvays
zat you eat somezing. You bring two apples into ze
class——.''

"No!" gasped Bessie. "There was only one
pear——.''

"But one pair, zat is two! You will trow bofe zose
apples into ze vaste-paper basket at vunce.''

"But I haven't—I didn't—I wasn't——," stuttered
Bessie. "I hadn't any apples, only a pear——.''

"Mon Dieu! I zink zat you understand ze English no
more zan ze French. If you have a pair, zat is two——.''

"C'est une poire, Mamselle,'' gasped Babs: and Bessie
held up the remainder of the pear as evidence.

Mamselle gazed at it.

"Ah ça! Une poire—maintenant je comprends. Take
zat poire and trow it into ze vaste-paper basket at vunce,
Bessie.''

Bessie Bunter rose reluctantly. For one brief moment
she had enjoyed life. Now all seemed weary, stale, flat,
and unprofitable, as she dropped the undevoured portion
of the pear into the waste-paper basket. She went back
to her place with a fat face from which all the joy had
departed.

After which, Bessie considered, Mamselle might at least
have left her alone and spared her French. But Mamselle
did not even think of sparing her French. Perhaps she
thought Bessie deserved it.

" Now you will go on, Bessie, from where Marjorie
leave off," said Mademoiselle Lupin, severely. " Parlez,
donc."

Bessie blinked at her book. It was rather unfortunate
that with her thoughts concentrated on the pear, she had
been quite unable to give any attention to the lesson. She
proceeded to stammer through the next sentence.

" Et s'il est d'une bonne famille——."

" Zat you translate! " snapped Mamselle. Mamselle's
little thin nose was growing red at the tip, a sign she was
getting " stuffy," and that detentions might be in the
offing.

" And——," stammered Bessie. Even Bessie knew
that " et " was " and." " S'il " bothered her for a
moment, but she got it. " And if he——." Bessie came
to a dead stop.

" Continuez! " rapped Mamselle. " And if he——."

" If he—if he—if he——," mumbled Bessie. Then she
had an inspiration. " Bonne" seemed plain enough——to
Bessie. She knew that a bonne was a servant in France.
For the moment she omitted to remember that bonne
was also an adjective, and that it meant " good." So she
rushed on triumphantly, " Et s'il est d'une bonne
famille——and if he is a family servant——."

" Ha, ha, ha! " came in a trill of merriment from the
Cliff House Fourth. Bessie was the girl for howlers: and
this was one of her best.

But Mademoiselle Lupin did not laugh. She gazed at
Bessie Bunter as the fabled Gorgon might have gazed.

" Assez! assez! " Mamselle almost shrieked.

Bessie blinked at her indignantly.

" Miss Bellew doesn't call us names in class," she
squeaked. " And Miss Primrose wouldn't like to hear us
called asses——."

" Ha, ha, ha! "

" Mon Dieu! Silence in ze class! Head of a pudding,
it is not zat I call you ass—I say assez, vich means enoff!

Do you not know enoff? Enoff! enoff! Zat is enoff!
Mon Dieu, but it is too much. Tais-toi, donc.''

Mamselle's nose was now quite crimson at the tip.

" Demain—to-morrow——you keep in, you Bessie, and
write out ze whole lesson. Zat is enoff.''

" But—but it's a half-holiday to-morrow, Mamselle——.''

" I say enoff! "

" I was going over to see my brother Billy at
Greyfriars——.''

" If you speak vun more word, you Bessie, I despatch
you to Mees Primrose.''

That was enough for Bessie. She had no desire whatever for an interview with Miss Penelope Primrose, the
Head of Cliff House. She relapsed into indignant silence,
while Clara Trevlyn carried on: fortunately without any
howlers, and the crimson gradually faded from Mademoiselle Lupin's nose-tip.

CHAPTER II

BESSIE KNOWS HOW

" MARJORIE——! "

" Yes, dear! Come in."

" Buzz off! "

" Scram! "

Bessie Bunter, looking in at the door of No. 7 Study in the Fourth, received those three replies all at once.

Marjorie Hazeldene gave the first, Clara Trevlyn the second, Dolly Jobling the third: but they all came together.

Marjorie and Co. were all occupied, when Bessie's plump figure filled up most of the doorway. Marjorie was looking through a letter she had taken from her bag. Clara, with her fair head a little on one side, and a pensive expression on her usually thoughtless face, was scanning a laddered stocking, considering deeply whether there was anything to be done about it. Dolly was filling a fountain pen from the study inkpot, her fingers gradually assuming the appearance of wearing a pair of black gloves.

None of the three had any use for Elizabeth Bunter. But Marjorie was always kind and patient. Clara and Dolly were kind enough, but much less patient. And quite a lot of patience was required in dealing with Bessie Bunter.

Bessie sniffed.

Of the three replies she received from No. 7 Study, she seemed to prefer Marjorie's. She neither buzzed off nor scrammed—she came in.

" I say, you girls——! " began Bessie.

" That stocking's a goner," said Clara, frowning. " Putrid, isn't it? "

" Oh, Clara," murmured Marjorie. " What would Miss Bellew say if she heard that? "

" I shouldn't say that to Miss Bellew, old dear. I should say to Miss Bellew that the stocking was unfortunately beyond repair. But as I'm not saying it to Miss Bellew, it's putrid! See? "

" I say——! " recommenced Bessie.

" I think this fountain pen leaks," said Dolly Jobling. " Look at my fingers."

" Behold, they are black but comely," said Clara.

" I say——! " howled Bessie.

" You still there? " asked Clara, looking round. " Fatima, you're de trop. That's a spot of French for you. Run away and ask Mamselle what it means."

" Minx! " said Bessie.

" What is it, Bessie? " asked Marjorie, hastily. " Put that cushion down, Clara. Now, Bessie——."

" What's a cat? " asked Bessie.

Three surprised stares were fixed on Elizabeth Bunter. She had a paper in one fat hand, and a pencil in the other, and had apparently come to No. 7 Study for assistance before putting pencil to paper. It was Bessie's way to seek information in the studies instead of looking it out in grammar or dictionary. It saved trouble—for Bessie. It might add trouble, for others—but that was a negligible consideration. But though Bessie was expected to ask questions, she was not expected to ask so extraordinary a question. Bessie had the most obtuse head at Cliff House School, and the number of things she didn't know would have filled whole libraries. But even Bessie Bunter was supposed to know what a cat was.

" Did you say cat, Bessie? " exclaimed Marjorie, blankly.

" Yes, cat. K-A-T, cat," added Bessie, spelling it out to make it quite clear.

" Oh, scissors," said Clara. " Like me to look it out in the dick for you, Fatima? "

" Yes, do," said Bessie.

" O.K.," said Clara, and she hooked a dictionary off the bookshelf, turned the pages to " CAT," and read out, " Cat—any one of the genus Felis, including Felis domesticus, or the domestic cat——."

" You silly chump! " hooted Bessie.   " What's the good of looking it out in that dick? 'Tain't there."

" No good at all," agreed Clara. " If you don't know what a cat is, go and speak to Matron—she's got a tabby one, and she will let you see it."

" Will you talk sense? " howled Bessie Bunter. " I say, Marjorie, I suppose you know what a cat is. It's something like shoot or shank or something."

" Oh! " gasped Marjorie. " Do you mean in French? "

" Eh? Of course I do. Think I want you to tell me what a cat is in English? "

" You didn't say so——."

" Didn't I? Well, what's a cat, anyhow? "

" Le chat—the cat," said Marjorie, smiling.

" Shah! " repeated Bessie, doubtfully.   " Sure it's shah? That sounds to me more like the Shah of Persia."

" That's right, Bessie," assured Marjorie.   " You don't sound the final T, you know."

" What kind of cat do you want? " asked Clara. " Chat is a boy cat. Chatte is a girl cat."

" Oh! " said Bessie. " Then its chatte I want. Sure that's right? "

" Quite," said Marjorie.   " What is it, Bessie—an exercise for Mamselle? "

" It's for Mamselle all right—but it's not an exercise," said Bessie, darkly. " She's a cat, and I'm going to tell her so."

" WHAT! " exclaimed all No. 7 Study, together.

" Look at the way she jumped on me in class! " said Bessie, indignantly. " Calling me an ass——."

" She didn't! " gasped Marjorie.   " Assez means enough, in French——."

" Ha, ha, ha! "

" Well, I believe she was calling me names," said Bessie. " Making out, too, that my translation was wrong——."

" But it was wrong——."

" Rot! " said Bessie. " Mean to say that bonne famille doesn't mean a family servant? "

" No, no, no! It means a good family——."

" Perhaps you know French better than I do," said Bessie, with a sniff. " I know French pretty well, I think, and I can write it, too, as Mamselle will find. I'd just forgotten what a cat was, that's all. I've got the rest all right. Did you say shock or shook, Clara? "

" I said chatte," chuckled Clara.

" Well, that sounds more like a cat than shah," said Bessie, and she put pencil to paper. " That's all right. Will Mamselle jump when she finds this on her study table? He, he, he! Giving me detention for to-morrow afternoon, when I've got to go over and see Billy! I'm going all the same."

" But you can't! " exclaimed Marjorie in alarm. " Mamselle will be furious if you go out of detention."

" I've got to," explained Bessie. " Billy's got tickets for the circus at Courtfield. Think I'm going to miss the circus to please Mamselle? "

" She will report you to Miss Bellew."

" Well, I'm always getting reported for something. They're all cats," said Bessie. " Besides, she mayn't find out."

" Now, Bessie dear——," urged Marjorie.

" I'm going," said Bessie, positively. " If there's a row, I can't help it—I never get justice, as you girls know. Now I'm going to put this paper on Mamselle's study table for her to find when she goes back from the Staff Room. He, he, he! "

" You'll be sent up to the Head if you call Mamselle a cat."

" Think I'm going to tell her it was me? " said Bessie, derisively.   " I've written it in capital letters." "

" And what have you written? " asked Clara.

" Mamselle Lupin est une chatte," said Bessie.   " That means ' Mamselle Lupin is a cat,' doesn't it? "

" For goodness sake! " exclaimed Marjorie, really alarmed for the fat junior.   " You mustn't, Bessie——.' "

" Mustn't I? " said Bessie.   " You'll see.   If she calls me an ass, I can call her a cat."

" But she didn't——! " shrieked Clara.

" I jolly well know what she meant," said Bessie, nodding a fat head.   " I'm going to stick this paper on her table now.   So she'll jolly well know what we think of her.   She won't know who wrote it—in capitals!   Look! "

Bessie Bunter held up the paper for No. 7 Study to see. They looked at it.   Then they shrieked.

Bessie had written—as she firmly believed—" Mamselle Lupin est une chatte."   But Bessie's spelling in French was on a par with her spelling in English.   The sentence in capitals that met the astonished eyes of Marjorie and Co was:

MADMORSEL LOOPANG AYTOON SHAT.

" Ha, ha, ha! " pealed from three almost convulsed junior girls of Cliff House.

Bessie grinned complacently.   She took that irresistible peal of laughter as a tribute.

" He, he, he! " she joined in.   " Fancy her face when she sees it!   What?   He, he, he! "

And Bessie Bunter rolled out of No. 7 Study, with the paper in her fat hand, satisfied in her fat mind that it was going to make Mademoiselle Lupin fearfully furious.   To No. 7 Study it appeared highly improbable that Mademoiselle Lupin would be able to make head or tail of it. But they couldn't have stopped Bessie anyway—they were laughing too much: and the happy possessor of the fattest figure and the fattest head at Cliff House rolled off triumphant.

CHAPTER III

BESSIE MEANS BUSINESS!

" Won't it be jolly! " said Marjorie.

Clara Trevlyn glanced at her chum with an amused glimmer in her eyes: and then winked at Dolly Jobling with the eye farthest from Marjorie.

Dolly just contrived to turn a giggle into a cough.

" Hazel will be here soon," added Marjorie.

The three juniors were walking in the quad after dinner the following day. It was a bright sunny day, and Marjorie Hazeldene's face, which was often grave and thoughtful, was as bright as the sunshine and the blue sky.

Marjorie was always pleased when her brother, Hazeldene of the Remove at Greyfriars, came over to Cliff House on a half-holiday. In the innocence of her heart she probably fancied that Clara and Dolly were equally pleased.

Which was not the case at all.

More than once, Clara had confided to Dolly her opinion that Marjorie's brother at Greyfriars was a " twerp," though she would not have let Marjorie hear that opinion for worlds. Dolly fully agreed that Hazel was a good deal of a twerp: but she, too, was very careful not to let Marjorie know what she thought of Hazel's twerpishness.

The news that Hazel was coming over that afternoon did not exhilarate Clara and Dolly at all.

In fact they would have liked that half-holiday much better without him. But they were prepared to play up, like good pals.

" What is he coming for? " asked Clara.

" To see me, I suppose," answered Marjorie, with a faint touch of reproach in her voice. " I've hardly seen him this term. And——."

Marjorie was interrupted.

The three girls were passing the windows of the Fourth Form room. The middle window was open. From that open window came a fat squeak that caused all three to look round.

A fat face and a large pair of spectacles looked out.

" I say, you girls! " squeaked Bessie Bunter.

" Come on," said Clara. " Mustn't speak to anyone in detention—and there may be a pre. about."

" Cat! " squeaked Bessie.

" Can't stop! " said Dolly Jobling.

" Minx! "

Marjorie Hazeldene hesitated.

" Let's stop a minute," she said. " What is it, Bessie? "

" Come closer to the window—I don't want to yell," said Bessie, peevishly. " I saw Stella Stone a few minutes ago—and you know what prefects are—always butting in. Come here, Marjorie."

Marjorie left her companions, and came under the window. Clara and Dolly remained where they were. It was strictly against the rules to speak to anyone in detention, and they did not want a spot of bother with a prefect, for the pleasure of conversation with Elizabeth Bunter. Such charms as Bessie's conversation had, had long since palled on the other girls in the Cliff House Fourth.

Bessie blinked down at Marjorie through her spectacles.

" Have you seen the cat? "

" Eh! No! If you mean the Matron's cat——."

" You silly donkey! "

" Oh! "

" I mean Mamselle," snorted Bessie. " I wish you had some sense, Marjorie. You're quite a nice girl in some ways, but you're silly."

" Thank you," said Marjorie, laughing.

" Well, have you seen that cat? " asked Bessie. " She's stuck me in here with six scenes from that putrid play to write out. I've got to go over to Billy's school, as I told you. Has she gone out?"

"Yes," answered Marjorie. "But——."

"Oh, good," said Bessie. "What about Miss Bellew? Have you seen her? Has she gone out too?"

"She went out with Mamselle——."

"Oh! Fine!" said Bessie. "I expect they told a pre., but never mind that. I can manage all right if both the cats are gone out."

"But you mustn't——."

"I told you Billy had tickets for the circus. I may get back before Mamselle comes in, and then it will be all right."

"But she will expect to find your detention task done, and if it isn't done, she will guess——."

"I shall tell her I had cramp in my hand, and couldn't write it out," explained Bessie.

"Oh!" ejaculated Marjorie.

"You wouldn't have thought of that, would you?" chuckled Bessie. "Not with your brains."

"I hope not," said Marjorie, "and you mustn't tell fibs, Bessie. And you will get into a row——."

"Well, I think even that cat ought to be satisfied with keeping me in for a half-holiday, without expecting a girl to write out six scenes from a rotten play when she's got cramp in her hand!" exclaimed Bessie, warmly.

"But you haven't got cramp in your hand!" gasped Marjorie.

"I wish you wouldn't argue. You're always arguing. I say, Mamselle hasn't said anything about that paper I left on her table yesterday. She's taking it lying down!" grinned Bessie.

"Perhaps she didn't understand it," said Marjorie, laughing.

"Well, I suppose she understands her own language, though she's rotten in English," said Bessie. "Mind, if she's after the girl that wrote it, mind you don't give me away. If she asks you if you know anything about it, you just tell her that you never saw it when I showed it to you."

" Oh, dear! "

" But never mind that now," said Bessie, briskly. " Now that both the cats are gone out, I'm going to scram. I don't want to be late for the circus. I——."

" Cave! " came a shrill whisper from Clara Trevlyn.

But the warning came too late. The tall figure of Stella Stone, of the Sixth Form, appeared in the offing. Marjorie looked round hastily, to find the Senior Prefect of Cliff House bearing down upon her.

Bessie's fat face vanished from the form room window. Marjorie was left, with reddened cheeks, facing Authority in the shape of Stella Stone.

Stella, tall and fair, marvellous at mathematics and chock-full of Greek, was a most important personage at Cliff House; and fully aware of her own vast importance. She walked and talked on terms of equality with the Staff, and was known to be perfectly at her ease even with Miss Primrose, the Principal. She did not need the " ash " of a Greyfriars prefect, a thing unknown and undreamt of at Cliff House. One glance from Stella's calm eyes would have quelled the wildest spirit in the Lower School.

She towered over Marjorie, almost petrifying her with that calm gaze, which was a little reminiscent of that of Medusa.

" I think you were speaking to a junior in detention, Marjorie," she said, in a calm voice that seemed to emerge from the uttermost depths of a refrigerator.

" Oh! Yes," stammered Marjorie.

" I must take your name," said Stella. " Now go away."

Marjorie went away, with dismayed face and crimson cheeks. Stella sailed on, lofty and stately, and forgot her existence.

" Chump! " said Clara, as Marjorie walked away with

her friends. " That means a report, and a paper to do for the Bellew."

" I'm afraid Bessie is going to ask for trouble with Mamselle——."

" Well, she's always asking for trouble, and now she's landed a spot of it on you, bother her."

Marjorie looked back at the form room window. Stella Stone had turned a corner of the school buildings and vanished. Once more a fat face and a large pair of spectacles adorned the open window, and this time a fat hand was waved, beckoning to the three girls in the distance.

" Bessie wants something," said Marjorie.

" Quite! " agreed Clara. " She wants her ears boxed."

" Perhaps I'd better cut back——."

" Perhaps you hadn't," said Clara. " One spot of bother with a pre. is enough for one afternoon."

" I—I think I'll chance it——."

" I think you won't," said Clara. " Take her other arm, Dolly."

She linked arms with Marjorie on one side, and Dolly linked arms on the other. Between them, Marjorie had no choice between going on and going back. She was walked onward by her loyal chums, out of the danger zone.

" Shall we get a spot of tennis if your brother comes? " asked Clara. " We can't go out of gates if he's coming."

" There's no ' if ' about it, Clara—he said he would come."

" Well, he's a bit uncertain, isn't he? "

" No, I don't think so. I mean——." Marjorie paused. If there was one thing certain about her brother at Greyfriars it was his uncertainty: and Marjorie could not help being aware of it.

" Well, let's go and bag a court, if we can, and then we shan't be wasting the afternoon anyway," said Clara.

" Yes, let's," said Dolly.

" I hope Bessie won't be so silly as to get out of detention——."

" What's the good of hoping she won't be silly, when she can't be anything else?   Come on."

Marjorie glanced back again.   She could not help feeling a little concerned about the fat and fatuous Bessie. And she had reason for concern, for her eyes fell upon a startling unaccustomed sight at the form room window in the distance.   What looked something like a barrage balloon was on the sill, with two plump legs dangling from it. But it was not a barrage balloon: it was Bessie Bunter clambering out of the window.

" Oh! " gasped Marjorie.   " Look! "

" Oh, my hat! " said the slangy Clara.   " She's hooking it."

" Little idiot! " said Dolly.

There was no doubt about it—Bessie Bunter was ' hooking ' it! She dropped, spluttering, from the sill. Then, gasping for breath, she blinked round her like an owl through her big spectacles. Then she bolted round the nearest corner, and was gone.

CHAPTER IV

NO CIRCUS FOR BUNTER!

" I SAY, you fellows! "

It was Bessie Bunter's brother Billy who was speaking, and he was addressing a group of five fellows in the quadrangle at Greyfriars School.

Harry Wharton and Co. were debating what they were going to do that half-holiday. The debate was interrupted by Billy Bunter, who rolled up to the group with a lugubrious fat face, and blinked at them dismally through the big spectacles that were so like Bessie's.

Billy Bunter looked as if he were understudying the Knight of the Sorrowful Countenance that afternoon. The Famous Five of the Remove were not particularly interested in Billy Bunter and his woes. Still, they were sympathetic, for Bunter was " gated " that afternoon, and they were not.

Not that " gating " was so severe on Bunter as it would have been on their more strenuous selves. A fellow who was gated could loaf about with his hands in his pockets, or frowst in an armchair in the Rag: and these were favourite occupations of William George Bunter. But for once, it it was tough on Bunter—as he had tickets for a circus in his pocket.

" Hallo, hallo, hallo, old fat bean," said Bob Cherry. " You look as if you've lost a sovereign and found a pound note."

" I say, you fellows, what's a fellow to do? " said Bunter. " You know I'm gated to-day——."

" The knowfulness is terrific," agreed Hurree Jamset Ram Singh. " The sympathise is truly great."

" Well, fancy wasting tickets for the circus! " said Bunter. " The pater sent them to me, to take Bessie—

and she's coming over. I can't take Bessie to the circus and stay in gates at the same time, can I? ''

'' Hardly! '' said Frank Nugent, laughing. '' Not too easy, anyway.''

'' Well, what's a fellow to do? ''

'' That's easy,'' said Johnny Bull. '' Some other fellow will go to the circus with Bessie if you give him your ticket. There's Hazel—mooching about with nothing to do. Ask him.''

'' Hazel's going over to Cliff House this afternoon,'' said Bob Cherry. '' I—I was rather thinking I might cut across with him, if you fellows don't specially want me——.''

Four fellows exchanged a grin.

'' Well, ask Squiff, Bunter,'' said Johnny Bull. '' He would do it.''

'' You silly idiot! '' ejaculated Bunter.

'' Eh? ''

'' I want to go to the circus. I don't want another fellow to go—I want to go myself! '' hooted Bunter.

'' Oh! '' said Johnny. He had supposed, for a moment, that Billy's concern was for Bessie: though he realised that he might have known his Bunter better.

'' It's pretty rotten of Quelch,'' went on Bunter. '' A fellow doesn't expect justice here, still, it's pretty rotten. Gating a fellow just because he skewed in con. Making out that I hadn't done my prep! Quelch all over.''

'' Had you done it? '' grinned Bob.

'' Yes, I had—and besides, Quelch couldn't know that I hadn't! Just guess-work! '' said Bunter, ''and here I am gated, and Bessie coming over for me to take her to the circus. So what's a fellow to do? ''

'' Get some practice at the nets——! '' suggested Harry Wharton.

'' Don't be a silly idiot, if you can help it. I want to go to the circus! '' yapped Bunter.

" I wonder——! " said Bob Cherry, thoughtfully—and paused.

" Go on, old chap," said Bunter, eagerly. " You wonder what can be done about it? If you can think of something——."

" Eh! No! I was wondering when Hazel is going to start——."

" Oh! Blow Hazel! " snorted Bunter. " What does Hazel matter? I say, Wharton, can't you think of something? "

Harry Wharton laughed.

" Well, you might put in a spot of exercise in the gym——."

" Do stop talking rot, for goodness sake. Don't I keep on telling you that I want to go to the circus? "

" Well, it's not much good telling us. Go and tell Quelch! " suggested the captain of the Remove. " He may change his mind, if you make him understand how important it is—perhaps."

" The perhapsfulness is terrific," murmured Hurree Jamset Ram Singh.

" Tell him Bessie's coming! " said Frank Nugent. " Quelch might stretch a point with a lady in the case! He's not a bad old bean, and he wouldn't like to disappoint a kid from Cliff House."

" Oh! " said Bunter. His fat face brightened. " I hadn't thought of that one."

" You would have," grunted Johnny Bull. " If you had been thinking about your sister instead of yourself."

" Yah! " retorted Bunter.

With quite a hopeful expression on his plump visage, Billy Bunter revolved on his axis, and rolled off to the House. Evidently he was going to try " that one " on his hard-hearted form master.

" Well, what about running out the old boat? " asked Johnny Bull. " Lovely afternoon for the river."

" Let's," agreed Nugent.

" O.K. " said Harry Wharton. " You coming, Bob? "

" Well, if you fellows don't mind——" hesitated Bob.

" Of course we don't, fathead! Give Marjorie our kind regards, ass! " And four fellows, grinning, departed, leaving Bob Cherry on his own with a rather red face.

Billy Bunter, feeling quite optimistic, rolled into the House, and tapped at the door of Mr. Quelch's study. Quelch was crusty, and Quelch was tough, but surely even a crusty and tough beak would relent, when he learned that an affectionate brother was sorely distressed about not being able to take his sister to the circus! Bunter hoped so, at least.

He expected to hear Quelch's crusty voice rap, " Come in! " As there was no rap, he opened the study door and blinked in.

The study was vacant.

" Beast! " breathed Bunter.

Quelch had left his study for something. It was very annoying to Bunter, when he wanted to speak to Quelch. Perhaps his view was that a form master ought to have remained a fixture in case Bunter might want to speak to him.

If that was Bunter's view, it was not Quelch's, for he was not there. But the fat Junior noted that a half-written letter lay on the blotting-pad on Mr. Quelch's writing-table, which indicated that Quelch had merely stepped out intending to return. So Bunter rolled in to wait for him—impatiently. It was not yet time to start for the circus at Courtfield, it was true: still, Bunter did not like wasting his valuable time hanging about waiting for a beak. However, as there was no help for it, he waited.

It was like Bunter to fill in time, while he waited, by glancing at the letter on the blotting-pad. Inquisitiveness was one of his besetting sins.

He blinked at the letter, and read:
"Dear Roger,

I am very pleased indeed by what you tell me, and certainly you may have the books you mention. I am sending you three £1 notes in this letter by registered post——."
That was all, so far. Quelch seemed to have been interrupted at that point, and had left the letter where it was, to finish when he returned to his study. Billy Bunter had just completed reading what was written there, and was about to turn prying eyes in other directions, when he suddenly became aware of a face at the doorway, and jumped away from the table as he realised that Mr. Quelch was looking in.

" Oh! " gasped Bunter.

Mr. Quelch rustled into the study. His face, always expressive, was more expressive than usual. His gimlet-eyes glinted. Only too plainly, those gimlet-eyes had detected Billy Bunter in the act of reading the letter on the blotting-pad.

" Bunter! " Quelch's voice was deep.

" Oh," stuttered Bunter. " I—I wasn't looking at that letter, sir——."

" I saw you reading it! " thundered Mr. Quelch.

" I—I—I—I wasn't, sir! I—I—I haven't read a word, sir——nothing about Roger, or—or about pound notes, or —or anything——I—I hope you don't think I would read your letter, sir——."

Mr. Quelch picked up a cane from the table.

" Bend over that chair, Bunter."

" Oh, crikey! I—I mean——."

" I have told you to bend over that chair, Bunter."

" I—I came to speak to you, sir! " gasped Bunter. " I—I had to wait, as you were not here! My—my sister Circus is coming over this afternoon——I—I mean——my circus Bessie is——."

" Bend over! " Quelch almost roared.

Billy Bunter bent over the chair. There was no help for it. Quelch's cane swept through the air.

Swipe! swipe!

" Wow! Whoooop! "

" Now leave my study! " snapped Mr. Quelch.

" Ow! wow! "

Billy Bunter trailed to the door. But at the door, he turned.

" If—if you please, sir——."

" Go! "

" If you'd let me off gating this afternoon, sir——."

" What? " exclaimed Mr. Quelch. " Upon my word! In no circumstances whatever, Bunter, will I rescind your punishment. Upon my word! "

" B-b-b-but, sir——."

Mr. Quelch picked up his cane again.

That was enough for Bunter. He fairly whizzed down the passage. Mr. Quelch, frowning, sat down to finish writing his letter, and to enclose the same, with three pound notes, in a registered envelope for the post. Billy Bunter rolled dismally out into the quad, wriggling. His visit to his form-master's study had earned him two swipes from his form-master's cane—merely that, and nothing more! And it was borne in upon his fat mind that instead of making matters better, he had made them hopelessly worse: and that, Bessie or no Bessie, there was no circus for him that afternoon.

CHAPTER V

TIT FOR TAT!

" WHERE's Billy? "

Bessie Bunter asked the question.

She asked it of a Remove fellow who was loitering in the quad with his hands in his pockets, and a moody look on his face. Hazel Hazeldene, of the Remove, did not look merry or bright that sunny afternoon. And he looked no merrier or brighter at the sight of a plump Cliff House girl, who blinked at him through spectacles just like Billy Bunter's, and squeaked at him with a squeak that was a twin to Billy's.

Bessie did not even notice that Hazel was looking morose and moody. She was not in the least concerned about Marjorie's brother: she was looking for her own. Hazel was interested in neither of the Bunters.

" Don't know! " was his reply, with Laconian brevity.

" I want him," explained Bessie. " I've come over from Cliff House to go to the circus with Billy. Well, where is he? "

Just as Billy Bunter seemed to consider that he was entitled to find Quelch in his study when he wanted to speak to him, so Bessie seemed to consider that any or every fellow at Greyfriars ought to know where Billy was when she wanted Billy. There was a great deal of family likeness about the Bunter clan.

" I expect he's in the House," said Hazel. " Here, Cherry, know where Bunter is?—his sister wants him."

Bob Cherry was coming towards Hazel, as if to speak to him. Hazel walked away and left him to Bessie. Bessie gave Bob a blink and a nod, as he jerked a cap from a rather untidy mop of flaxen hair.

" Where's Billy? " demanded Bessie.

" He was in the quad a few minutes ago," answered Bob. " I think he went into the House——."

" Take me to him," said Bessie.

" Oh! All right! "

Bob was rather anxious to settle matters with Hazel, before that youth started for Cliff House. Still, Hazel showed no sign whatever of starting, so far: and Bob was always a polite and obliging fellow where girls were concerned. So he obeyed Miss Elizabeth Bunter's behest, without demur.

Billy Bunter was discovered in the Rag. The fat junior had that apartment to himself, no other Remove fellow being indoors that sunny afternoon. He was sitting, or more accurately sprawling, in an armchair—but not, apparently, with comfort. Every now and then he gave a sort of spasmodic wriggle, and his fat face was lugubrious.

" Hallo, hallo, hallo! " Bob Cherry roared, at the doorway. " Here's your sister Bessie, Bunter."

Bessie rolled in, and Bob departed, to look for Hazel again. Billy Bunter blinked at Bessie, but his fat face did not clear: the sight of Sister Bessie did not seem to cheer him much.

" Well, aren't you getting ready? " demanded Bessie, fixing her spectacles on him. " It's time we started for Courtfield."

" I can't go! " grunted Bunter.

" Rot! " said Bessie. " You've got the tickets."

" I'm gated."

" You shouldn't be gated when you've got tickets for a circus."

" Well, I am! " yapped Bunter.

" What are you gated for? "

" Oh! Quelch! " said Bunter, bitterly. " He made out that I hadn't done my prep—as if he knew I hadn't! "

" What are you wriggling like an eel for? Got pins and needles? "

"No, I haven't! Quelch whopped me in his study,"
snorted Bunter. "He made out that I was reading a letter
on his table, just because I was looking at it! That's the
sort of justice we get here!"

"Well, I've come over to go with you to the circus,"
said Bessie, crossly. "I may get into a row for coming,
as that cat Mamselle gave me a detention task. Now you
tell me you're gated and can't come. Look here, you go
and tell Mr. Quelch that I've come over specially, and he
will let you off."

"That's what I went to his study to tell him," groaned
Bunter. "Only he came back suddenly and saw me reading
his letter—I mean, just glancing at it."

"Go and ask him again."

Bunter shook his head, promptly.

"No fear! He's jolly shirty! He might whop me
again."

Miss Bunter gave an angry sniff.

"But I'll tell you what," said Bunter. "You go and
ask him. Quelch is a beast, but we would have to be civil
to a girl. He can't whop you, anyhow. He might let
me off if you ask him. It's a chance."

Bessie Bunter nodded.

"That's a good idea," she agreed. "I know he's a
crusty old stick, but even a crusty old stick might stretch
a point for a pretty girl."

"Eh! What? Oh! Yes!" gasped Bunter. "Well,
you go and try it on—you know his study."

Bessie Bunter rolled out of the Rag, leaving her brother
only moderately hopeful. It was a chance: but it was
quite possible that Quelch would only be made shirtier by
a Cliff House girl butting in.

Bessie tapped at Mr. Quelch's study door. Like her
brother half-an-hour ago, she received no reply to that tap.
So she opened the door and rolled in, with her sweetest
smile turned on for Mr. Quelch.

That proved to be a sheer waste; for, like Billy again, she found that Mr. Quelch was not in the study.

" Oh, bother! " breathed Bessie, crossly.

Mr. Quelch was not there.   Having finished and sealed his letter, he had left the study again, no doubt tempted out of doors by the bright weather.

Bessie Bunter blinked round the study with an irritated sniff.   Her blink fell on the registered letter lying on the blotting-pad, sealed ready for post.   Bessie was as inquisitive as Billy, but as the envelope was sealed, her inquisitive blink was rewarded only by the name and address on the outside.

She gave another sniff, and rolled out of the study again, to seek the Remove master elsewhere.

" Where's Mr. Quelch? " she asked, coming on Squiff of the Remove near the House doorway.

" Squatting on a bench under the elms, swotting over Form papers," answered Squiff, and Bessie rolled out into the quad.

She soon found Mr. Quelch.   The Remove master was seated on one of the old benches, under a shady elm, his back to the massive ancient trunk, shady branches over his head.   He had a pile of Form papers on his knee, a pencil in his hand, and a concentrated expression on his face. Quelch was enjoying the open air and sunshine while he worked at correcting the papers for his form, as he often did in fine weather.   He had quite a number to do, before he was at liberty to take a walk abroad, and post his registered letter at Friardale post office.   And he did not seem pleased by the interruption when Bessie Bunter hove into the offing.

" Please, Mr. Quelch——! " said Bessie, again turning on her sweetest smile.

The Remove master looked up.   His expression did not indicate that he was charmed by a pretty face.   It was impatient.

" Well? " he said.

HE DID NOT SEEM PLEASED BY THE INTERRUPTION

" I'm Bunter's sister——.''

" I am aware of that."

" I've come over to go with Billy to the circus, but he says he's gated. Please will you let him off? "

" I am sorry," said Mr. Quelch, in a tone and with a look, that revealed more annoyance than sorrow. " That is quite impossible."

" But——! " said Bessie.

" Kindly say no more."

" But——."

" I have told Bunter," said Mr. Quelch, in a deep voice, " that in no circumstances whatever will I rescind his punishment. It was impertinent of him to ask you to speak to me on the subject. Now please go away."

Evidently the pretty face of Elizabeth Bunter had no effect whatever on the crusty old stick!

" But——! " recommenced Bessie.

" Go away at once! " said Mr. Quelch. And he dropped his gaze to the Form papers, and resumed marking the top one on the pile, with a complete and total disregard of Miss Elizabeth Bunter.

Bessie breathed hard through her little plump nose. Evidently there was nothing doing. Perhaps Mr. Quelch considered that it was impertinent on the part of a Cliff House junior girl to butt into Greyfriars affairs. Anyhow he was not going to let Bunter off—that was certain. Bessie, breathing hard, gave the top of his bent head an inimical glare. She would have liked to smack that head! Seldom or never had Bessie felt so extremely exasperated.

She walked back to the House, with a frowning brow. It was quite likely that trouble awaited her at Cliff House, for breaking detention: and it was all for nothing because a crusty old stick wouldn't let Billy off a gating. Bessie Bunter really would have liked to scratch him! At the very least she would have liked to upset the inkpot in his study over his papers! She had done that once in

Mademoiselle Lupin's study at Cliff House, with quite satisfactory results—to Bessie, not to Mamselle!

As that thought came into her mind, Bessie blinked about her, through her big spectacles, in a rather stealthy way.

She remembered that there had been nobody about in Masters' quarters when she had gone to Mr. Quelch's study. If there was still nobody about——.

Nobody was, when she blinked into the passage. A few moments more, and she was back in the Remove master's study. Her eyes gleamed behind her spectacles. An upset inkpot was a just retaliation for a crusty old stick knocking out that excursion to the circus!

But as she reached a fat hand towards the inkpot, she noticed the registered letter again, on the blotting-pad.

That put a new and much brighter idea into her mind.

She did not overturn the inkpot. She picked up the registered letter, stepped to the bookcase, and dropped the letter behind a row of books!

Quelch could look for it when he wanted it!

By the time he found it, perhaps he would be sorry for himself! He was not likely to find it in a hurry!

" He, he, he! " Bessie chuckled softly.

It was tit for tat—a Roland for an Oliver. Circuses, it seemed, were off; but Fatima of Cliff House was feeling somewhat consoled, as she rolled away from Mr. Quelch's study—it was quite exhilarating to think of the crusty old stick hunting all over his study for that registered letter, and not finding it perhaps for hours and hours!

CHAPTER VI

TOO LATE!

" OH! Bessie! " ejaculated Billy Bunter.

He sat up in the armchair in the Rag as the plump junior of Cliff House rolled in.

He blinked at Bessie with a guilty blink.

There was a change in Bunter since Bessie had left him there. He was sticky. Billy Bunter generally was sticky when he was in funds, for his funds were immediately expended upon something of a sticky nature. That day Bunter hadn't been in funds, so he hadn't been sticky. But he was sticky now—awfully sticky.

His fat fingers, his wide mouth, and his podgy chin, were all sticky. An empty toffee packet lay near him on the floor. Evidently, toffee had happened, since Bessie had left him in the Rag. Bunter was, in fact, disposing of the last chunk, when the Cliff House junior came back.

" I—I—I say, what did Quelch say? " asked Bunter, anxiously.

" He said no! " snapped Bessie.

" Oh, good! "

" What? "

" I—I—I mean, rotten! " said Bunter, hastily. " Awfully rotten! We—we shan't be able to go to the circus now, Bessie."

Bessie eyed him suspiciously.

It was Bunter who had suggested that she should try Quelch. He had hoped for the best, though with a very faint hope. But something had happened, in the meantime, to change his views. It was a relief to him to hear that Bessie's mission had failed. It was perplexing, but it was plain: Bunter was relieved to hear that Quelch had said no!

" Don't you want to go to the circus? " demanded Bessie.

" Oh! Yes! Rather! But——."

" Well, let's go! " said Bessie. " I got out of detention, and you can get out of a gating. Quelch won't stop you—he's sticking under a tree squinting over a lot of silly papers. Hook it, see, same as I did."

" I—I couldn't! " gasped Bunter. " Girls don't get whopped! Boys do! Quelch would give me six! "

" It's worth it, if he does," said Bessie, encouragingly. " Bob Cherry wouldn't funk a whopping."

" Well, he's tougher than I am," said Bunter. " Besides, it—it—it's wrong, Bessie. I couldn't do it! It's wrong to be disobedient."

" Wha-a-a-t? "

" Very wrong," said Bunter, shaking his head. " I—I want to go to the circus of—of course——I—I'm awfully sorry I can't take you, Bessie——but—but I couldn't do anything wrong you know."

" Have you lost the tickets? " asked Bessie.

" Oh! No! I—I haven't lost them."

" Then what do you mean? "

" Oh, really, Bessie! I'm bound to respect my formmaster," explained Bunter. " If I cut, it would be disrespectful to Quelch. I couldn't do it."

Bessie breathed hard.

What her brother Billy stated was, no doubt, quite right. But it was also quite new. This was the very first time that William George Bunter had expressed such highminded views. She gazed at him, not admiringly.

" The best thing you can do, is to cut back to Cliff House at once," went on Bunter. " It's rotten about the circus, but it can't be helped. It was wrong to get out of detention, Bessie, just as it would be if I cut gates."

" Well, if you funk it——" said Bessie.

" Tain't that! But, you see——."

" If it isn't that, what is it? "

" Oh, really, Bessie——."

" Well, look here," said Bessie. " You've got pals in your form, I suppose? "

" Lots! " said Bunter. " I've always been the most popular chap in the Remove. What about that? "

" Well, you can give one of them the tickets, and he can take me to the circus," said Bessie. " Frank Nugent is a very nice boy——."

" He—he—he's gone out."

" Well, Wharton, then——."

" He's gone out with Nugent."

" Well, there's that nice Indian boy——."

" He's gone out with Wharton and Nugent."

" Bob Cherry, then——."

" He—he's gone out with Wharton and Nugent and Inky——."

" He hadn't," said Bessie. " I spoke to him when I came, and he came to this very room with me."

" I—I mean, he's gone out since——," stammered Bunter.

Bessie's gaze at the fat junior in the armchair grew more and more suspicious. It was getting clearer and clearer that, for some mysterious reason, Billy Bunter had changed his mind about the circus at Courtfield. He did not want to go, himself, and he did not want Bessie to go.

" Mean to say there's nobody? " demanded Bessie.

" Nobody at all! " said Bunter. " Awfully sorry, old girl—but there it is! You'd better cut back to Cliff House——."

" Give me the tickets! "

" Eh? "

" If you're not going to the circus, you won't want your ticket," said Bessie. " Give them both to me."

She held out a plump hand.

Billy Bunter blinked at it. But he did not place a couple of circus tickets in the plump palm. His aspect grew more and more uneasy, and more and more guilty. But he made no move to produce circus tickets.

" Wha-a-at do you want them for, Bessie? " stammered the fat Owl.

" I'm going to the circus."

" But—but you can't——."

" I'm going to. Where are those tickets? "

" I—I—I——I jolly well knew that Quelch would say no——."

" Where are those tickets? "

" I—I swopped them——." gasped Bunter.

" What? " shrieked Bessie.

" I knew Quelch would say no," gasped Bunter. " So I—I swopped them for a packet of toffee with Skinner——."

It was out now! Billy Bunter's sticky state was accounted for. Perhaps, had Bessie not wasted time in giving Mr. Quelch tit for tat, by hiding the registered letter behind the books in his study, she might have been in time to save the circus tickets! As it was, she was too late! She gazed at the guilty fat Owl, her very spectacles gleaming with wrath.

" Has Skinner gone? " she gasped.

" Yes—he went off at once with Snoop——."

" Where's the toffee? "

" The—the toffee! " stammered Bunter. As the circus tickets were beyond recovery, Bessie apparently was thinking of putting in a claim on the toffee, but she was too late for that also.

" Yes, the toffee! Where is it? "

" I—I—I've eaten it."

Words failed Elizabeth Bunter. Besides, words were useless. No words, however expressive, could bring back either the circus tickets or the toffee. Words being superfluous, Bessie Bunter went into action.

Smack!

The plumpest hand at Cliff House established sudden contact with the fattest head at Greyfriars School.

" Yarooooh! " roared Bunter.

Billy Bunter had not expected that! Really, he might have—but he hadn't! But expected or unexpected, he had had it! He roared.

" There! " snorted Bessie.

And she whirled out of the Rag, leaving the fat Owl rubbing a fat head and spluttering. It was a wrathful Bessie that rolled back by the lanes to Cliff House, rather wishing that she had delivered another smack before departing. Bunter, on the other hand, was quite satisfied with one.

CHAPTER VII

CAUGHT!

" Babs! Mabs! I say——! "

" Oh! " ejaculated Barbara Redfern.

" Oh! " echoed Mabel Lynn.

Barbara and Mabel—more often called Babs and Mabs in the Cliff House Fourth—stared blankly at Bessie Bunter. They had not expected to see anyone, when they came round the gardener's shed: but if they had expected to see anyone, Bessie was the last person they would have expected to see.

Bessie was supposed to be under detention in the form-room, writing out six scenes from " La Poudre aux Yeux." Marjorie, Clara and Dolly knew that Elizabeth Bunter had bolted—Babs and Mabs did not. So they were quite startled at the sight of a fat face, and two little round eyes blinking at them through a large pair of spectacles, as they came round the shed in search of a lost tennis ball.

" You little donkey! " exclaimed Babs. " What are you doing here? "

" You've got out of detention! " exclaimed Mabs.

Bessie sniffed.

" I've been over to Greyfriars," she answered. " Now I've come back. I say, I dodged behind this shed when I saw the Bull. Is the Bull coming this way? "

" The Bull " was Miss Bullivant, games-mistress at Cliff House. She was, at the moment, almost as alarming a sight to Bessie Bunter as any Durham bull could have been.

A girl who had bolted out of detention, and hoped to get back undiscovered, couldn't walk in at the school gates, under the eyes of Piper the porter, and dozens of other eyes. Bessie had to be cautious. She had clambered over a little gate in a privet hedge, and was threading her way by the path through the kitchen gardens, where no eyes were likely to fall upon her, unless the gardener happened to be there. Luckily, he did not happen to be there; but all of a sudden three figures appeared from the direction of the tennis courts. Two of them were junior girls, who did not matter—but the third was the stocky, muscular figure of the Bull; and Bessie had promptly hunted cover. Babs and Mabs, coming round the shed to ascertain whether that lost ball might have dropped there, came on her suddenly.

"Is she coming?" breathed Bessie. "Look here; Mamselle and Bellew have gone out, and if I get back in time, they won't know I scrammed, see? But if the Bull sees me——!"

"I—I think she was looking among the cabbages," said Barbara. "But——."

Barbara stepped back to the corner of the shed, and surveyed the kitchen gardens. At a little distance was the stocky figure of the Bull, bending and scanning the ground. She was not looking towards the shed, but she was coming directly towards it. Her progress was slow, but sooner or later, it was clear, she would pass the little building, and then everything behind it would be in her view.

"She's coming!" said Babs, turning back.

"Oh! The cat!" breathed Bessie. Everybody who caused Bessie Bunter discomfort was, according to Bessie, a "cat." Sometimes it seemed that from Bessie's point of view, the population of Cliff House was almost wholly feline.

"She won't be here for two or three minutes," said Babs. "But she's coming. You shouldn't have got out of detention, Bessie."

"Do talk sense!" snapped Bessie.

Barbara laughed.

"Isn't that sense?" she asked.

" Oh, do be quiet! Look here, I'm not going to let the Bull spot me, if I can help it. I daresay you'd like me to be sent to the Head! " snorted Bessie.

She blinked round her anxiously through her big spectacles in search of more secure cover. But there was no cover available. There were several trees at hand, but none with a trunk massive enough to screen Bessie Bunter. Then she blinked at a little window in the back wall of the shed, and her fat face brightened.

" I can get in there! " she breathed. " Go round and go in and open that window, Babs! Quick. The Bull won't look in the shed. She won't think a tennis ball has dropped inside a shed. Quick."

" But——! " gasped Barbara. It was a small window —a very small window. A slim girl like Babs, or Mabs, could have negotiated it without much difficulty. But Bessie Bunter was not slim. She was far from slim. It was easy enough to go round and open the window. But how Elizabeth Bunter's ample form was to pass through it, when opened, was a mystery to Babs and Mabs.

" Will you be quick! " hissed Bessie.

" But you couldn't get through, Bessie," gasped Barbara.

" Cat! "

" You couldn't really, Bessie——! " urged Mabs.

" Minx! "

A voice—a very powerful voice—came from the distance, beyond the gardener's shed.

" Barbara! Mabel! Have you found that ball? "

" Oh, dear! " murmured Barbara. She stepped into view round the corner of the shed, and called back, " Not yet, Miss Bullivant—we're looking."

Miss Bullivant, so far, had no suspicion that there was a third person behind the shed. But she was coming nearer and nearer!

Bessie caught Mabel Lynn by the arm.

" Go round and open the window, quick! " she breathed. " I can get in at the window—don't be a cat, Mabel. I can hide in the loft, if the Bull looks into the shed. Quick! "

" Oh, all right! " said Mabs. She hurried round the shed, and disappeared.

Bessie waited anxiously. But Mabs was quick: in less than a minute, there was a creak, as the little window opened from within. Bessie gasped with relief. The way of escape was open.

" Help me up, Babs! "

" Oh, dear! " said Babs. But she gave a helping hand. Bessie clutched, and clambered, and Barbara hoisted and pushed.

" Help me in, Mabs! " gasped Bessie. " You pull while Babs pushes. It's easy enough. Tain't as if I was fat."

" Oh, dear! " said Mabs.

But they were good-natured girls, and they did their best. Mabs caught hold of plump shoulders and pulled, and Barbara, from astern, pushed. Head and shoulders went in successfully, and then Bessie jammed. She gave an anguished squeak, and strove to struggle through. But it booted not. The little window was not so wide as Elizabeth Bunter: it would have been as easy for a camel to pass through a needle's eye, as for Bessie Bunter to pass through that window. Half-way there was, so to speak, a traffic jam.

" Oooooogh! " squeaked Bessie.

" It's no good, Bessie—you can't get through——." gasped Mabel.

" Ow! Cat! Wooogh! "

" Better get back——."

" Urrggh! Minx! Ooooh! "

" Oh, scissors! " ejaculated Barbara. " Here comes the Bull! "

She ceased to shove at the fat figure jammed in the window. A stocky figure came past the end of the shed, and Miss Bullivant glanced round, and gave quite a jump at what she beheld. Quite forgetful of lost tennis balls, the Bull came up with her long strides.

" What—what—what is that? " she exclaimed.

" I—I—I think it's Bessie, Miss Bullivant," stammered Barbara.

" Ooogh! Ow! I'm being pinched! Oooogh! " wailed Bessie. " I've got a pain in my ribs! Oooogh! "

" Upon my word! " exclaimed the Bull. " Bessie, why are you not in the form-room? Get down from that window at once."

" I—I—I kik-kik-kik——."

" What? " thundered Miss Bullivant. " If you dare to kick, Bessie——."

" Oh, crikey! I—I——I kik-kik-kik-can't! " shrieked Bessie. " I—I kik-kik-kik-can't get out! Oh, lor'! "

" Get down at once."

" I—I kik-kik-can't! I'm stuck! " wailed Bessie. " I kik-kik-can't get in, and I kik-kik-can't get out! Ow! Help! "

Bessie was fairly caught. She struggled wildly, two plump legs thrashing the air. But it was in vain. She could neither advance nor retreat. She was stuck fast in the window.

" Ow! ow! ow! Help me out! " shrieked Bessie. " Wow! I've got a pain! Ow! Will you help me out! Ooooooh! "

" Upon my word! " exclaimed Miss Bullivant. Her powerful hands grasped Bessie Bunter, and she pulled. Yell after yell came from Bessie, as she was slowly, but surely, extracted, like a cork from a bottle.

" Ow! ow! ow! ow! " wailed Bessie, when she was landed at last. " Ow! ow! ow! I've got a pain—wow! "

" Come with me," said Miss Bullivant. " I shall take

you back to the House at once!   Barbara, there is nothing
to laugh at! ''

" Oh! no, Miss Bullivant! " gasped Barbara.

" Come! " snapped the Bull.

" Ow! ow! ow! ow! wow! "

Bessie rolled dismally away with the Bull.   She
squeaked as she went.   Barbara looked at Mabel, and
Mabel looked at Barbara.

" Oh, dear! " said Babs.   " Ha, ha, ha! "

" Oh, scissors! " said Mabs.   " Ha, ha, ha! "

They resumed hunting for that lost ball, with smiling
faces.   But Bessie was not smiling, as she trailed away with
the Bull.   She seemed to be understudying that ancient
king who never smiled again!

CHAPTER VIII

TROUBLE FOR HAZEL!

" HALLO, hallo, hallo! "

Mr. Quelch frowned.

That cheery and powerful voice, echoing among the old elms, was quite a cheerful sound, really. But it interrupted Quelch. And he was not in the best of tempers anyhow. Billy Bunter had irritated him—Bessie Bunter had added to his irritation—and he was getting a little tired of Form papers, anxious to get through and go for his walk.

In that secluded spot in the shade, almost hidden from view by the old trees, Quelch expected quiet. So Bob Cherry's vigorous voice, booming only a few yards away, was not music to his ears.

Still, Quelch was a reasonable man. He did not expect youth to observe a Trappist silence, simply because a form-master had taken his work out into the open air. He knew, too, that Bob would have subdued his stentorian tones had he been aware that his form-master was in the offing. Evidently, Bob did not know that he was there, as he hailed some other fellow under the elms.

" Trying to keep that tree up, Hazel? " went on Bob's voice.

Hazeldene, it seemed, was leaning on one of the old trunks. Mr. Quelch's frown deepened. He had already noticed Hazeldene, of his form, that afternoon, loafing about with a discontented face. Now, it seemed, Hazel was leaning on a tree. Quelch did not approve of loafing, of discontented faces, or of leaning about in a slack manner.

A grunt was all the answer Bob Cherry received from Hazel. That grunt sounded as if Hazel was still feeling as discontented as he had looked when Quelch had noticed him half-an-hour ago.

" Starting for Cliff House pretty soon, old scout? "
went on Bob.

" Eh! Oh! Bother Cliff House."

" Weren't you going over to see Marjorie this afternoon? "

" Oh! Yes! "

" Like me to run across with you? "

" If you like."

" If you're going on your bike, I'll get the jiggers out,
if you like," said Bob.

Mr. Quelch ceased to mark Form papers. It was
simply useless to try to carry on, with a conversation going
on, on the other side of his tree. He was tempted to call
out to the juniors to go away. But, as a reasonable man,
Quelch had to admit that schoolboys had a right to talk
in the quad if they liked. Quelch was, perhaps, crusty,
but he was just. He waited for golden silence to accrue.

" I'm not going yet," grunted Hazel.

" Oh! " said Bob. " Not much good hanging about,
old chap."

" Look here, Cherry——." Hazel paused.

" Go it," said Bob.

" I—I'm in rather a scrape. Look here, you might
help, if you liked. I—I've had a bet on with a man in the
Fourth, and—and he's dunning me for a quid. Could
you lend me a quid? "

" Oh, my hat! " said Bob Cherry. " You must be an
awful ass, Hazel——."

" Never mind that! Can you lend me the quid? "
snapped Hazel, irritably. " I lost it, and I've got to pay,
and I'm stony. I was going to ask Wharton, but you
know what he thinks about a fellow having a bet on——."

" I think the same as Wharton does, about that," said
Bob, drily.

" Oh, don't give me one of his sermons at second-
hand! If you can't, or won't, help a fellow out, clear off
and leave a fellow alone, at any rate."

" Well, I can't," said Bob. " Quids don't come my way very often. I've got ninepence, if that's any use."

" Oh, don't be an idiot."

Mr. Quelch, on his side of the big elm, was sitting bolt upright, with an expression on his face that was reminiscent of the fabled Gorgon. He seemed almost paralysed by what he heard. But at this point he came to himself, as it were, and rose to his feet.

Quelch was not the man to take heed of words spoken inadvertently in his hearing. But this was much too serious a matter to be passed over. Quelch's face was thunderous with wrath as he rose.

" Well, what about getting out? " Bob was going on. " Won't do any good to mooch about——! "

Bob was interrupted at that point. An awful figure whisked round the big elm, and a pair of gimlet-eyes were fixed on the two juniors.

" Oh! " gasped Bob.

Hazel's eyes popped at his form-master. His weak, good-looking face became almost white. He had not had the remotest idea that Quelch was anywhere near at hand. It flashed through his mind that Quelch must have heard what he had said, and he was almost sick with dismay and apprehension.

" Hazeldene! " thundered Mr. Quelch.

Hazel did not speak; he could only stare. Bob stood silent, a picture of dismay.

" I heard what you said to Cherry, Hazeldene! "

Hazel was still dumb.

" I am amazed—shocked—disgusted! I shall inquire into this," said Mr. Quelch. " Go to my study, Hazel-dene, and remain there till I come in."

" I—I——! " stammered Hazel.

" You need say nothing now, Hazeldene. I shall question you in my study. Go there at once, and wait for me."

Hazel slowly detached himself from the trunk on which

3

he was leaning. There was sullen resentment in his face, as well as apprehension. Like many weak natures, Hazel had a strain of sullen obstinacy in him.

"It's a half-holiday, sir," he muttered.

"What? What? Go to my study at once, Hazeldene."

Hazel slouched away towards the House, Mr. Quelch's gaze following him, as he went, with a thunderous frown.

"If you please, sir——!" murmured Bob.

"What? What? Did you speak, Cherry?"

"Hazeldene was going to Cliff House, sir," ventured Bob. "I—I think his sister may be expecting him——."

"Take fifty lines, Cherry!"

"Oh! Yes, sir!"

Bob realised that he had better say no more. He backed away, and Mr. Quelch, still thunderous, circumnavigated the elm again, and resumed his seat and his Form papers.

Bob Cherry followed Hazel to the House. The culprit scowled as he joined him.

"Precious row you've landed me in," he snapped.

"I!" exclaimed Bob.

"I suppose you didn't know Quelch was there——."

"Of course I didn't! You didn't! You might have been a bit more careful though before you yowled out about making bets with a man in the Fourth."

"I shouldn't have said anything if you hadn't come up and started jawing. Now I'm booked for a sermon from Quelch, and a whopping to follow up the pi-jaw," said Hazel, savagely.

"I came to speak about going over to Cliff House—I never expected you to talk about your silly betting——."

"Well, you've done it now, whatever you expected! I've got to wait in that old goat's study—on a half-holiday ——well, I shan't wait long, anyhow. If he keeps me waiting long I shall clear."

Bob looked alarmed.

"For goodness sake, Hazel, don't play the goat," he

exclaimed, earnestly. " Quelch has got his rag out—don't make matters worse. Look here, shall I cut over to Cliff House, and tell Marjorie that you can't come this afternoon? "

" You can mind your own business."

With that Hazel tramped into the House, and went to his form-master's study. He left Bob Cherry breathing hard. Hazel, in his concentration on his own dingy troubles, obviously did not think, or care, anything about Marjorie at Cliff House. Bob did think, and did care; and he felt rather like punching Hazel's sulky head.

Hazel, scowling in Mr. Quelch's study while he waited for his form-master, gave neither Bob nor Marjorie a thought. He had himself to think about!

Quelch was going to ask him questions, give him oceans of " pi-jaw," and wind up with a caning. That was the programme—not a happy one to which to look forward. Waiting for it made it worse: and gradually Hazel's sulky resentment gained the upper hand of his apprehension. It wouldn't have been so bad, if Quelch had got it over. But he had to wait for it—sticking in a study on a sunny half-holiday. He grew more and more resentful and angry with every passing minute.

Several times, as he loafed wearily about the room, he turned towards the door, hesitated, and turned back again.

Still Quelch did not come.

Four o'clock sounded from the clock-tower. Hazel set his lips. He had been waiting more than half-an-hour— how long did Quelch think that he was going to wait? He walked to the door and opened it.

A portly figure was in the passage. It was not Quelch; it was Mr. Prout, master of the Fifth, going to his study.

Prout glanced at the Junior in Quelch's doorway. Hazel took no heed of him. Was Quelch coming?

There was no sign of Mr. Quelch. Hazel waited for several more minutes. Then he walked out of his form-master's study, and went off.

CHAPTER IX

LOST BROOCH!

" Babs! "

" Well? "

" Seen my brooch? " asked Bessie Bunter.

" Lots of times," answered Barbara. " It's rather difficult not to see, when you've got it on."

" Sort of leaps to the eye! " remarked Mabs.

" Well, I've lost it! " snapped Bessie.

" Bang goes saxpence! " said Barbara.

Bessie Bunter's spectacles fixed on Babs with a withering glare.

" That brooch was worth pounds and pounds," she said. " Think I got it in a Christmas cracker? "

" Didn't you? " asked Babs, sweetly.

" No! " hooted Bessie. " I didn't! My Uncle Carter gave me that brooch on a birthday. It's real emeralds. Big ones! "

" Quite big! " agreed Barbara.

" Awfully big! " agreed Mabel.

" That makes them more valuable," explained Bessie. " Miss Bellew won't let me wear it if she can help it. I expect she's jealous about it."

" Oh! " said Babs and Mabs.

" But the trouble is, it's lost," went on Bessie. " I know I had it on when I went out this afternoon. The pin was a bit loose. It must have fallen off."

Bessie's fat face looked worried. Babs and Mabs did their best to look sympathetic. But really, they could not feel that it was an overwhelming loss. It was true that the emeralds in that brooch were very big ones. But it was also true that they looked suspiciously like green glass. The value of that brooch really was not in proportion to its size.

The three junior girls were in their study, No. 4 in the Fourth. The summer dusk was falling, and it was close on lock-up. Babs and Mabs were talking tennis when Bessie announced her loss. Babs rose from her rocker with a resigned sigh.

"Let's look round the study for it," she said.

"That's no good," said Bessie. "It was dropped out of doors. I couldn't go out and look for it, as I had to go into detention. But I know where it must have dropped —when I was climbing in the shed window, and Mabel clawing at me——."

"Was I?" ejaculated Mabs.

"Yes, you were!" yapped Bessie. "I expect you clawed it off. I asked you to help me in, not to claw at me like a cat."

Babs and Mabs exchanged a glance, and laughed. Both of them had been lectured by Miss Bellew for having tried to help the truant escape the eagle eye of the Bull. This was Bessie's own inimitable way of expressing thanks for services rendered.

"That's where it must have happened," resumed Bessie. "The pin was a bit loose—but it wouldn't have dropped off if I hadn't been wriggling in that beastly window, and Mabel clawing at me. It's lying in the gardener's shed now. Which of you is going to fetch it for me?"

"Neither," answered Babs, promptly. "It's lock-up now—there goes the bell."

"You'd better go, Mabs, as you clawed it off——."

"It's all right till to-morrow," said Mabs. "If it's there, it won't walk away."

"Suppose the gardener found it?" said Bessie, darkly. "Or suppose he trod on it! I'm not going to leave it out there all night, I can tell you."

"Well, go and fetch it, if you want to risk a row for going out after lock-up," said Barbara.

"I'm not going to get into another row. I'm in rows enough already," said Bessie, indignantly. "I've got an

extra detention for going out to-day. Perhaps you'd like
me to lose some more half-holidays! ''

" I'd like you to give us a rest! " sighed Barbara.

" Yes, do! " urged Mabs.

" If you won't go——! " said Bessie.

" No ' if ' about it,'' assured Barbara.

" Then I'll go and ask Marjorie.''

" Look here, you little duffer, don't go bothering Marjorie,'' exclaimed Babs. '' Marjorie's down in the mouth
about that precious brother of hers not turning up this
afternoon. Leave Marjorie alone.''

" Cat! " was Bessie's polite reply to that. And she
rolled out of No. 4, and headed for No. 7.·

There she found Marjorie and Clara and Dolly. Clara
and Dolly smiled as she came in. All the form, by that
time, had heard about Bessie's wild adventures in the
window of the gardener's shed, and seemed to think it
funny.

Marjorie's face was a little clouded. Hazel had not
come over that afternoon, as promised, and she wondered
whether that meant that he was in some trouble at his
school. Often and often was Hazel in trouble of some
kind or other; and it was always, according to Hazel,
somebody else's fault. A fellow in whose character stub-
born obstinacy was mingled with weak vacillation, sulky
temper with irresolution, was always likely to be a worry
to a relative who cared about his well-being, as Marjorie
did.

" I say, you girls——,'' began Bessie. She frowned
at two smiling faces, blinked at a serious one, and went
on, '' I've lost my brooch. It must have fallen off when
I was in that window——! ''

" Ha, ha, ha! " trilled Clara and Dolly.

" Oh, laugh! " snorted Bessie. '' Funny, wasn't it,
to be stuck in a window, with a silly girl clawing at me,
making out she was helping me in. Well, she made me

drop that brooch with her clawing, and it's in the gardener's shed now. I say, Marjorie———."

"Did you see my brother at Greyfriars this afternoon,
Bessie?" asked Marjorie.

"I don't remember. Now, about my brooch———."

"But you must remember if you saw him," said
Marjorie.

"Eh! Oh! Yes, I did! I asked him where Billy was,
and he scowled at me," answered Bessie. "That's all I
saw of him."

"He wasn't in detention or anything?"

"He couldn't have been, as he was loafing about scowling. But never mind him," said Bessie, impatiently.
"You never can stick to a subject, Marjorie. I'm talking
about my brooch. That's important."

"Much more important that your brother, Marjorie,"
remarked Clara, sarcastically, and Dolly giggled.

"It's lying in that gardener's shed now," said Bessie,
unheeding sarcasm. "It must be lying just under the
window inside, as I must have dropped it there. Will you
go and fetch it for me, Marjorie?"

"It's lock-up," answered Marjorie.

"I've had that from Babs," yapped Bessie. "I don't
want to know whether it's lock-up, as I can hear a bell just
as plainly as you can. I want to know whether you'll
fetch my brooch."

"And why can't you fetch it yourself?" demanded
Clara, warmly, while Marjorie hesitated.

"I don't want to get into a row with Bellew."

"And doesn't it matter if Marjorie gets into a row with
Bellew?" exclaimed Clara. "You're not going, Marjorie."

"We're not allowed out after lock-up, Bessie, you
know," said Marjorie, mildly. "Better leave it till the
morning."

"I shan't leave it till the morning. It's easy enough
to go—the lobby door is never locked till after call-over,

and there's tons of time before that. I wish you wouldn't be selfish, Marjorie.''

" Well, it wouldn't take a few minutes——! " said Marjorie, hesitating.

Clara gave an emphatic sniff.

" You're not going! " she said. " I wouldn't, and Dolly wouldn't——.''

" No fear! '' agreed Dolly Jobling.

" Oh, do be quiet, you two! '' exclaimed Bessie Bunter. " It's all right for you, Marjorie. If Stella Stone or some beastly pre. spots you going out, you needn't say you were going as far as the kitchen gardens. You can say you dropped your handkerchief just outside the lobby door, see? ''

" Oh! '' gasped Marjorie.

" I wonder if that little fat animal has ever heard of telling the truth! '' exclaimed Clara. " You must have heard it spoken of, at least, Bessie.''

" Cat! '' said Bessie. " That's just like you, Clara. Bellew makes out that I tell fibs. So does Mamselle. And so do you! Plain girls are always catty with pretty girls! I expect it.''

" Oh, ye gods and little fishes! '' said Clara.

Marjorie smiled.

" I think I might go, Clara——! '' she said.

" And I think you mightn't! '' said Clara. " If Fatima wants her brooch, she can go and fetch it, and get into a row with Bellew herself. You're too soft, Marjorie. You're just not going to do it, see? ''

" You leave Marjorie alone, Clara——'' hooted Bessie.

" Bow-wow! '' said Clara. " Likewise, rats! ''

" You'll go, won't you, Marjorie? ''

" She won't,'' said Clara, determinedly. " Marjorie, if you take a step out of this study before the bell goes for roll, I'll hold on to your hair.''

Marjorie laughed.

" Leave it till morning, Bessie,'' she said.

" Cat! " said Bessie.

And Bessie Bunter rolled out of No. 7, where it seemed that there was nothing doing. In the corridor she came on Gwendoline Cook, Bridget O'Toole, and Grace Woodfield, chatting in a group. She paused and blinked at them.

" I say, you girls——! " she began.

That seemed to be enough for Gwendoline, Bridget, and Grace. They faded away down the staircase, leaving Bessie blinking.

" Cats! " breathed Bessie.

She went down the stairs, and on the middle landing encountered Margaret Lennox. Margaret had no chance to fade away—Bessie clutched her by the sleeve.

" I say, Margaret, I want somebody to go down to the gardener's shed and find my brooch I lost there——."

" Then I hope you'll find somebody! " said Margaret, cheerily; and she jerked her sleeve away and escaped.

Bessie breathed hard through her plump little nose. It was borne in on her fat mind that if anybody was going down to the gardener's shed for that brooch, it had to be Elizabeth Bunter herself. And at length Bessie made up her mind to it, and rolled away to the junior lobby to let herself out in the thickening dusk.

CHAPTER X

A SCARE IN THE DARK!

SCREAM!

" Goodness gracious! " ejaculated Miss Bellew.

Scream!

" Mon Dieu! " exclaimed Mademoiselle Lupin.

Scream!

Grunt, from Miss Bullivant.

The three members of the Staff were standing in the old stone porch of the House, in the light of the open doorway, chatting. Within, all was light; but outside the dusk had thickened to dark. The bell had not yet rung for roll, and the three were at leisure, enjoying the balmy summer evening as they chatted. All was calm and peaceful—till suddenly, unexpectedly, startlingly, those piercing screams came ringing from the dusky quad.

One of the Cliff House girls, evidently, was out of the House after lock-up: and judging by the sounds, that one was in a state of terrified fright. The Fourth-form mistress, the French mistress, and the games mistress, all stared out with startled eyes.

" Who——? " exclaimed Miss Bellew.

" Vat——! " exclaimed Mademoiselle Lupin.

Miss Bullivant stepped out, scanning the dusky spaces.

Scream!

A sound of rapidly pattering footsteps came with the scream. Miss Bullivant turned in the direction of the sound, as a fat figure, with hair blown out in the wind, and terrified eyes popping through a large pair of spectacles, came shooting out of the dark.

Bump!

Bessie Bunter did not even see the Bull—and the Bull did not see Bessie in time to avoid a collision. The fattest

THE FATTEST FIGURE AT CLIFF HOUSE SCHOOL CRASHED
INTO THE GAMES MISTRESS

figure at Cliff House School crashed into the games mistress; and powerful and muscular as Miss Bullivant was, she staggered under the shock.

" Ooooh! " gasped Miss Bullivant.

" Ow! Help! " shrieked Bessie Bunter.

Even as she staggered, the Bull clutched. Her strong hand closed on a fat shoulder, and Bessie was captured. But she struggled wildly in that clutch, not recognising the Bull in her terror.

Scream! scream! scream!

" Be silent, Bessie! " thundered the Bull. " You absurd child, be silent! Do you want to alarm the whole school? "

Scream!

" What has happened? " exclaimed Miss Bellew.

Scream!

" Mon Dieu! Cette Bessie! " exclaimed Mademoiselle Lupin.

Scream!

" You have been out of the House after lock-up, Bessie! "

Scream!

"The silly child has been frightened," said Miss Bullivant, and she hooked Bessie Bunter into the porch with a swing of her powerful arm, and with another swing, landed her inside the lighted doorway. "Bessie! Be quiet! "

Bessie Bunter blinked like an owl in the light. Her fat cheeks, which generally resembled ripe apples, were like chalk. Her eyes popped. Evidently Fatima of Cliff House had been badly scared—though by what, it was difficult to imagine. There was nothing within the high walls of Cliff House School calculated to scare Bessie or anyone else—so far as anyone knew, at least.

But even Bessie was reassured as she found herself in the lighted hall, with a startled crowd of girls of all forms gathering round her and realised that it was the Bull's grip that was on her plump shoulder. The hefty Bull was reassuring, in a moment of peril.

" Whatever has happened, Bessie? " exclaimed Marjorie Hazeldene.

" Ooh! It was all your fault! " gasped Bessie.

" Mine! " exclaimed Marjorie, blankly.

" Yes, it was! You know I asked you to go and fetch my brooch, and you wouldn't," gurgled Bessie. " So I had to go! Oh, dear! "

" You went out of the House after lock-up, Bessie! " exclaimed Miss Bellew.

" Oh! No! I—I mean, I had to go and fetch my brooch—I lost it in the gardener's shed this afternoon! " wailed Bessie. " I didn't know anybody was there! Ooooooh! "

" You have been to the gardener's shed? But what has frightened you, you stupid girl? " exclaimed Miss Bellew.

" Somebody was there, and—and I—I walked right into him—oooooooooh! "

" Do you mean the gardener? "

" No! It wasn't Potts. Potts wouldn't be there in the dark. And he would have spoken, if it had been Potts. Ooooooh! It was—was—was somebody——and I—I walked right into him——ooooooh! "

Bessie shuddered from head to foot. She gave scared blinks at the open doorway, and clung to the Bull's stout right arm.

" I—I—I was frightened," she stuttered. " It—it was dark in the shed, and I—I hadn't a torch, and I—I never thought of taking any matches, and—and—and it was dark, and I didn't know he was there, and—and—— ooooooooooh! "

" Nonsense! " said the Bull, decisively. " Nobody could be in the shed but Potts, and he would not be there without a light. The silly girl has been frightened by the dark."

" I—I haven't! " wailed Bessie.   " I tell you, I touched him——walked right into him—and he jumped ——and—and so did I——!   I—I—I think it was a burglar! Oh, dear! "

Snort, from the Bull. A burglar in a gardener's shed, early in the evening, did not seem probable to the Bull.

" Or—or—or a tramp! " gasped Bessie. " Perhaps it was a tramp! I know it was somebody——."

" If there was anyone, did you not see him? " demanded Miss Bellew.

" I can't see in the dark——I'm not a cat! " wailed Bessie.   " But I touched him——ooooh!——oh, dear! I was s-s-s-so fuf-fuf-frightened! I—I—I screamed, and —and ran away——ooooh! "

" Marjorie, take Bessie away," said Miss Bellew. " You will come to my study after call-over, Bessie. There is no occasion whatever for alarm," added the Fourth-form Mistress, sharply. " I have no doubt that what Bessie touched was a potato sack, or something of the kind."

" It wasn't—it was him——."

" Silence! Go away at once! " snapped Miss Bellew. " Disperse, all of you—there is no occasion whatever for excitement."

Marjorie led Bessie away, still spluttering: and though Miss Bellew had stated that there was no occasion whatever for excitement, the Cliff House girls seemed to think that there was, all the same.   Quite an excited crowd of Third, Fourth, and Fifth surrounded Bessie in the junior common-room, eager for details—even tall girls of the Sixth lent an ear at the doorway.   But there were few, if any, who took Bessie's strange story with much seriousness. Bessie was the girl to be scared in the dark, and to fancy the rest; and really it seemed very improbable thåt any extraneous person could be lurking in the dark in Potts' shed, among the lawn-mowers, garden-rollers, picks and spades, and sacks of potatoes.

While Bessie was spluttering out her story, over and over again, to the crowd in the common-room, Miss Bullivant took a torch and a hockey-stick and went to investigate. Those who saw her go, did not feel any apprehension for the Bull, if a tramp happened to be there. It was rather for the tramp to be apprehensive. The Bull was fully equal to dealing with the most truculent tramp that ever trudged on the King's highway.

Miss Bullivant came back in ten minutes, with a frowning brow and an unused hockey stick.

"Nobody there, of course?" asked Miss Bellew.

"Nobody!" grunted the Bull.

"Of course there could not have been anyone."

"Of course not."

And that was that!

CHAPTER XI

MARJORIE'S DISCOVERY!

" LET'S all go! " said Barbara.

" Oh! Yes, let's! " sighed Mabel. " We shall never hear the end of it till it's found."

" Why not have a whip-round, and buy Bessie a new one? " inquired Clara Trevlyn. " A penny each——! "

" Ha, ha, ha! "

" I say, you girls, that brooch is worth pounds and pounds and pounds! " declared Bessie Bunter. " You've all seen it——."

" We've all seen it a mile off! " agreed Clara.

" Well, let's all go and look for it, and we're bound to find it, if it's in the shed at all," said Marjorie. " Lots of time before class."

" Come on," said Bessie, briskly.

In the bright and sunny morning, Bessie had lost her terrors of the shed in the kitchen garden. If a burglar or a tramp had been there, even Bessie did not suppose that he was still there! She led the way, and Marjorie and Clara and Dolly, Babs and Mabs, followed on—rather anxious to find that lost brooch, if only to hear an end of the subject.

Nobody but Bessie believed in the great value of that brooch with its big emeralds. Perhaps Bessie did not quite believe that it was worth pounds and pounds and pounds. Still, it was hers, and that made it important.

As the girls came round the school buildings, to the kitchen gardens, they had a view of considerable stretches of cabbages, beans, and potato plants, with Mr. Potts at work in the distance, doing some early hoeing. But Mr. Potts was a good way from the shed, and did not even look round; and Marjorie lifted the latch, and they all entered the shed.

All sorts of gardening implements were stacked in the shed, as well as an assortment of vegetables. But the space under the little window was clear, and upon that spot, six pairs of eyes fixed, in search of the lost brooch.

Bessie had no doubt that it must have dropped off while she was wriggling in the window, and it seemed quite probable. But six pairs of eyes, aided by one pair of spectacles, failed to discern it anywhere on the brick floor.

For several minutes the schoolgirls searched, till every available inch of floor had been scanned. But there was no glimmer of rolled gold and green glass to reward them. The brooch was not to be seen.

"No luck, Fatima!" said Babs.

"It's a goner, old dear," said Clara.

"That tramp must have had it!" exclaimed Bessie.

"What tramp?"

"Oh, really, Clara! You know there was a tramp in the shed last night, when I came to look for the brooch——."

"I know there wasn't," said Clara.

"Well, there was!" said Bessie, positively. "He must have had it! He must have come in to pinch something, and if he found a valuable brooch, of course he would pinch it. He had it! Shall I ask Miss Bellew to telephone to the police station, Marjorie?"

"Oh, my summer bonnet!" ejaculated Clara. "I can see the Bellew phoning up the police to look for an imaginary tramp and a brooch out of a Christmas cracker——."

"Ha, ha, ha!"

"It wasn't out of a Christmas cracker!" shrieked Bessie. "And my Uncle Carter gave at least ten pounds for it."

"Then they did him out of nine pounds nineteen and six!" said Clara.

"Don't be a cat, Clara Trevlyn! I'm not going to lose that brooch to please you!" hooted Bessie Bunter.

" I shall go and ask Miss Bellew to phone up the police station. I know that tramp had it."

" But, my dear Bessie——! " said Marjorie.

" Don't you be a cat like Clara, Marjorie. I know there was a tramp here, or else a burglar, because I walked into him, in the dark. Who could it have been if it wasn't a tramp or a burglar? "

" There wasn't anybody," said Dolly Jobling. " You were frightened in the dark, you little fat goose, and that's all."

" So would you be frightened if you walked into a bamp—I mean a trurglar—I mean a tramp or a burglar——."

" Ha, ha, ha! "

" Well, if the tramp had it, he's gone off with it," yawned Clara. " May have sold it by this time and bought a car with the loot——."

" Ha, ha, ha! "

" Anyhow, he's not here now," said Clara. " Not much use us being here either. Coming, Marjorie? "

" Well, we can't do anything more," said Marjorie. " We can't find the brooch——."

She was suddenly interrupted by an exclamation from Clara.

" What's that? What the dickens is that, in the loft? " Clara stared up, with startled eyes, at the wooden ceiling of the shed.

All the girls stared upward at the same moment. There was a sound from the loft above the gardener's shed, as if something had stirred there. It was quite startling.

That loft, so far as the schoolgirls knew, contained nothing but some old boxes and sacks, as the time had not yet come for storing apples. Mr. Potts, certainly, was not there, as they had seen him at a distance with his hoe.

Bessie Bunter gave a scream.

" Ooooooh! He's still here—that tramp! He's in the loft! He's got my brooch, and he's in the loft! Oooooh! "

" Nonsense," said Marjorie.

" Bosh! " said Clara.   " It did sound like somebody, but——."

" Listen! " said Mabs.

All the girls listened, but there was no repetition of the sound.   Mabel made a step towards the ladder in the corner.   But she stopped.

" Can't be anybody there," she said.

" Of course there can't," said Babs.

" Must have been a rat, I think," said Marjorie. " But it did sound like somebody moving in the loft, for a moment."

" I say, you girls——."

" Nobody's there, Bessie," said Marjorie, soothingly.

Clara whistled—a boyish way she had.

" I say, suppose a tramp did dodge in, after dark, looking for a night's lodging," she said.   " It's possible. Bessie thinks she ran into somebody——."

" I didn't think! " howled Bessie.

" My mistake," said Clara.   " I know you never think, old dear.   Bessie fancies she ran into somebody. Well, it might possibly have happened, although Bessie says it did."

Marjorie laughed.

" It's all nonsense, Clara.   A tramp wouldn't have the nerve to climb over the wall, and camp out for the night in this shed.   It was only Bessie's fancy——."

" Minx! "

" Might as well look into the loft," said Clara. " Who's going up that ladder to look into the loft? "

" Echo answers, ' who '! " said Mabs.   " If there's a tramp there, I don't want to walk into him as Bessie did— if she did! "

" I say, you girls, let's call Potts——."

" He would think us a lot of silly geese, calling him here for nothing," said Marjorie.   " There cannot be anybody in the loft.   I'll look, if you like."

Marjorie crossed to the ladder in the corner.

" I—I say, though," said Clara. " If there should be somebody——."

" There isn't," said Marjorie. " I'll just look."

She mounted the ladder clamped to the wall in the corner, till her fair head almost touched the trap-door that gave access to the loft. Babs and Mabs, Clara and Dolly and Bessie watched her, all feeling a little excited. It seemed highly improbable, but there was perhaps a chance that some wandering tramp had sought a night's lodging in the precincts of Cliff House School, and that Bessie's strange tale of what had happened in the shed was not wholly unfounded.

Marjorie put a hand to the trap-door, and pushed it up. It rose under the push, and leaned back against a beam.

Mounting the steps further, she put her head through the opening, and glanced round the dusky loft.

It was very dusky indeed, as it had no window, though gleams of sunlight came in here and there through small interstices. Marjorie was very watchful, prepared to beat a prompt retreat, if she spotted some Weary Willy or Tired Tim in the loft.

But no such tattered figure met her gaze. There were several boxes, a pile of sacks, and several old packing-cases which Potts had parked there out of the way. Unless somebody was hidden out of sight behind them, there was no one in the loft.

" See anybody, Marjorie? " called out Clara.

" No! Not even a rat," called back Marjorie. " I'll look round while I'm up here, but of course there's nobody."

She stepped from the ladder to the plank floor of the loft. There she was out of sight of the girls gazing up from below. She was not feeling the slightest trepidation, being quite assured that there was no one in the loft. But as she stepped along towards the packing-cases, she gave a sudden start, and the blood thrilled to her heart. From the dusky corner behind the packing-cases came a sound —the undoubted sound of a movement; and Marjorie catching her breath, realised that someone was there.

She stood, startled, too startled to stir. And as she stood, a head rose above the packing-cases, and a face, as white as chalk, looked at her—and Marjorie Hazeldene, with starting eyes, gazed at her brother, Hazel of the Greyfriars Remove.

CHAPTER XII

A SECRET TO KEEP!

MARJORIE stood dumb.

It was Hazel.

She could scarcely believe her eyes. But it was Hazel, staring at her white-faced from the dusk of the apple-loft.

If she had been thinking about Hazel, she would have supposed that he was at his school, waiting with the others for the bell to ring for classes. And he was here—here, hidden in the loft over the gardener's shed, peering at her from the dusk with scared eyes.

She could not speak or stir. She could only gaze at that startling apparition, overwhelmed.

But her thoughts raced. She had had a vague uneasiness, the previous day, that the wayward junior might be in some trouble again. Now she knew that he was in trouble—more seriously and terribly than she could ever have surmised or dreamed. Something had happened—something terrible—he was not at his school, he was here—in hiding! Hiding—from what?

It was only a matter of moments, but it seemed an age to Marjorie that they stood, their eyes fixed upon one another, in silence.

The silence was broken by the voice of Clara Trevlyn, calling from below.

" Found anybody, Marjorie? "

Then there was a laugh from Babs.

" If there's a tramp up there, Marjorie, chuck him down, and we'll catch him as he comes."

" I say, you girls, he may be there, you know. I know that he had my brooch——."

"If he had your brooch, Fatima, he wouldn't hang about here with it—he would rush off at once and sell it for a thousand pounds."

"Ha, ha, ha!"

Marjorie panted. The careless voices and laughter from below, contrasted strangely with the scene in the loft above—the white, scared face staring at her from the dusky corner. Her heart beat painfully.

As her lips moved to speak, Hazel leaned over the packing-case behind which he had crouched and hidden, making signs to her to be silent. He dared not speak, lest his voice should be heard below—but Marjorie understood, and was silent too. He was in hiding—why, she could not begin to guess, except that something terrible must have happened, and he was in terror of being discovered. One word reaching the schoolgirls below, and the discovery would have been made.

"Are you going to produce that tramp, Marjorie?" Clara called up the ladder from the shed.

Marjorie made a reassuring sign to Hazel, and turned towards the opening in the floor. She tried to make her voice casual as she answered Clara.

"There's no tramp here, Clara, of course."

"Well, I didn't think you'd really make a catch," said Clara. "Nothing but a spider or two, anyhow. Shall I come up?"

"Oh!" Marjorie gasped. "No!"

"I say, Marjorie." It was a fat squeak. "Have you looked all over the place? He might be hiding, you know. I say, Babs, you go up and see."

"You go up and see, Fatima!"

"Fatima couldn't—not without a steam crane!"

"Ha, ha, ha!"

"I'm coming up, Marjorie," called out Clara, and she began to mount the ladder.

Marjorie caught her breath.

She made an almost frantic sign to Hazel.   The Grey-friars junior ducked down and disappeared from sight behind the packing-cases.

What she could do, what she should do, in those strange and startling circumstances, Marjorie simply did not know. But she knew, at least, that she could not betray the wretched fellow who was in hiding there. Whatever he had done—and she knew, only too surely, that he must have done something—he was her brother, and in his fear he was appealing to her for help. It could only be for her help that he had come to Cliff House at all—he could have found other hiding places, if that had been all he wanted. Often enough, when his weakness or folly had landed him in trouble, he had come to Marjorie for help, and her quiet calmness and steadiness had helped him.   Now, in some unimaginable disaster that had befallen him, it was her help he wanted—and her only thought was to help him— to save him, though from what, she did not know.

Clara's golden head rose into the loft, and her blue eyes danced round its dusky recesses.

" Nobody at home! " she said.

Marjorie's heart was like lead.   She had to keep Clara out of the loft—the most casual search would have revealed the wretched schoolboy hiding and trembling in the corner behind the packing-cases.

" No tramps—no burglars, Clara." She tried to speak lightly.   " Let's go down."

" You've looked round? "

" Yes, I've looked round. Let's go down—Potts wouldn't like us up in his loft, if he came in."

" And Bellew would bark, if she saw us scrambling about here," chuckled Clara.   " But it did sound as if somebody moved, up here, all the same.   You're looking as pale as a sheet, Marjorie—were you afraid that there might be a tramp up here after all? "

" Oh! No! I knew there wasn't, or I wouldn't have

come up. But let's go down now—there are no tramps, but there are spiders.''

'' Ooooooh! '' said Clara. And to Marjorie's immense relief, she descended the ladder.

Marjorie gladly followed her. She had to see Hazel again, to learn what had happened, what he wanted, and how she could help him. But that had to wait. For the moment, the urgent thing was to get everybody away from the gardener's shed, and prevent the possibility of a chance discovery.

It was a relief to close down the trap over her head. She breathed quickly as she descended, and stepped off the ladder.

Babs and Mabs were already strolling out of the shed. Dolly Jobling was waiting in the doorway for her friends. Bessie Bunter blinked anxiously at Marjorie through her spectacles.

'' Sure there was nobody there? '' she asked.

Marjorie coloured. She could not answer that question directly. The more talkative Clara saved her the trouble.

'' That tramp's one of the has-beens—if he isn't one of the never-was's,'' she said. '' Ten to one he's chartered a plane before this, to get your brooch out of the country—it will make him rich for life in South America.''

'' Cat! '' howled Bessie.

'' Come on, Marjorie.'' Clara caught her friend's arm, and marched her out of the shed. '' If Fatima wants to root about any more, let her root. The bell will be going soon.''

Marjorie stopped at the doorway, in spite of Clara's pull on her arm. She did not want to leave Bessie Bunter in the shed. Certainly it was unlikely that Bessie would attempt to carry her considerable weight up an almost perpendicular ladder. Neither was she likely to penetrate into any spot where she had the faintest idea that there might be a tramp. But Marjorie was in fear of even unlikely contingencies.

" Come on, Bessie," she called.

" I say, you girls, let's have another look round for my brooch. If the tramp never had it, it must be lying about."

" We've looked everywhere——."

" Well, now let's look everywhere else," yapped Bessie. " If that valuable brooch belonged to you, you wouldn't want it to be lost."

" I'll give you the next one I get out of a cracker! " said Clara.

" Minx! "

" Well, I'm going," said Clara. " Come on, Marjorie, I tell you."

" Do come, Bessie," urged Marjorie.

" Shan't! "

" I've got some toffee in my study."

" Oh! " Bessie Bunter gave a last blink round. After all, the search had been thorough, and it was improbable that the brooch was lying about the shed. And toffee was toffee! Bessie rolled out.

Marjorie shut the door, and fastened the latch. She gave an uneasy glance at Mr. Potts, still hoeing industriously in the distance, quite unconscious of the attraction his shed had had for half-a-dozen girls of the Cliff House Fourth that morning. Potts came to that shed three or four times a day, at least, and Hazel was hidden in the loft over it! But Potts was unlikely to hoist his ancient joints up the ladder to the loft unnecessarily, and he had no use for the loft at the present time. Anyhow that chance had to be taken—there was nothing that Marjorie could do about it.

She walked away with her friends, her face as calm and composed as she could make it, but her heart beating unpleasantly. The first and most urgent thing was to keep Hazel's secret, and she had contrived that, so far. From whatever it was that he had fled, he was safe for the moment. But what was it—what had happened—what

could have happened—what dreadful tidings was she to
hear from him? It was not easy to keep up an aspect of
unconcern, with that weight on her mind and her heart.

" Penny for 'em! " said Clara, suddenly, when they
were in the quad, among a crowd of other girls.

Marjorie started, realising that she had not spoken a
word since leaving the gardener's shed. Both Clara and
Dolly were glancing at her curiously.

" Oh! What? " she stammered.

" Penny for your thoughts," explained Clara. " Or
as they seem so jolly deep, I'll make it three ha'pence.
Is it a go? "

Marjorie tried to laugh.

" But I know what you're thinking about," added
Clara, with a sniff.

" Clara! What do you mean? What——? "

" That precious brother of yours," said Clara.

Marjorie's heart almost ceased to beat.

" He didn't come over yesterday, so you think his bad
old beak has been keeping him in, or something." Another
sniff. " As he never does anything wrong himself, it must
be his beak's fault."

" Clara! "

" Let's go in and ask Bellew to let us use her phone,"
went on Clara.

" What for? " asked Dolly Jobling.

" To phone up Mr. Quelch at Greyfriars, and tell him
to be more careful with Marjorie's brother, because he's
such an angel that it's very wrong and wicked to keep him
in on a half-holiday."

Dolly trilled with merriment.

" Oh, Clara! " said Marjorie, reproachfully.

Bessie Bunter tugged at Marjorie's sleeve.

" Look here, Marjorie——."

" Oh, don't bother, Bessie! " exclaimed Marjorie, for
once impatient with the fat junior. She really had enough
to bear, just then, without Elizabeth Bunter added.

" Well, I like that! " exclaimed Bessie, indignantly. " You said you had some toffee in your study. If you didn't mean that you were going to give me some——."

" Oh! " Marjorie had forgotten the magnet with which she had drawn Bessie out of the gardener's shed. " Oh! Yes! I'll get it for you, Bessie." She went into the House, rather glad to get away from her friends for a time.

Bessie Bunter promptly followed her in. Bessie was anxious about that toffee. Clara and Dolly exchanged an eloquent look.

" That twerp——! " said Clara, with a deep breath. " I knew Marjorie was worrying about that twerp."

" Don't let Marjorie hear you calling him a twerp! " murmured Dolly.

" I wouldn't! But—I hope the trouble is that Quelch has whacked him," said Clara, quite viciously. " I jolly well hope that Quelch has whacked him, and whacked him jolly hard, so there! "

Bessie Bunter emerged from the House with a red cheek bulging. But Marjorie's chums did not see her again till the bell was ringing, and she joined the Fourth Form crowd heading for the form-room.

CHAPTER XIII

TROUBLE IN THE FORM-ROOM

Miss Bellew frowned.

It was but seldom that frowns came Marjorie's way. She was careful in class, as in other things; and always attentive. She was not, perhaps, so brilliant as Barbara, who seemed to learn without effort, and to be able to dash off a Latin paper almost without looking at it. But the form-mistress of the Fourth was always satisfied with her, or almost always—and that, possibly, added to Miss Bellew's annoyance on this particular morning, when one of her best pupils seemed to have suddenly become one of her worst.

From Bessie Bunter, Miss Bellew expected obtuseness and made allowances for the same. From Clara Trevlyn she expected a happy mixture of cleverness and careless-ness. From Barbara Redfern, brilliance with an occasional lapse into thoughtlessness—from Dolly Jobling, a plump slowness—from Mabel Lynn, just as much work as Mabs thought would do. From all her girls, in fact, Miss Bellew knew what to expect. But this morning she had the unexpected from Marjorie Hazeldene.

Twice she spoke to her without even receiving a look in reply, and at the third time of asking, Marjorie coloured, and stammered, " Yes, Miss Bellew." And as Miss Bellew's third remark had been, " Have you become deaf, Marjorie? " such a reply was plain evidence that Marjorie's thoughts were wandering.

So it was no wonder that Miss Bellew frowned, while the whole Form stared, and Bessie Bunter giggled.

" Marjorie! " rapped Miss Bellew. " What do you mean? "

Marjorie's face, already pink, became crimson. She

had caught her name without catching the question: her thoughts had been, not in the Fourth-form room, but in the apple-loft with a frightened hidden schoolboy. She realised that she had blundered somehow.

" I—I mean——! " she stammered. " I—I——."

" So you have become deaf? " asked Miss Bellew, with sarcasm. Bellew could be quite sharply sarcastic at times: though Marjorie Hazeldene seldom had the benefit of it.

" Oh! No! " Marjorie was giving attention now. " Not at all, Miss Bellew."

" Then why did you answer in the affirmative when I asked you if you had become deaf? "

" Oh! " gasped Marjorie. " Did—did I? I—I mean ——I never meant——."

" You mean that you did not hear when I asked you? "

" Oh! Yes! "

" You are thinking of other matters," suggested Miss Bellew. " Something much more important, perhaps, than such a trivial thing as attending to instruction from your form-mistress? "

" Oh! Yes! I—I mean no," gasped Marjorie. " I—I am sorry, Miss Bellew——I—I was not giving attention."

" I am aware of that, Marjorie. May I suggest," went on the sarcastic Bellew, " that you should endeavour to give a little attention while in the form-room? It makes things so much easier."

Poor Marjorie's face was burning by that time. Bellew seldom or never " ragged " her in class, and it was a new and painful experience. Marcia Loftus winked at Freda Foote. Marcia often had the sarcastic edge of Bellew's tongue—and deserved it. Now she was rather pleased to see Marjorie getting it for once. But most of the girls were sympathetic, only wondering what was the matter with the usually circumspect Marjorie.

" I—I—Oh! Yes! Certainly, Miss Bellew," murmured Marjorie. " I—I—I am very sorry I—I was not listening."

Miss Bellew seemed satisfied with that—perhaps having enjoyed her own sarcasm—and the lesson went on—Marjorie endeavouring, as Bellew had so sarcastically suggested, to give a little attention.

But it was not easy.

In spite of herself, in spite of her strong desire not to draw anyone's attention to her distress of mind, she simply could not help her thoughts wandering to the apple-loft. Her brother was there, in hiding—from what was he hiding? What had he done? What dreadful calamity had happened at Greyfriars? Hazel was weak in character, over-sensitive and sulky: he could not face up to punishment like such a fellow as Bob Cherry, for instance. But this could not be an ordinary case of some punishment that daunted him—he was weak and wilful, but he could not be so weak and wilful as to run away from school to escape a caning, or even a flogging. It was something more serious than that—something much worse than that. What had he done?

She had to know—she had to see Hazel, and hear what he had to tell her. She had to know how she could help him.

But there were endless difficulties in the way of even that. Potts might be about the shed any time during the day, and Potts must not be allowed to have the faintest suspicion that anyone was hidden in the apple-loft. She would have to find some time when the gardener was not about. Even so, she would have to elude Clare and Dolly; and they, not having the faintest idea that they were being eluded, would not be easy to elude.

She had a secret to keep, and it was not easy for a frank girl like Marjorie to keep secrets.

Another thought, too, had come into her mind—Hazel must have been all night in the apple-loft. It was plain enough that Hazel's was the unseen figure into which Bessie Bunter had walked in the dark—it had not been imagination, after all, on Bessie's part—Hazel must have been

there. Bessie had almost discovered him, before he had
hidden himself in the loft—had the fatuous fat junior had a
light, she would infallibly have discovered him. He must
have spent the night sleeping on the sacks in the loft; and
—he must be hungry. Perhaps that was partly why he
looked so white and wretched. And when that thought
came into Marjorie's mind, she realised that it was not
merely a matter of keeping the secret—she had to get food
to him somehow. If he remained in hiding he must eat.
And yet—he could not remain in hiding—how could he?
And why—why—why was he in hiding at all?

It seemed to the poor girl that her head must turn
round, as she tried to think it out.   No wonder Miss
Bellew's voice came to her like a distant drone that was
merely faintly irritating.

That distant drone suddenly became near and emphatic.
Marjorie became aware that her thoughts had gone hopelessly wandering again, and that Miss Bellew was speaking
to her.

" Marjorie! Have you fallen asleep in class? "

This time Marjorie did not answer " Yes, Miss Bellew "
without stopping to think. She tried to collect her scattered
thoughts.

" I—I—I——No, Miss Bellew," she stammered.

" You are merely bored? " asked Miss Bellew, with
almost ferocious sarcasm.

" Oh! No! "

" Well, if you are neither asleep nor bored, perhaps
you will construe, as I have already told you twice to do."

" Oh! " gasped Marjorie. " Yes, Miss Bellew." She
stared almost blankly at her book.   Eutropius was not
really a difficult author, but just then, as Marjorie stared
at the page, he might have been as full of snags as Livy.
The lesson had been prepared, and Marjorie was always
careful in prep; but now the Latin page seemed to have
lost any meaning it might have had when she had tackled
it in prep.

" I am waiting! " said Miss Bellew, ominously.

" Yes, Miss Bellew. I—I——."

" Have you lost your place? "

" Yes," said Marjorie, desperately.

" You have not been following the lesson? "

It was not to be denied. Marjorie certainly hadn't been following the lesson; she had forgotten the existence of Eutropius, almost forgotten that she was in the form-room at all. She could only stammer.

" You will show Marjorie the place, Clara."

Clara gave her chum an anxious look. She could not guess what was the matter with Marjorie that morning.

" Pull up your socks, old girl," she whispered. " Go on from ' Dum bellum in Numidia contra Jugurtham geritur——.' "

Marjorie stammered.

" While the war in Numidia——! " whispered Clara, greatly daring. It was not safe to whisper tips under the eagle eye of the Bellew.

" Clara! " came a sharp rap.

" Oh! Yes, Miss Bellew! " moaned Clara.

" Are you giving Marjorie the translation? "

" I—I—I——just a word or two, Miss Bellew——."

" Take fifty lines, Clara."

" Oh! Yes, Miss Bellew."

" Marjorie! Perhaps you will have the excessive kindness to construe, and not waste further the time of the class," suggested Miss Bellew—all sarcasm now from top to toe.

Marjorie stammered over a passage that would hardly have bothered Bessie Bunter. The poor girl felt more like crying than construing, but she would not let the tears come to her eyes.

Miss Bellew interrupted, with a rap as sharp as a postman's knock.

" That will do, Marjorie! You will stay in after the hour and write out the lesson."

5

Marjorie almost fell on her form in dismay. After third hour was her chance to see Hazel, if Potts had gone to his lunch.

" Oh, Miss Bellew! " she gasped.

The dismay in her face touched Miss Bellew. She was a kind-hearted woman; though she had polished her weapons of sarcasm so long, at the expense of the Fourth, that she really could not refrain from using them. She said no more, and turned to Gwendoline Cook for " con."

But when the hour was up—they still called it an hour at Cliff House from ancient usage, though it lasted only forty minutes—and the girls filed out, Marjorie remaining miserably behind, Miss Bellew gave her a not unkindly glance.

" Marjorie! "

" Yes, Miss Bellew," said Marjorie, heavily.

" You may go! "

" Oh! " Marjorie brightened. " Thank you, Miss Bellew. I—I am so sorry that I was inattentive, Miss Bellew."

" Well, well, we will forget all about it," said Miss Bellew, quite graciously; and Marjorie, in great relief, followed the other girls from the form-room.

CHAPTER XIV

WHAT HAPPENED TO HAZEL

" Seedy? " asked Clara.

" No—no."

" Then what's the matter? "

" N-nothing."

" Rot! " said Miss Clara, decisively. " You've been a perfect idiot in class this morning. Bessie was quite bright compared with you. Why did you muddle up your arithmetic in first hour? "

" Did I? "

" Did you? " said Clara. " Did she, Dolly? "

Dolly Jobling giggled.

" You couldn't have told the Sharper how many beans make five, if she'd asked you," said Clara. " And in second hour, what did you mean by telling Moce that the Spanish Armada blew in in 1688? "

" I—I meant 1588," stammered Marjorie.

" And then going to sleep in third hour——.''

" I didn't go to sleep," protested Marjorie.

" You might as well have, for all the sense that the Bellew could get out of you. You can construe Eutropius on the back of your neck, if you like. Why did you get the Bellew's rag out? "

Marjorie was silent.

Her two friends were concerned about her. They just could not make Marjorie out that morning. One of the brightest girls in the Fourth seemed to be bent on contesting Bessie Bunter's distinction of being the dunce of the form. It was really hard to understand.

" You've been in a maze ever since we went to Potts' shed this morning," continued Clara. " Hasn't she, Dolly? "

" She has! " agreed Dolly.

" I say, you girls——! " It was a fat squeak.

" Oh, run away and play, Bessie! " exclaimed Clara, exasperated. " Look here, Babs and Mabs room with you—go and bother Babs and Mabs."

" I've asked Babs and Mabs, and they won't listen to a word about my brooch,". said Bessie Bunter, indignantly. " They just ran away when I said ' brooch '——."

" Good idea," said Clara. " Let's do the same, you two! Come on, Marjorie! Come on, Dolly! Luckily, Bessie can't run! "

And Clara and Dolly scampered off, laughing. Marjorie made a step to follow, and then stopped. Certainly, she was as tired as any other girl at Cliff House of the subject of Bessie's lost brooch. But it came into her mind that this was an opportunity to get to the gardener's shed without exciting attention and comment. In the circumstances, Bessie's absurd brooch was something in the nature of a windfall.

" I'll have another look for it, if you like, Bessie," she said. " I'll go round to the shed again now. You sit down and wait for me."

Nothing could have suited Bessie Bunter better. She wanted that brooch hunted for, but her disinclination for personal exertion was very strong. To sit on a bench under a shady tree, while another girl looked for the lost brooch, seemed to Bessie a very sound idea.

" Mind you look everywhere," was her parting injunction, as she deposited her weight on the bench, and Marjorie departed.

There was nobody near the gardener's shed when Marjorie arrived there. Mr. Potts had gone to his lunch, and the coast was clear for some time to come.

Marjorie went into the shed, with beating heart.

But she did not immediately approach the ladder in the corner. She had told Bessie that she would look for the brooch, and she did so, carefully and conscientiously.

As there had been quite a thorough search already, the missing article was not likely to be found. But there was a possibility that it had fallen somewhere out of sight, if a remote one; and Marjorie hunted industriously among potato-sacks and agricultural implements. She would have been quite glad to find the wretched thing, to please Bessie, and to hear the last of it. But it was not to be found: and having satisfied her conscience by making quite an extensive search, she went to the ladder, at last, and mounted the steps.

Her heart beat painfully as she lifted the trap.

All was silent. Hazel, no doubt, had heard all that had been said in the shed early that morning, and realised the peril of making a sound, when anyone was below. But Marjorie, as she peered into the dusky loft, wondered whether he was still there, or whether, perhaps, he was gone.

Standing on the ladder, with her head in the loft, she whipered:

" Hazel! "

Then there was a movement. Hazel was still there. His head rose into view over the packing-cases. Evidently he had dodged into that recess, when he heard movements in the shed, fearful of someone coming up the ladder.

" Marjorie! " he breathed.

Marjorie stepped into the loft, and shut down the trap. Hazel came out of his hiding-place. His untidy, unkempt look, the miserable pallor in his almost effeminately good-looking face, touched Marjorie's heart with a pang. Hazel was always neat and clean, even a little dandyish. Now he looked a good deal like a tramp.

" Hazel! Now tell me——."

He interrupted her.

" Yes, yes! But—have you got anything to eat? " His voice was husky. " I—I'm famished! I've never been so hungry, Marjorie."

" Yes, I thought of that," whispered Marjorie.
" Here! " She opened her little bag, and Hazel almost
snatched at biscuits, a sandwich, and a bar of chocolate.
" That was all I could manage—but later——."

He did not even hear her. He was devouring the food
like a hungry animal. She waited in silence till he had
finished.

" That's better," said Hazel, at last. He sat down on
a box. " That makes a fellow feel better. I—I say, nobody knows I'm here? "

" Nobody."

" Those silly chattering girls don't suspect anything? "

Marjorie set her lips a little. That was Hazel's des-
cription of her friends in the Cliff House Fourth. Girls
did not amount to much in Hazel's valuable estimation.
That he was there, helpless, to seek help from a girl,
made no difference to that.

" Nobody has any idea that you are here, Hazel,"
said Marjorie, quietly. " That is all right—so far, at
least."

" For goodness sake, keep it dark," muttered Hazel.
" If I'm found, I shall be sent back to Greyfriars. I can't
go."

" But——! " said Marjorie.

" I don't know what to do! " There was almost a
wail in his voice. " I'm up against it, Marjorie. I had
to get away——had to! I—I thought of you, of course
——I wanted to see you——but I couldn't come up to the
school, you see——I had to hang about——and then I
remembered this shed, and dodged in over the wall after
dark, and got here. And then——." He shivered.
" Some fool barged in, in the dark, and ran into me——
some fool of a girl who ran off screaming——I was afraid
that it was all up——."

" It was Bessie—she came to look for something——."

" That ass Bunter's sister? Did she expect to find
anything in the dark? "

" She forgot a light——."

" Yes, that's like Bunter," sneered Hazel. " The sort of thing that fat ass would do. Silly idiocy runs in the family, I suppose. Still, it's jolly lucky she hadn't a light —she would have seen me. I dodged up into the loft— and afterwards, I heard somebody rummaging about the shed——."

" That was Miss Bullivant. Bessie thought it was a tramp, so Miss Bullivant came to look——."

" That old sketch! I was afraid every minute whoever it was might come up the ladder. But it was all right. Oh, Marjorie, I had to sleep last night on that heap of sacks! I hardly slept a wink. I—I wondered and wondered how I could get word to you——and I couldn't think of a way——not without showing up. And then I heard a lot of silly chatter down there, early this morning——."

Hazel broke off.

" But I haven't told you what's happened. Marjorie, I don't know what to do. I've been in rows before— things have always been against me, somehow—I get into rows when other fellows don't. Some fellows are lucky. Wharton or Bob Cherry would never land in a scrape like this."

Marjorie was too tactful to point out that Wharton or Bob Cherry would not be likely to do whatever it was that had landed Hazel in this scrape.

"Look at Smithy," went on Hazel, bitterly. " Why, Smithy's a regular blackguard—but they never nail him. He can look after himself. And then Quelch jumps on me because I had a bet with a man in the Fourth——."

" A bet! It is betting then——" faltered Marjorie.

" No! No! That was only the beginning! It was what happened afterwards." Hazel paused, and cocked his ear to listen, like a hunted animal. " I say, is anybody likely to come to this shed? If they heard us talking——."

"Speak low," said Marjorie. "But nobody's likely to come just now—Potts will be at his lunch. Tell me, Hazel—tell me what it was you did."

"That's just like a girl, isn't it?" said Hazel, resentfully. "You think at once that I've done something—as if a fellow never had injustice."

"Do you mean that you have done nothing?" asked Marjorie, blankly.

"Nothing at all—at least, not what they think. I don't know anything at all about a registered letter in Quelch's study——never set eyes on it——I don't believe it was on his table at all, or I should have noticed it while I was kicking my heels in his study for nearly an hour—— more than half an hour, anyway——but—but—but——." Hazel's voice became a husky whisper. "Quelch said it was gone, and he asked me——and—and they believe——."

Marjorie's face was white.

She had wondered and wondered: but never in her worst fear, had she thought of anything so bad as this.

"Hazel! A registered letter——."

"Yes," breathed Hazel.

"With money in it?"

"Quelch said there was money in it."

"It is missing?"

"So Quelch said."

"You were in his study?"

"I couldn't help that! He sent me there, and told me to wait for him—how could I help being in his study——?"

"But you were?"

"I've told you I was."

"And—and nobody else——?"

"Not that anybody knows of. I wish I'd waited now till he came in—but—I didn't. He couldn't have said it was me, if I'd been there when he came in. Only——I wasn't. And—and when he questioned me, I—I got scared, and said I hadn't been there——."

" Hazel! "

" And—and he found out for certain that I had, and so——."

" Hazel! "

" Don't look at me like that, Marjorie! Do you believe that I touched the rotten thing? " Hazel's voice was shrill. "Oh, good heavens, no wonder they believe it, if my own sister does."

" No! No! No! " Marjorie panted. " No! No! But—but it was madness to run away——to hide——anything was better than that——."

" I had to." Hazel spoke in a husky whisper. " It—it—it was the police, Marjorie. I—I dared not wait for that! "

CHAPTER XV

BROTHER AND SISTER

MARJORIE HAZELDENE leaned on the wall of the apple-loft, with a feeling that all the strength had gone out of her. Her face was as white as chalk, her eyes dilated. She could only gaze at her brother, overcome with horror and dismay. Her worst fears could never have envisaged anything like this. For a long minute, she was too utterly overwhelmed to speak.

Hazel watched her anxiously, almost furtively. He was not thinking of the distress he was causing her. He wanted her to believe in him—to help him somehow. Instinctively the weak character leaned on the strong. If anybody could help him, Marjorie could. She would try, at any rate—nobody else would even try. Nobody cared for a fellow who was down and out!

She found her voice at last.

" Hazel! I can't understand all this—tell me what's happened, from the beginning. There's some dreadful mistake—it can be put right! "

" Yes, there's a mistake," muttered Hazel. " That old fool Quelch——."

" Mr. Quelch is not a fool, Hazel. And he is a just man. He is a wise man and a just man," said Marjorie, sharply. " He must have some reason—what seems to him a good reason——tell me how it happened."

" It was that fathead Cherry's fault in the first place——."

" Bob Cherry! What had Bob to do with it? "

" Oh, I mustn't call him a fathead to you, I suppose—

you think a lot of the lumbering ass——," muttered
Hazel. " More than you do of me, I daresay."

" What had Bob to do with it? "

" Oh! Nothing! Only he came up to speak to me, and
neither of us knew that Quelch was in hearing——."

" It could do no harm if Bob spoke to you in Mr.
Quelch's hearing. Bob would never say anything that
anyone might not hear."

" Oh, I know that," said Hazel, irritably. " But that
did it, all the same, because I asked him to lend me a
pound, to settle a bet with a man in the Fourth, and
Quelch heard me——."

" Is that what you call Bob Cherry's fault? "

" Oh, don't jaw a fellow, for goodness sake. Haven't
I got it bad enough already? That started it, because
Quelch went off at the deep end, and ordered me to his
study, to wait for him to come in——."

" And you waited? "

" I waited over half-an-hour," said Hazel, sullenly.
" I wasn't going to wait longer than that, Quelch or no
Quelch. Why should I, on a half-holiday? "

" You left the study before Mr. Quelch came in,
then? "

" Yes, I did! I knew I was due for six, anyway. I
don't see why a fellow should wait about for it."

" You should have waited for him, Hazel. Any form-
master would be angry at such disobedience."

" Oh, I know that! If I'd known what was coming,
I'd have waited in the study, if he hadn't come in till roll,"
snapped Hazel. " But how could I know? I tell you I
never even saw a registered letter on his table. I don't
believe Quelch left it there, either."

" If he said he left it there, Hazel, he did leave it
there."

" Oh, take his side! Quelch can't make a mistake, and
I'm in the wrong. Go it! " sneered Hazel. " I'm always
in the wrong, of course."

" Tell me, what happened after that? "

" Quelch sent for me after tea.   Of course, I thought it was about that silly bet, what I'd said to Bob Cherry, with something extra for not waiting in his study as he told me. I never dreamed of anything else.   But—he had a face like a gargoyle.   Then I knew that something was up— something awfully serious—though I couldn't guess what. You believe me, Marjorie? "

" Yes, yes, yes—go on."

" He told me that a registered letter had been on his study table, ready for post—he had been going down to Friardale with it, it seems, when he'd got through a lot of Form papers.   He said it was not there when he came back to his study and, as I had been in his study waiting for him, he wanted to know if I knew anything about it."

" Did he suspect you? "

" Well, more or less, I think.   You see, he had heard me say that I owed money on a bet, and couldn't pay up, so he knew I was hard up.   Anyhow, he wanted to know, and I—I—I got scared——."

" What did you say? "

" What would any fellow say, when he was going to be suspected of pinching a registered letter? " muttered Hazel. " I knew that nobody had seen me coming to the study— everybody was out, on a half-holiday—not a soul about the place when I went there——and Quelch didn't know I'd waited, as I was gone before he came in, so I—I—I said I hadn't gone to the study at all."

Marjorie was silent.

" I—I know you wouldn't have, Marjorie," Hazel almost whimpered.   " But—but your old girls here are nothing like Quelch——his eyes were boring into me—— and—and I thought of going up to the Head and—and I lost my nerve——it seemed so jolly easy just to say that I hadn't been in the study at all, as—as nobody knew I had——and there was an end of it——see? "

" Did Mr. Quelch believe you? "

" I—I think he did! He ain't a suspicious man, like Hacker. He can take a fellow's word. He thought I was sulky and disobedient and hadn't obeyed his order to go to the study. But—but you know old Quelch——he's so jolly careful——he never lets anything slip. He told me to leave his study for the present, and I hoped it was all over, but—but——."

" But what then? "

" I—I suppose he began to make inquiries, anyhow it came out about Prout——! " muttered Hazel.

" Mr. Prout? "

" Yes—the Fifth Form beak. I'd forgotten that that old goat was in the passage, when I looked out to see whether Quelch was coming," groaned Hazel. " I—I hardly noticed him at the time, you see, and forgot all about him. But when Quelch started asking questions, Prout told him that he'd seen me there——and that put the lid on."

" Oh, Hazel! " breathed Marjorie.

She understood now, only too well. Like the weak and irresolute fellow he was, Hazel had landed himself in trouble by sheer wilfulness, lied as the easiest way out of it; and that lie had fastened suspicion on him, as nothing else could have done.

" Quelch sent for me again," Hazel mumbled on. " He told me that Prout had seen me in the study, and—and I had to own up that I'd been there. That settled it with Quelch. I could see in his face what he believed."

Marjorie sighed. Hazel spoke resentfully, but Marjorie, bitterly distressed and dismayed as she was, could see no cause for resentment. What Mr. Quelch believed, in the circumstances, was inevitable; he could hardly have believed anything else.

" And then? " asked Marjorie, quietly.

" Quelch asked me whether I had anything to confess.

I—I told him I'd done nothing——never even seen the rotten thing——and him standing there with a face like a gorgon. He let me run on——not believing a word of it, as I could see. At last he said——Oh, Marjorie! "

" What did he say? "

" He said that the registered letter had been taken, that it contained money, and that the pilferer had to be found. So—so—so it would be necessary to send for a police-officer from Courtfield."

Hazel's voice died away, huskily.

" That is quite natural, Hazel," said Marjorie. " Any-one might have taken the letter—someone must have taken it—and it would have to be investigated. If Mr. Quelch could not find out who had taken it, he would send for a police-officer as a matter of course."

" I—I know!   But—but don't you see——." Hazel groaned. " What's the policeman going to think, when he hears that I was in the study, and denied having been there, till it was found out that I had? "

" Oh, Hazel! If you had only told the truth——."

" What's the good of saying that now?   I was scared, and I'd forgotten all about that old goat Prout seeing me there.   I should have come off all right but for that. Anyhow, it's done."

" Yes, it's done," said Marjorie, heavily. " Do you know whether Mr. Quelch did send for the police-officer? "

" I don't know!   I—I suppose he did!   I know I wasn't going to wait, to feel a policeman's hand on my shoulder.   I cleared out as soon as I got away from Quelch."

" But—it's useless," said Marjorie. " They must be looking for you now. Hazel, you ought to go back to Greyfriars, and face it out——."

" Are you mad, Marjorie? " panted Hazel. " I've got to keep clear.   Why, I should be run in—put in a cell —are you mad? "

" It couldn't come to that. But you're making matters worse by running away and hiding. Don't you see that? " said Marjorie, earnestly. " Running away from it looks like guilt—what else can it look like? "

" I won't go back."

" But, dear Hazel——."

" You don't care, of course! You don't care what happens to me, so long as I don't worry you with it. I know! I was a fool to come here at all, I know that. I thought you might be able to help—to advise me what to do. And that's all you want—just to get rid of me." Hazel's voice broke, in a burst of self-pity, and the tears came into his eyes.

Marjorie hardly noticed, and did not heed, the ingratitude and injustice of her brother's words. She was only thinking of trying to help and comfort the wretched boy for whom her heart ached.

" Dear Hazel, what I advise is the sensible thing," she urged, earnestly. " There can be no proof that you did what you did not do—think of that. You are not really in danger, if you could only see it. But if you will not go back to your school——."

" I won't! I won't! "

" Then you must go home. Father will know what is best to be done——."

" Oh, you fool, you fool! That's the first place they'll look for me. I daren't go home! "

" But what can you do, Hazel? " exclaimed Marjorie.

" I don't know! I've got to get somewhere. I've got to hide till I can think of somewhere to go. I don't know."

" But you cannot——."

" I won't go back to school, and I won't go home! You can turn me out of here, if you like——go and tell all those chattering minxes that I'm here, and I shall be turned out fast enough. That's what you want, I suppose! "

Marjorie did not reply to that. The wretched boy was almost in hysterics, and it was futile to argue with him.

" I thought you might be able to help," muttered Hazel. " But you don't care——."

" Don't say that, Hazel! I shall help you all I can. I—I don't see what can be done, but I—I shall think it over——I'll do all I can. But——Oh! be quiet."

There were footsteps in the shed below.

Brother and sister remained perfectly still and silent. Someone had come into the gardener's shed—more than one. Marjorie was glad that she had closed the trap. A voice floated up.

" Still looking for that benighted brooch, Marjorie? Why, she's not here! Bessie said she came here to look for that idiotic brooch." It was Clara Trevlyn.

" Well, she's gone, if she did," came Dolly's voice.

" Well, where has she gone? Marjorie's jolly queer this morning—getting into rows in class, and now dodging her old pals. I wonder if she's still bothering her head about that twerp."

" If she is, I'd like to smack his head."

" So would I—hard! Come on, she's not here, anyhow."

The two girls were heard to leave the shed again. Marjorie did not stir till they were gone. Then she rose from the box on which she had been seated. Hazel caught her by the sleeve.

" Are you going? "

" They will be looking for me," whispered Marjorie. " I shall have to be very careful—if you stay here. I must get some food somehow, and bring it to you as soon as I get a chance."

" You'll get into a row if you're spotted." For once, Hazel seemed to have a glimmer of thought for some person other than himself. " I don't want to get you into a row with those old cats, Marjorie."

" I shall be careful," said Marjorie, quietly, " and—
and I will try to get some news from your school, Hazel
——it may not be so bad as you think——anyway I will
find out, and we shall see. Now I must go."

She lifted the edge of the trap, and peered down into
the shed. It was vacant: and she descended the ladder,
Hazel closing the trap after her. Her heart was like lead,
as she hurried away.

CHAPTER XVI

A FRIEND IN NEED

How she got through class in the afternoon, Marjorie
hardly knew. There was a French set, and her troubled
mind was more impenetrable to French grammar than it
had been to Latin in the morning. Her ramblings among
the irregular verbs caused the sharp tip of Mademoiselle
Lupin's nose to grow perfectly scarlet.

But it was over at last, and she was free.

Clara Trevlyn and Dolly Jobling linked arms with
her when they came out. The three chums of No. 7
Study were almost inseparable, which had always been very
pleasant—till now. Now Marjorie wanted almost feverishly
to be alone—but it was not easy to be alone in the Fourth
Form at Cliff House. Bessie Bunter, no doubt, could have
had all the solitude she wanted, if like the sages she had
found charms in the face of solitude—which she never did.
Marcia, with her sharp temper and acid tongue, would
have found it quite easy to be left alone. But it was not
easy for the most popular girl in the form, especially as
Clara was a little proprietary in her friendship, and plump
little Dolly a devoted ally who followed her almost like a
faithful dog.

It was an immense relief to the troubled girl when Babs
and Mabs, having " bagged " a court, claimed two of
them for tennis. The two claimed were Clara and Marjorie; but Marjorie pleaded that she did not feel up to it,
and passed it on to Dolly. Of which, fortunately, Clara
was pleased to approve.

" Marjorie's no good to-day," said Clara. " She's
been turning Mamselle's hair grey, and her nose red, in
the French set. She can't do a thing to-day. Come on,
Dolly."

98

Marjorie was alone—for a minute. Then a fat hand clutched her sleeve.

" You didn't find my brooch," squeaked Bessie Bunter.

" No! I looked everywhere."

" Well, you can't have looked everywhere, or you'd have found it," said Bessie, argumentatively.

" I don't think it's there at all, Bessie."

" It's no good telling me you don't think it's there, when I know it is. Are you going to look again? " inquired Bessie.

" Some other time——."

"You've got nothing to do now," said Bessie. " You're not playing tennis. Are you going to score for them? "

" N-no! But——."

" Then you've got nothing to do. Look here, come and look for my brooch again, and I'll help! " said Bessie, in a burst of generosity.

" I can't just now——."

" Why can't you, when you've got nothing to do? "

" Because I don't want to, Bessie! " said Marjorie, goaded; and she shook off a fat and somewhat sticky paw, and escaped from Elizabeth Bunter.

Bessie blinked after her in surprise through her large spectacles. She was surprised, and she was annoyed. Hitherto, Bessie had made an exception in Marjorie's favour in a form which, according to Bessie, consisted mainly of " cats." Now she was driven to the conclusion that Marjorie, after all, was a " cat " like the rest of the Fourth—and that she, Bessie Bunter, was the only really nice girl.

To which Marjorie was quite indifferent, for a few moments later she had quite forgotten the fat existence of Bessie Bunter.

She walked down to the gates, which stood open after class, until one of the innumerable bells of Cliff House should announce that it was time for Piper to shut them.

In the gateway were Gwendoline Cook and Katie Smith. It was just impossible for Marjorie to walk out unheeded.

" Going for a walk? " asked Gwendoline.

" Yes, I—I think so."

" We'll come! Come on, Katie! "

It was so natural for other girls to join up with Marjorie, that there was nothing she could say or do. She walked out between Gwendoline and Katie, down the lane towards the village of Friardale.

" Let's go on the cliffs," suggested Gwendoline.

" Yes, let's," assented Katie.

" You two go on the cliffs," said Marjorie, hopefully. " I have to go to Uncle Clegg's in Friardale."

" Oh, we'll come to Friardale, then," said Gwendoline. " We'll pick up something to take in for tea."

" Old Clegg has jolly good home-made jam! " remarked Katie.   " Better than we get at the school shop."

Marjorie walked on, silent between two care-free schoolgirls, chattering across her. She had to get food to take to the hidden fugitive in the apple-loft, but she did not want other eyes on her shopping at the village shop. And she had a hope of coming upon one of her friends in the Greyfriars Remove, from whom she would be able to learn more than Hazel had been able to tell her.

It was not—it could not be—so bad as Hazel feared. All that he had told her was coloured by his terrors. A few words with Harry Wharton, or Bob Cherry, or Frank Nugent, would at least enlighten her as to how matters actually stood. It was quite likely that one or another of them might be in the village after class, and a few words would be enough. But she did not want those few words to be uttered in the hearing of other ears from Cliff House.

But Gwendoline and Katie, quite unsuspicious of what was in her mind, had no idea of parting with her.

They arrived at the village shop together. As they stopped at the door, Gwendoline glanced at a figure on a bicycle in the distance, coming into the village street from the lane that led to Greyfriars School.

" That's Cherry," she said. " You know him, don't you, Marjorie? "

Marjorie caught her breath. It was exactly what she wanted—if she had been alone.

" Oh! Yes," she said. " He's a friend of my brother's." She looked at Bob, and saw him give a little start, as he caught sight of the three schoolgirls at the shop doorway. She saw, too, that he coloured, and that the bicycle slowed down. She could read in his honest, rugged face that he was wondering whether she knew about Hazel.

" Well, let's go in," said Katie, and the schoolgirls went into the shop, where Uncle Clegg, behind his dusky counter, ducked his ancient head to them.

Katie secured her pot of home-made jam, and Gwendoline a bag of oranges. Marjorie had more extensive shopping planned, but she could not quite carry out her plan in the circumstances, under two pairs of eyes. Gwen and Katie certainly could not have guessed that she was shopping for a hidden refugee in the apple-loft, but they would have wondered. As it was, the extent of her purchases did not pass unnoticed.

" Sandwiches—cake—biscuits—scones——I suppose you're having Bessie to tea," said Gwendoline, laughing.

Marjorie laughed, too, without replying. She was carrying quite a large parcel when the three girls left Uncle Clegg's shop.

" There's Cherry," said Gwendoline, and Marjorie's face brightened. She had wondered whether she would see Bob again—and there he was, evidently waiting. He held his bike with one hand, and raised a cap from a mop of flaxen hair with the other.

" Jolly seeing you here, Marjorie," he said. " I say, let me carry that parcel for you."

" Are you going our way? " asked Marjorie, at which Gwendoline and Katie exchanged a smile.   They were aware that Bob Cherry always went Marjorie's way if he could contrive it.

" Oh!   Yes!   I'm going along to the Cliff road," answered Bob.

" But you're riding."

" No—I'd rather walk the jigger for a bit."

Bob took the parcel and hooked it on his handle-bars. They walked out of the village together in the direction of Cliff House.   Marjorie's lips were a little set.   If only Gwen and Katie had been out of hearing, she could have asked Bob what she so anxiously wanted to know.   But Gwen and Katie had not the remotest idea of getting out of hearing.   They chatted on cheerily, Marjorie quite silent, and Bob making perfunctory remarks, till suddenly his bike slipped on a   stone, and nearly crashed into Gwendoline.

Gwendoline jumped clear just in time.

" Oh!   Sorry! " ejaculated Bob, and he grabbed the machine round, with the result that it nearly crashed into Katie.

Katie bounded in her turn.

Gwen and Katie, with rather expressive expressions on their faces, accelerated a little and walked on ahead.   They seemed to have had enough of Bob Cherry's bike, and his clumsy handling thereof, at close quarters.

" I say, Marjorie," Bob spoke in a low voice.   " We can speak now—I say, have you heard anything——? "

" Oh! " exclaimed Marjorie, in astonishment.   She had never dreamed that Bob Cherry could be diplomatic, but she realised now that that clumsy handling of the bike had had an object.

Bob coloured a little under her surprised glance.

" I—I just had to speak to you, Marjorie," he said. " I was going to loaf about hoping I might see you.   I—I——."

"I JUST HAD TO SPEAK TO YOU, MARJORIE," HE SAID

He broke off; and Marjorie at once came to the rescue.

" I know about my brother," she said.

" Oh! " said Bob.   " Well, I thought most likely you did—I jolly well guessed that he would let you know first thing, but I couldn't be sure.   I—I knew you'd be awfully knocked over, if you knew, so I——."

" I understand," said Marjorie, softly.   " It was kind of you, Bob.   Tell me——is it so bad as he thinks——is it the—the—the——."   She could hardly utter the word. " Is it the—police? "

" No! " said Bob, and Marjorie felt as if an overwhelming and unendurable weight had been rolled from her heart.

CHAPTER XVII

UP TO BOB!

BOB CHERRY wheeled the bike on, Marjorie walking by his side, under the leafy trees in the lane. Gwendoline and Katie, a little way ahead, were talking nineteen to the dozen, discussing the hat Mademoiselle Lupin wore on great occasions—agreeing that it wasn't a hat, and that if it had been a hat it wouldn't have suited Mademoiselle Lupin. This interesting topic quite absorbed them, and they seemed to have quite forgotten that Bob and Marjorie were walking on behind. It was an immense relief to Marjorie—just what she wanted; yet she hesitated to speak, now that the opportunity had come. But she broke the silence at last.

" Bob! You wouldn't believe that Hazel——? " she faltered.

Bob coloured uncomfortably. In a rather timid, boyish way, he thought the whole world of Marjorie; but he would not have liked to tell her what he thought of her brother.

" Hazel's been an awful ass," he said, awkwardly.

" I know he's often in trouble, Bob, and he's thoughtless—and—and wilful, but he wouldn't—he couldn't ——you couldn't believe——."

Bob's colour deepened. He did not speak.

Marjorie's face hardened a little.

" If you think that Hazel did what they suppose, Bob, it's not much use talking," she said, quietly. " I'll go on and join my friends."

" Hold on," said Bob. " I—I don't believe it, Marjorie. I don't——anyhow, I won't. I—I think it can be explained somehow, though goodness knows how. It looks bad, but—but——." He stammered.

Marjorie smiled faintly.   Bob wanted, at least, to believe as she believed, and he was doing his best.

" You've seen Hazel, of course? " said Bob.

" Yes, I've seen him, and he's told me." She did not intend to tell even Bob where she had seen Hazel, or where Hazel was now.   That was a secret that had to be kept.

" I guessed that," said Bob.   " I was sure of it, really.   When he was missed, it came into my head at once that he'd cut across to see you.   He's the sort of chap to——! "   Bob checked himself just in time.   He had been going to say that Hazel was the sort of chap to land his troubles on a girl!

" What were you going to say? "

" I—I mean, he knows you've got more sense than he has, and I was sure he would come to you," amended Bob. " I thought you'd advise him to come back, but he never came."

" I know."

" It was awfully silly to cut like that," said Bob.   " Of course, he had the wind up, and I dare say hardly knew what he was doing."

" But what was it exactly that happened? " asked Marjorie.

" They haven't let out all the particulars," answered Bob.   " Some money is missing from Quelch's study, and they think Hazel had it.   Don't blame old Quelch for that, Marjorie—he had something to go on——."

" He heard Hazel ask you to lend him money to settle a bet," said Marjorie.

" Oh!   Hazel's told you that?   Well, after that, you see, Quelch missed money from his study and Hazel was there.   It's come out that he denied having been there, and then it turned out that a beak saw him there——he must have been an awful fool to tell crammers about it ——but he did——and—and—and that seems to have settled it, for Quelch."

"It was wrong and weak and foolish of him," said Marjorie. "I can't wonder that Mr. Quelch thinks what he does, but Hazel never touched the money, Bob."

"No!" said Bob, as sincerely as he could.

"Do try to believe in him, Bob."

"I—I will, Marjorie——I mean, I do!" said Bob, sturdily. "It looks pretty bad, but—but there must be some way out. Only, you see, the money's gone, and somebody must have shifted it."

"Couldn't someone else have gone to the study?"

"Well, yes: Quelch was in the quad for a long time, and there was hardly a soul about the place. I—I suppose anybody could. But—but——." Bob gave a sort of wriggle of discomfort. "You see, it seems that Quelch left the money in an envelope on the table. Well, who'd know it was there——except a fellow sent to the study, who happened to see it?"

"If some other boy was sent to the study——."

"Nobody was."

"Someone may have gone in for something——."

"Well, fellows don't go to a beak's study unless they're told," said Bob. "But—but——perhaps—perhaps somebody might——."

Marjorie felt her heart sinking.

"They've been asking questions, of course," said Bob. "Nobody went near the study, from what they say. Hazel's known to have been there, and to have told a lie about it. It's that that fixes it on him. If he'd only had sense enough to tell the truth——."

"He was scared," said Marjorie. "He was afraid of being suspected, and thought it the easiest way out."

Bob made no reply to that. He did not want Marjorie to hear his opinion of a fellow who resorted to lying as the "easiest way out."

"Don't think I defend that," said Marjorie, wincing again. "But that was all he did, Bob——he has told me that he never even saw the money there, and I believe him.

He thinks, too, that Mr. Quelch is mistaken in supposing that he left it there.''

Bob shook his head.

'' That's tosh,'' he said. '' Quelch couldn't make a mistake like that. I dare say Hazel never saw it, but Quelch left it there all right. I think he'd got the letter ready for post, or something—that's how it was. It was there, and it was gone when Quelch came in. If Hazel had stayed in the study, as he was told, it would have been all right. He could have turned out his pockets if Quelch had wanted him to. But he'd cleared off. Then afterwards he denied having been there at all, and that did it. And—and after that, he cut——the silliest thing he could have done.''

'' That was because Mr. Quelch spoke of calling in a police-officer, Bob.''

'' Well, Quelch would have to do that, if they couldn't spot the man,'' said Bob. '' You see, it might have been one of the servants, or even some sneak-thief from out-side—it had to be looked into. A thing like that can't pass and nothing done.''

'' No! '' said Marjorie.

'' But now they know it was a Greyfriars man, of course it won't go so far as that. I—I—I mean——.'' Bob stammered. '' I mean now that they think it was a Grey-friars man, of—of course.''

'' Do you know what is going to be done about it, Bob? ''

'' Well, not exactly: they're making an awful fuss about Hazel running away, and—and I suppose they'll let your people know. The prefects were out looking for him last night——but they never found him. I suppose he's gone home——I don't see where else he could go. Did he tell you, when you saw him yesterday? ''

'' He told me that he would not go home.''

Bob whistled.

" I don't see what else he can do.   Poor old Hazel—he must be in an awful state.   I—I wish I could do something to help, Marjorie."

" Perhaps you could, Bob—if you would."

Bob was all eagerness, at once.

" If I would! " he repeated.   " Marjorie, you know I would, don't you?   Tell me anything I can do, and I'll do it like a shot."

" First of all you can believe in Hazel——."

" Oh!   Yes!   Of course."

" If you believe in him, you must believe, from that, that it was another person who did—what was done."

" Oh! " said Bob.   " I—I—I see!   Yes? "

" And you might be able to find out who it was."

" Oh! " said Bob, again.

" Bob," said Marjorie, earnestly.   " It wasn't Hazel! I know his faults as well as you do—I know only too well how weak, and wilful, and obstinate he is——I know he is weak and foolish enough to tell a lie to get out of even a small trouble, let alone a big one——but he wouldn't, he couldn't, be a thief, Bob.   That's impossible.   No more than I could, Bob."

Bob Cherry drew a deep breath.

" I believe you're right, Marjorie.   I—I'm sure you're right."

" I know I'm right in that, Bob.   It is Hazel's own fault that he is suspected—I know that.   But he never did it.   And if you'd help——."

" I'll try," said Bob.

" Someone else must have gone to the study.   That is certain.   It must be possible to find out who it was.   Oh, Bob, if you could do that——! " breathed Marjorie.

" They've asked everybody, you know——."

" I know!   But—there must have been somebody, you see; and if you could find him out, think what it would mean for Hazel—and for me."

" I'll jolly well try," said Bob. " I'll get my pals to help me, and we'll jolly well go after it like a dog after a bone, Marjorie."

They were almost at the gates of Cliff House now. Gwendoline and Katie had gone in. Bob halted the bike, and Marjorie took her parcel.

" Leave it to us," said Bob. " I'm not fearfully bright myself, Marjorie—but Wharton's as brainy as you like, and old Inky's as sharp as a razor. If there's anything to be rooted out, you can bank on it that we'll root it out— Marjorie, perhaps I'll have some good news for you next time."

Marjorie stood and watched him career away on his bicycle; and when he was gone, she went in at the gates, with a glimmer, at least, of hope to comfort her.

CHAPTER XVIII

NOTHING FOR BESSIE

" Oh! " gasped Bessie Bunter.

She jumped.

Considerable as Bessie's weight was, she almost lifted it from the floor of No. 7 Study.

Bessie was taken by surprise.

Elizabeth Bunter had, of course, no business in No. 7 Study at all, especially when the proprietors of that apartment were absent. Bessie's study was No. 4, with Babs and Mabs. But Elizabeth Bunter was often in places where she had no business.

There was a cupboard in No. 7, and Bessie was standing in front of that cupboard, searching the interior with eager eyes and spectacles. Many things met her gaze— such as maps, books, papers, stationery, a half-knitted jumper on which Clara Trevlyn had been at work, a pair of slippers belonging to Dolly Jobling, two or three tennis balls, a couple of rackets, some sewing materials, and so on. Bessie, like Gallio of old, cared for none of these things. There was a shelf in the cupboard that often contained things for which Bessie did care—and now it was, to Bessie's surprise and annoyance, bare.

Cliff House girls were permitted to supplement the school fare with additions of their own, at their own expense. Sometimes those additions were taken to the common tea-table, at other times there were study teas. Bessie Bunter had no doubt that a study tea was toward in No. 7—to which Marjorie and Co., doubtless because they were " cats," had not remembered to ask Bessie.

She had seen—actually seen, with her own eyes and her own spectacles—Marjorie Hazeldene come in from Friardale with a parcel. She had seen that Gwendoline Cook had a bag of oranges, and Katie Smith a pot of jam—so there was not much doubt what Marjorie's parcel contained. Bessie's interest in that parcel was deep and intense.

Bessie was prepared, if asked, to share the feast. She had not been asked. So she was prepared to share it unasked.

Having seen Marjorie, Clara, and Dolly in the junior common-room, with a crowd of other Fourth Form girls, Bessie naturally supposed that the coast would be clear in No. 7 Study. So there was Bessie at the study cupboard—expecting, naturally, to discover the shelf, on which comestibles were usually kept, well laden. Had Marjorie's recent purchases been placed there, Bessie would not have been more than a minute in the study—it would not have taken her longer than that to load herself with all she could conveniently carry, and roll off with it. But there was nothing on that shelf—absolutely nothing! Which was surprising and annoying, and caused Bessie to remain in the study longer than she had planned.

She blinked to and fro, and up and down, and round about. Whatever Marjorie's parcel had contained was there—it had to be there—it must be there, though not stacked on the accustomed shelf. Possibly the " cats " had packed it out of sight, suspecting that Bessie might have a hungry eye on it—they were capable of it, Bessie thought.

But no amount of blinking to and fro, up and down, and round about, could discover anything in that cupboard of an edible nature; and minutes were passing, many minutes; and so it came about that Bessie Bunter was still standing at the study cupboard, in exasperated quest of what was not there, when three girls came in at the doorway—and a sarcastic voice—Clara's—inquired what Bessie was looking for. And Bessie, startled, jumped, or rather, bounded.

She spun round and blinked at Marjorie and Co. Marjorie smiled faintly; she was accustomed to Bessie's ways, and was patient with them. Dolly Jobling gave her a glare—Clara a sniff.

"Oh!" gasped Bessie. "I—I wasn't looking for anything. If you girls think I was looking for anything——."

"Then what are you up to?" asked Clara.

"Nothing! I mean, well, n-nothing! I never knew you were going to have a feast in the study, of course. I never saw Marjorie come in, and never noticed that she had a parcel under her arm, and I never knew she had been shopping at Uncle Clegg's in Friardale."

Marjorie coloured.

That parcel had been deposited in a secluded spot, to wait till an opportunity came for conveying it unseen to the apple-loft. Clara and Dolly knew nothing of it, and were not intended to know. But she had not counted on the inquisitive eyes and spectacles of Bessie Bunter, and Bessie's deep and abiding interest in food.

"Oh, we're going to have a spread, are we?" said Clara. "Good egg! I hope you've brought in something better than the wishy-wash and marge in hall, old dear."

"She jolly well has," declared Bessie. "It was a big parcel."

"Marvellous!" said Clara. "Bessie knows that it was a big parcel, without ever having seen it. How do you do these things, Bessie?"

"Oh! I—I—I mean——."

"You mean you thought Marjorie had parked the things in that cupboard, and you came here to scoff them before we came up? Lucky you didn't, Marjorie, or the spread would have been a goner."

"But where is it, then, if it isn't in the cupboard?" asked Dolly.

"I say, you girls, I'll fetch it if you like," said Bessie, eagerly. "Where did you leave it, Marjorie? Downstairs in the lobby?"

7

Three pairs of eyes, and one pair of spectacles, were fastened on Marjorie's confused face.

"Cough it up," said Clara. "It's just on tea-time—and anything in the study is better than the scrum in hall."

"I say, I'll go and fetch it——."

"You won't!" said Clara. "It wouldn't get very near this study if you did."

"Cat!" squeaked Bessie.

"We'll all go, and march it home in state!" said Clara. "If there's enough to go round, we'll ask Babs and Mabs."

"And me!" hooted Bessie.

"No need to ask you—you'll barge in anyway. Where is it, Marjorie? Don't say that Matron pounced on it. She's nosey sometimes."

"Oh! No!" stammered Marjorie. "But——."

"But me no buts!" said Clara. "I get hungry towards mealtimes, if you don't! I know it's frightfully unladylike to get hungry, and I wouldn't admit it outside Cliff House for worlds; but I don't mind letting you know, as a pal. Where's the provender?"

"Bessie's mistaken," stammered Marjorie. "I never brought in anything for tea."

"Oh, my only summer hat and pink sunshade!" ejaculated Clara. "What a swizz! Bessie, you benighted little idiot, what do you mean by tantalizing famished schoolgirls in this way? Raising our hopes of something better than wishy-wash and marge, and then dashing them to the ground!"

"What a sell!" sighed Dolly.

"But I say," gasped Bessie. "Marjorie did bring in a big parcel. I tell you I saw it under her arm——."

"A minute ago you told us you didn't."

"Oh, really, Clara——."

"So Marjorie brought in a parcel, and you fancied there was tuck in it, and you came here to scoff it; and when you got there, the cupboard was bare, and so the poor dog had none! " said Clara. " Well, I'm going to give you something out of this cupboard, Bessie."

" There's nothing to eat there," said Bessie. " I've looked."

" There's one of Dolly's old slippers," said Clara.

" Eh! I don't want one of Dolly's old slippers."

" You do, and you're going to have it! " Clara picked up the slipper, and flourished it in the air. " Now, where will you have it? "

" Wow! Keep that slipper away, you cat! " roared Bessie. She made a wild bound for the doorway, and disappeared into the passage.

" Come back and have this slipper, Bessie! "

" Cat! " floated back from the passage. And Elizabeth Bunter was gone.

Clara laughed, and tossed the slipper back into the cupboard. Then she glanced at her little wrist-watch.

" Just time to do that putrid spot of arithmetic for the Sharper before tea, Marjorie," she said. " Sit down and pile in—I'm going to chuck it when the tea-bell goes, whether it's done or not."

The three girls sat down round the study table. It was a great relief to Marjorie that the subject of the parcel was dropped. She had a slightly guilty feeling about it, but she could not explain, and so the less that was said about it, the better. She was rather glad to plunge into arithmetic—not in itself very attractive—so that the subject would not be revived. But it was destined to be revived: once more she counted without Bessie Bunter.

Five minutes later the study door reopened, and a fat face looked in. Bessie Bunter blinked at three bent heads through her spectacles—warily, perhaps uneasy that the slipper might come on the scene again.

" I jolly well knew! " squeaked Bessie. Her fat face was pink with indignation, and her fat squeak thrilled with it. " I knew all the time; there was tuck in the parcel, as I jolly well knew, and Marjorie's keeping it for herself, so yah! I've asked Katie, and she says there were sand-wiches, and cake, and biscuits, and scones, and a pot of jam, so there! ''

Clara laid down her pen, and picked up the inkpot.

The fat face vanished from the door, and it banged after Bessie Bunter.

Clara put down the inkpot again, and looked curiously at Marjorie. Dolly Jobling looked at her.

Marjorie did not raise her head from her work, and did not speak. She seemed unconscious of the curious gaze of her friends, but her ears were burning.

Clara opened her lips—but closed them again. She looked at Dolly, and Dolly looked at her; then they resumed their work, without a word. Arithmetic proceeded in No. 7 Study in a somewhat uncomfortable silence.

CHAPTER XIX

IN THE NIGHT!

MARJORIE sat up in bed, and listened.

From the two other beds in No. 7 came the sound of regular breathing, with an occasional hint of a snore from Dolly.

The summer stars glimmered in at the window. It was past eleven—an hour at which all Cliff House School was fast asleep. Probably, in all the great building, Marjorie Hazeldene was the only one with open eyes at that hour.

But Marjorie had not closed her eyes since " dorm."

She did not dare to sleep, lest she should not wake in time. There was little repose for her that night.

The knowledge of what she was going to do almost made her tremble. But she had to do it—there was no choice.

She knew that one other, at least, could not be sleeping —her brother, hidden in the apple-loft over Potts' shed. The long hours of the day, in hiding and solitude, must have been heavy and dreary to him—but it was not likely that the night had brought sleep, unless in fits and starts. Except for the trifles she had been able to take to him at midday, he had had no food since running away from his school—and he had to have food. There was no one to help him but his sister—and she had to help him.

The parcel from Uncle Clegg's had been safely hidden in a shrubbery, ready to be picked up when opportunity came. But no opportunity had come. Once after tea, and once just before supper, Marjorie had succeeded in eluding other eyes, and scouted near the gardener's shed to ascertain whether the coast was clear—but neither time had it been clear—Potts had been in or about the shed each time. In despair she had given it up, and at " dorm " she had gone to bed with the rest of the Fourth—but without closing her eyes. She had to go to Hazel—and there was only one way. The thought of breaking House bounds, of stealing out on tiptoe in the night, was almost overwhelming to her. But she had made up her mind to it, since there was nothing else to be done.

Her heart beat painfully as she sat in bed and listened.

Clara and Dolly were fast asleep. That was a comfort. The Fourth Form rooms were mostly " threebedders "; studies by day, dormitories by night. She had no fear of being heard or seen by girls in the other rooms. But if either Clara or Dolly had been awake——.

Luckily, both were sleeping. Dolly was not likely to wake, even if a noise should be made—she was almost as sound a sleeper as Bessie Bunter. Marjorie was not so sure of Clara. But Clara, at all events, was sleeping now.

Softly, silently, Marjorie crept from her bed, and dressed in the dim glimmer of starlight from the window. She put on a pair of old well-worn tennis shoes, that made no sound as she moved. Silently, she flitted to the door.

Before she reached it, she suddenly stopped, her heart beating almost to suffocation. There was a sound from Clara's bed.

Marjorie heard a low murmur, and a rustle as Clara, half-awake, turned. But she settled down again, and her breathing was regular once more.

For long minutes Marjorie stood, with beating heart. But all was still, and she stirred at last.

The door opened, and closed, without a sound. Marjorie trod silently down the dark passage to the stairs.

There was no glimmer of light in the building, save here and there from the stars at the windows. But she knew her way well enough; and in a few minutes she was in the junior lobby, turning a key and withdrawing a bolt with a stealthy caution that was quite foreign to her nature. But she had to be cautious—terribly cautious. What would happen if she was discovered leaving the House in the middle of the night, she could hardly imagine: but one thing she could not doubt—the next day would be her last at Cliff House School. That was the risk she was running for the wretched schoolboy in the apple-loft.

The lobby door opened, and the fresh night wind blew in her face. She stepped out, closing the door softly behind her.

The night was light and starry. She would have been glad had it been darker. It seemed to her that the many windows that glimmered in the starlight were so many eyes watching her.

She almost ran to the shrubbery where she had hidden the parcel. She drew it from the shrubs, glancing round her fearfully in the shadows. Then she hurried round the school buildings to the kitchen gardens.

Once there, she felt more at ease, though her heart was still beating painfully. She was at a distance from the House, now, and there was no danger, unless she was missed from her room and looked for. And that was not likely to happen.

She reached the gardener's shed, and silently lifted the latch. Within, all was as black as pitch. She stepped in, into the thick darkness, and drew the shed door shut, and latched it again.

Not till then, did she turn on the light of a tiny flash-lamp. The beam glimmered on sacks and boxes and gardening implements, and on the ladder in the corner that led up to the loft.

She mounted the ladder, panting.

The trap above lifted under a push from her hand. She had little doubt that Hazel would be awake—probably expecting her, as she had not come earlier. She whispered softly:

" Hazel! "

Then she heard a movement. A whisper followed:

" Is that you, Marjorie? "

" Yes! "

" Oh! I'm glad you've come."

He came into the beam of the lamp, and lifted the trap.
Marjorie stepped into the loft, and he closed the trap again.

In the glimmer of the flash-lamp, his face was white
and haggard, and his eyes seemed sunken. They turned
almost wolfishly on the parcel she carried.

He took it from her hand, and tore it open.   In a
moment, he was crunching sandwiches.

Marjorie did not speak. She placed the flash-lamp on
a little ledge, where it shed a patch of light on them. Then
she sat down on a box, to wait till her brother had taken
the sharpest edge off his appetite.

Uncle Clegg's sandwiches disappeared very quickly.
Then Hazel, his mouth full of biscuits, spoke at last.

" I'm just famished, Marjorie! I thought you'd come
sooner than this. Couldn't you get here? "

" I tried, but I couldn't! Not without being seen."

" It's awfully late now—it must be."

" Half-past eleven."

" Oh, Marjorie! " He ceased to eat, for a moment,
and stared at her. " Marjorie! Then you've got out of
dorm—why, they'd sack you if they knew——."

" I know," she said, quietly.

" I shouldn't have come here," muttered Hazel. " It's
been awful—awful—sticking here all day, trembling whenever anybody came into the shed—and now—now you've
had to run this risk. I'm a brute to let you do it."

" No, no," whispered Marjorie.

" But—but there's nobody to help me but you! " Hazel
groaned. " I'm done for, if you let me down."

" I shan't let you down."

" I know you won't, Marjorie. Oh, what rotten luck
I've had—I've done nothing—nothing—and now all
this! "

Marjorie did not answer that. She was well aware
that her brother, so far from having done " nothing," had
been wilfully and recklessly disobedient, and had lied to

his form-master—and that it was for these two reasons that he was under suspicion, and in his present situation. But she had not come there to argue with him, or to hurt him. She was there to help.

" Have you had any news? " he asked. " Anything from Greyfriars——? "

" I met Bob Cherry after class to-day——."

" Oh, that fathead! " grunted Hazel. " It was all his fault——but never mind that. Did he give you any news? Are they at the school——the—the—the police, I mean?" His voice was husky.

" No! "

That reply seemed to relieve him for a moment; but only for a moment.

" That means that they've fixed it on me," he muttered. " If they didn't know who it was—I mean, if they didn't fancy they knew who it was—they'd call in a police-officer, of course."

Marjorie sighed.

" I'm afraid it was your running away that has made them so certain, Hazel. If you'd faced it out——."

" How could I? " he muttered. " After I'd told Quelch that I wasn't in the study at all, and he found out that I was, it was all up. Nobody but me ever has such awful luck."

Marjorie was silent again.

" Did Cherry tell you anything else? " Hazel peered at her. " Does he believe I did it? But I needn't ask— of course he does! They all do."

" No! " said Marjorie. " Of course, he knows how it looks. But Bob doesn't believe you did it, and he's going to help if he can."

Hazel sneered.

" Help! That lumbering fathead! I'd like to know what he can do. He can knock a ball for six, if that's any good."

"It's something if he believes in you, Hazel, against all the evidence," said Marjorie, with a note of sharpness in her voice.

"Oh, I dare say! I don't feel awfully obliged to him for believing what is true. But what does the lumbering ass think he can do?"

Marjorie breathed rather hard. But she went on, quietly.

"Don't you see, Hazel? Something is missing from Mr. Quelch's study, and you did not touch it. That means that somebody else went there."

"I suppose it does! What about it?"

"Well, if he could be found——."

"Bet you he'll keep it jolly dark, if he had Quelch's money," jeered Hazel. "A detective might find out who it was! Is Cherry going to set up as a detective?"

"Don't you want him to help you, Hazel, if he can?"

"Oh! Yes, of course. But he can't do anything."

"He will try."

"A pretty rotten reed to lean on," said Hazel. "I've got more brains in my little finger than Bob Cherry has in his head, and I can't think of a thing. I've been thinking it over and over, who could have had that money—somebody must have if Quelch really left it on his table as he fancies——."

"That is certain, Hazel."

"Well, then, somebody had it——but who? I've thought of everybody. There's Bunter——he would pinch anybody's tuck. But—but——I can't see him doing that. There's Smithy——he's just the man to lark in Quelch's study whilst he's out——but he wouldn't be such a fool as to lark with money. I've thought of every man in the form, but I can't make it out——I'm just beat! I don't fancy that that fathead Cherry will see any clearer than I can."

"It's something, Hazel, at least, if Bob tries to help."

"Oh, yes, I suppose so," grunted Hazel, ungraciously.

" I don't suppose he would, on my account—he's doing it for you, I expect.   That's the sort of ass he is."

Marjorie made a movement.

" I must go now, Hazel!   I'll try to come again when Potts is at his lunch to-morrow.   I—I hope that Bob may have some luck.   I'll leave you the flash-lamp——but be careful about the light.   Good-night, Hazel."

" You're in a hurry to be gone," said Hazel, discontentedly.   " I've been stuck here all day without seeing a soul, and now——."

" If I should be missed from the House——."

" Oh, all right!   You'd better cut, I suppose.   I dare say I can sleep, now that I've had a feed.   Good-night, Marjorie."

The trap-door closed over Marjorie's head again, and she flitted from the shed in the starlight.   Keeping in shadow as much as she could, she made her way swiftly back to the House.   Every minute outside the House, at that hour of the night, was a dread to her; and she was deeply glad and relieved when she stood in the lobby again with the door locked and bolted once more.

All was still and silent as she stole up the stairs.   No. 7 was silent, as she softly opened the door, save for a faint snore from Dolly's bed.   Marjorie stepped in and closed the door; and then her heart seemed suddenly to cease to beat, as she glimpsed a figure in pyjamas in the glimmer from the window.   She leaned back, panting, against the door, as Clara Trevlyn's voice came, shaken and almost husky:

" Marjorie!   Are you mad?   You've been out—out of the House—it's nearly midnight—Marjorie!   Are you mad? "

CHAPTER XX

BESSIE KNOWS!

" HE, he he! "

Bessie Bunter giggled.

Bessie's eyes, and spectacles, were fastened on three girls in the quad, in the sunny morning. The amiable Bessie seemed amused, as she scanned Marjorie and Clara and Dolly.

The Cliff House girls were out in break. Generally, the three chums of No. 7 Study were together. Often they came out with linked arms. Always they were on the best of terms. In other studies, there were sometimes rows—Babs and Mabs sometimes argued, Bridget O'Toole was sometimes heard to slang Cissy Train in No. 5, and in No. 8, Vivienne Leigh occasionally would not speak to Meg Lennox, or Meg would not speak to Vivienne; and at times Gwendoline Cook was stuffy with her dearest friend Katie, or Katie was stuffy with her dearest friend Gwendoline. There were little storms in little tea-cups in the Cliff House Fourth, from time to time. But never in Study No. 7, where Marjorie's sweet temper, and Clara's boyish high spirits, and Dolly's plump good-nature, always kept the peace—perfect peace. Now it seemed that there was a change—which Fatima of Cliff House seemed to find amusing.

Marjorie's face, often grave, was graver than usual. Clara's, often expressive, was more expressive than usual. Dolly's plump visage was puzzled.

The three came out into the sunshine—but not together. In the quad, Clara walked away from the other two.

Then she turned her head, and called:

" Coming, Dolly? "

Dolly looked at her, and looked at Marjorie. A faint flush came into Marjorie's grave face, and she too walked away, on her own. Poor Dolly was left standing, undecided which to follow, until both were gone.

" He, he, he! " giggled Bessie.

There was a spot of trouble in the study where hitherto peace, perfect peace, had reigned. Several other girls noticed it, though they did not giggle, like the fat and fatuous Bessie. If there had been a quarrel in No. 7, nobody could begin to guess the cause—excepting Bessie Bunter. Bessie had little doubt—or rather, none—that she knew.

She rolled after Clara. Clara, catching sight of her with the corner of her eye, accelerated; not, apparently, desiring the charms of Bessie's conversation that morning. But it was not easy to shake off Bessie Bunter. Bessie accelerated, too, and caught Clara's sleeve in a fat paw.

" I say, Clara——! " she squeaked.

Clara jerked her arm loose. Then she took out her handkerchief, and carefully wiped her sleeve, where the fat paw had clutched. Which rather pointed action indicated that Miss Trevlyn was not in her sunniest temper.

" Oh, really, Clara——! " squeaked Bessie.

Clara walked on, quickly.

Bessie trotted.

" I say, you needn't be stuffy with me, because you're stuffy with Marjorie," protested Bessie. " I jolly well know why, Clara."

Clara Trevlyn stopped dead.

" What? " she ejaculated.

Her look at Bessie's fat face was startled. How Bessie could know anything about the strange scene in No. 7 last night, was a mystery to her—and rather an alarming one. She might be " stuffy " with Marjorie, but probably friendship survived stuffiness, for she certainly did not want Marjorie's midnight adventure to become the talk of Cliff House. And if Bessie Bunter knew, it was not likely to be long before it was common property in the Fourth, and other forms too.

Bessie chuckled.

" Think I don't know? " she grinned.

" How do you know anything about it, you prying little sausage roll? " asked Clara, acidly.

" Well, of course I do, as I saw her," said Bessie.

Clara jumped.

" You saw her? " she exclaimed.

" Of course I did."

" You saw Marjorie——?" gasped Clara.

" Yes, I did. I know why you've rowed in your study, and I don't blame you," said Bessie. " I'd have rowed with any girl in my study who did the same. Not that Babs or Mabs would, you know."

Clara stood looking at her, full of dismay. She was utterly puzzled, mystified, and a good deal alarmed, by Marjorie's adventure the previous night. Marjorie had quietly, but resolutely, refused to explain. Dolly, fortunately, had not awakened, and knew nothing of the incident—and Clara did not intend to tell her, or anyone else. But she was alarmed, troubled—and angry. And like the prophet of old, she felt that she did well to be angry! Marjorie had done a mad thing, and refused to utter a word in explanation—which was more than enough to make a good pal angry. Nevertheless, the bare idea of Marjorie's escapade becoming known, chilled Clara with dismay. Chattered up and down the school, it must sooner or later reach official ears; and it was quite terrifying to think of the outcome if Miss Bellew, or Miss Locke, or Miss Primrose, heard of it.

Clara stood speechless, gazing at Bessie Bunter. Bessie rattled on:

" Of course Babs or Mabs wouldn't do such a thing, Clara! You wouldn't, would you? I know I wouldn't! I'm quite surprised at Marjorie! Ain't you? "

" How did you know? " gasped Clara.

" I tell you I saw her——."

" Where? " breathed Clara. " When? "

" Eh! When she came in, of course."

" But you must have been asleep——."

" Oh, really, Clara! Of course I wasn't asleep! How could I be asleep in the quad? " exclaimed Bessie, staring at her.

" In the quad! You were out of the House too? " stuttered Clara.

" Of course I was! I couldn't have seen her come in from Friardale if I had been indoors, could I? "

" From—from Friardale! " Clara knew that Marjorie had been out of the House in the night. She had not dreamed that Marjorie had been out of gates, too! " Did—you say Friardale? You mean Marjorie went to the village? "

" Of course she did. She couldn't have got it anywhere else, could she? "

" She couldn't have got what? "

" What she brought in with her."

" Did she bring something in with her? She never brought anything up to the study."

" No, I know she didn't! She didn't mean you and Dolly to see it—I can see that now. Hid it away, somewhere," said Bessie, with a scornful sniff. " I know her game—greedy! Keeping it all for herself! Not the sort of thing I would do! "

Clara felt as if her head was turning round. She had wondered and wondered what could have caused Marjorie's action—but certainly had never dreamed that her object could have been to smuggle in tuck. That was wildly impossible—yet, according to Bessie, that was it. And Bessie said that she had seen her bring it in!

" Mean, I call it," went on Bessie. " Stingy! Greedy! If I had a parcel of tuck, I'd ask my friends to whack it out. And it was a jolly big parcel—sandwiches, and cake, and buns——."

" Oh! " gasped Clara. A sudden light dawned on her mind, as she remembered Bessie's words at the door of No. 7 Study the previous day. " You dithering little dunderhead——.''

" Oh, really, Clara——.''

" You—you—you concentrated quintessence of idiocy, when did you see Marjorie coming in with that parcel of tuck? ''

" Eh! I told you yesterday, didn't I?—when she came back from Friardale with Katie and Gwendoline——.''

Clara gasped with relief.

It was only a misunderstanding. Bessie knew nothing about that midnight adventure. Bessie's mind was running on tuck—as usual. She fancied that Clara was " stuffy " with Marjorie on account of that parcel of tuck!

" You—you—you little idiot! " breathed Clara.

" I don't think you ought to call me names, when I'm backing you up,'' said Bessie, warmly. " I don't wonder that you've quarrelled with Marjorie about it——.''

" You unspeakable little chump, I haven't quarrelled with Marjorie about it,'' hooted Clara.

" Eh! Everybody can see that you two are stuffy,'' said Bessie, " and I jolly well know why. If Babs or Mabs had a parcel of tuck and hid it away——.''

Clara gazed at her—or, rather, glared at her. She had had some moments of real terror, in thinking that Bessie knew of the previous night's happenings. And Bessie didn't know a thing—she was only thinking about food! Clara's temper was on edge that morning. Now it failed her.

She reached out, and grasped two fat shoulders, and shook. Bessie Bunter emitted a startled, breathless squeak, as she was shaken.

" Oooooooh! ''

Shake! shake!

" Ow! Leggo, you cat! Ooooh! ''

Shake! shake!

" Wooooooooooooh! "

Shake!

" There! " gasped Clara.   " There, you fat thing! There! I haven't quarrelled with Marjorie——."   Shake! " I don't believe there ever was a parcel of tuck——." Shake!   " And if there was, I don't want to know anything about it——."   Shake!   " There! "

And having administered a final and extremely vigorous shake, Clara released the fat shoulders, turned, and walked away; leaving Bessie Bunter spluttering and spluttering and spluttering for breath—too winded even to ejaculate " Cat! "

CHAPTER XXI

BACK UP!

" WHAT's the game? " asked Johnny Bull, of the Grey-friars Remove, as he came into No. 1 Study in the Remove passage.

Harry Wharton and Frank Nugent were in that study. They shook their heads in response to Johnny's question.

" Bob said there was a meeting here," said Johnny.

Harry Wharton laughed.

" He told us the same," he answered. " That's all we know."

" But the meeting must be about something, I suppose," said Johnny, puzzled.

" Probably! I dare say Bob will tell us, when we're all gathered in the fold," said Frank Nugent, laughing.

" Here's Inky—perhaps he knows."

A dusky face glimmered in the doorway, and Hurree Jamset Ram Singh came in. He glanced round inquiringly at the three faces.

" The esteemed Bob remarked that there was an idiotic meeting in this absurd study," said the nabob of Bhanipur, in the English he had not learned at Greyfriars. " What is the upfulness, my preposterous chums? "

" Nobody seems to know, so far," grunted Johnny Bull. " We ought to be getting down to the nets——."

" Hallo, hallo, hallo! " Bob Cherry came in, with the heavy tread that sometimes reminded his friends of the " huge earth-shaking beast " in Macaulay. " All here? Good." Bob kicked the door shut. " Now we'll go ahead."

" Is it about the cricket? " asked Johnny.

" No, ass."

" Well, what's up, then? "

" Hazel is—for the sack."

Four fellows stared blankly at Bob Cherry. They had wondered why Bob had called that meeting in No. 1 Study, but they had not surmised that it was about Peter Hazel Hazeldene.

" Hazel! " repeated Johnny Bull. He gave an expressive grunt. " We're not here to talk about that chap, I suppose."

" We are," said Bob.

" Then we may as well get along to the nets. We're wasting time. Hazel's got it in the neck, and serve him jolly well right, after what he did. No need for us to chew it over, as far as I can see."

" Which isn't very far, as a rule," said Bob.

" Look here——! "

" My esteemed chums," murmured Hurree Jamset Ram Singh. " Let not the exacerbation of arguefulness cloud the idiotic smile of ludicrous friendship. Speech, my esteemed Johnny, is silvery, but silence is the bird in hand that spoils the broth, as the English proverb remarks."

Johnny Bull grinned. That English proverb seemed to have the effect of restoring what the nabob called the idiotic smile of friendship.

" Well, what about Hazel, Bob? " asked Harry.

" I know he's rather a twerp," said Bob. " But—but he's had jolly hard luck, I—I don't believe he did it."

" Rot! " said Johnny.

" Hem! " murmured Nugent.

" Quelch seems to think so, Bob," said Harry Wharton, drily.

" I know! I'm not blaming Quelch! Hazel asked for it—sat up and begged for it, like a dog for a biscuit. He's only got himself to blame. All the same, if he never did it——."

" The if-fulness is terrific," murmured Hurree Jamset Ram Singh.

" Look here, talk sense," said Johnny Bull.   " Hazel
was hard up, owing to his silly putrid betting. He let
Quelch hear him say so.   Then he's sent to the study,
where there's money on the table. He clears off, against
orders, before Quelch comes in.   He's gone—and the
money's gone.   Then he tells lies and says he wasn't in
the study at all. It's proved that he was. If you want
evidence clearer than that——! "   Johnny wound up with
a snort.

" That's common sense, Bob," said Wharton.

" On top of it all, he runs away from the school," went
on Johnny.   " Looks sort of innocent, doesn't it? "

" It doesn't," said Bob, quietly.   " It looks a clear
case—as clear as a magistrate could want in a court of law.
But I don't believe that Hazel did it, all the same."

" And why don't you? "

Bob hesitated a moment.

" I've had a talk with Marjorie——! " he said.

" We're all sorry about that, Bob," said Harry
Wharton.   " We know how this will hit Marjorie.   I
wouldn't like to be the chap to tell her what's happened.
But facts are facts, old fellow."

" Marjorie knows," said Bob.   " Hazel told her—he
must have cut across to see her when he left here.   I
thought he would—doesn't he always land all his troubles
on her? "

Snort, from Johnny Bull.   That snort expressed, very
expressively, Johnny's just opinion of a fellow who landed
his troubles on a girl.

" I know he's a twerp," said Bob, impatiently. " He's
got himself to blame all along the line.   But—Marjorie
believes in him, all the same."

" She would! " said Frank Nugent.   " But that doesn't
alter facts, old bean."

" The question is, whether those facts are facts at all,"
said Bob.   " I—I believe in Hazel, too."   He coloured
as he saw involuntary smiles dawn on four faces.   " I tell

you, I believe that Hazel never did it——I believe
that——."

" Since you had a talk with Marjorie? "

" Well, yes."

" Goodness knows we all feel it, on her account," said
Harry. " But Marjorie's bound to stand by her brother—
she couldn't get it into her head that he's done what he's
done—but——."

" Marjorie's got her head screwed on the right way,"
said Bob, " and she's got more sense in it than we have in
ours."

" Hem! "

" Well, that's the idea," said Bob. " Marjorie made
it much clearer than it had looked before I spoke to her
about it. She pointed out that, if Hazel hadn't done it,
somebody else must have gone to Quelch's study that afternoon——."

" That didn't need an awful lot of pointing out,"
remarked Johnny Bull. " Nobody supposed that Quelch's
money walked away on its own."

" And she said that a fellow on the spot might be able
to find out who it was," went on Bob, unheeding, " and
I said I'd try, and that my pals would help me."

" So that's what the jolly old meeting is about? " asked
Johnny.

" Yes, that's it."

" We're to believe in a chap who's got the knock on
the plainest evidence, and find out somebody else whom
there's no evidence against? "

" Oh! " said Bob, rather taken aback. " That's not
how Marjorie put it."

" Probably not! " agreed Johnny Bull, drily. " But
that's the programme, as far as I can make out—which
of course, isn't very far," he added, sarcastically.

" We—we'll all help, of course, if you think there's
anything doing, Bob," said Harry Wharton, slowly.

" We'd all be glad——and Quelch would be jolly glad——
to set it right, if there's been any mistake. But——."

" But——! " murmured Nugent.

" The butfulness is terrific, my esteemed Bob," said
Hurree Jamset Ram Singh, with a shake of his dusky head.

" I know it's not going to be easy. But just take it,
for a minute, that Hazel wasn't the man," said Bob.
" That means that some other man went to Quelch's study
on Wednesday afternoon. Any man might have, as it was
a half-holiday, and practically nobody about. Man might
not have been seen."

" Hazel thought he hadn't been seen, but it turned out
that Prout saw him," said Johnny. " Still, I suppose it
might have happened."

" Well, if it did happen, we want to spot who it was,"
said Bob. " He's keeping it jolly dark, whoever he is,
and that can only mean one thing. If we find out that
somebody was in that study while Quelch was out, we've
got him."

Harry Wharton nodded.

" I suppose that's so," he added. " But nobody can
have seen him, or it would have come out before this, as it
did about Prout seeing Hazel there. The man's only got
to keep mum—as he's done so far."

" And even if we got on his track—supposing he
exists," said Johnny Bull, " he would deny having been
there, wouldn't he? "

" Well, if he told lies about it, that would fix it on
him," said Bob. " An innocent chap doesn't tell lies."

" Oh, my hat! Didn't Hazel tell lies about it? "

" Oh! " said Bob, taken aback again. " Oh! yes! I—I
suppose so! Yes." As he realised that he had, out of his
own mouth, condemned the fellow whose cause he was
trying to champion, a hopeless look came over Bob's
rugged face. " I—I—I suppose you fellows think it's all
rot! Perhaps it is! But——I've promised Marjorie to
help if I can. She believes in that miserable fool——he's

her brother. If I had a sister, I hope she'd stand by me, if I was in a jam. I'm going to help——somehow."

"My dear old chap, we'll all jolly well help," exclaimed Harry Wharton. "There's a chance—if it's a thin one. There may be something doing."

"And—and Hazel's telling lies doesn't really fix it on him," said Bob, catching at straws, as it were. "He's told lies before, when he was in a scrape, but that doesn't make him out a thief. Bunter tells lies all over the shop, but he wouldn't pinch Quelch's cash to save his fat carcase. We're not trying to find out whether Hazel tells lies when he gets a scare——we know that already. We always knew he was a bit of a skunk. But that's different from what he's accused of. Look here, if you fellows back me up, we may find out what really happened."

"We'll back you up, old bean."

"The backupfulness will be terrific."

"It's all rot," said Johnny Bull, stolidly. "But we'll back you up all the same."

Bob's face brightened.

"Well, if we all go to it, something's bound to come of it," he said. "If—if there's anything to be found out, we can find it out, if we all go to it. Let's begin at once. Now, what's going to be the first step?"

Bob looked round at his friends. They looked at him, and at one another. Bob was eager—and his friends were willing. But no one spoke. Nobody seemed quite to know what the first step was going to be.

There was a long, long silence in No. 1 Study. And it was borne in upon Bob Cherry's mind that the task Marjorie had set him was going to be an uphill one—very steeply uphill!

CHAPTER XXII

A RIFT IN THE LUTE

" Marjorie dear——."

" Yes, Dolly? "

" What's the row? "

" There isn't any row."

" Then why aren't you speaking to Clara? "

Marjorie's knitting needles ceased to click, and a little pucker came into her forehead. Dolly, sitting on a corner of the study table, with her little plump legs dangling, gazed at her a good deal like a distressed owl.

There was a rift in the lute in No. 7. It worried poor Dolly. She was almost equally attached to both her friends. She would never have dreamed of being " stuffy " with either of them. So long as they weren't stuffy with one another, all was well: and Dolly was happy and contented. But her little world seemed to fall to pieces when there was trouble between her friends—and it was the first time she had known it to happen.

She was in the study with Marjorie after class. Dolly had difficulties with a jumper she was knitting for herself, and which was not going according to plan. Under Dolly's plump hands, it seemed to be growing more and more like a sack. What was wrong Dolly didn't quite know: but it seemed that Marjorie did, and Marjorie had done quite a lot of unpicking, and started again at the spot where Dolly had gone off the rails. Dolly was sitting on the table, watching her, when Clara Trevlyn looked in at the doorway.

Clara gave only one glance into the study—and walked on, leaving Dolly staring, and Marjorie with a red spot in either cheek.

Dolly Jobling was not very quick on the uptake. She always followed Marjorie's lead in everything, which saved the trouble of thinking, which was not Dolly's long suit anyway. If Marjorie was not available, she followed Clara's. Now she had some thinking to do for herself, and found it rather hopeless. It was plain even to the unobservant Dolly that Clara had walked on because Marjorie was in the study. She wouldn't come in because Marjorie was there. It was a situation with which Dolly could not deal.

She spoke at last. But Marjorie seemed to have no reply to her question ready. Dolly continued to regard her with an owl-like stare.

" You didn't speak to Clara! " she resumed, at last.

Marjorie smiled faintly.

" Clara didn't speak to me," she said.

" Well, why didn't she? "

" Nothing to say, perhaps," suggested Marjorie.

" That's rot," said Dolly. " Clara's always talking, whether she's got anything to say or not. She talks more than you and I put together. You don't say more than one word, and I don't say more than two, to Clara's dozen. Do we? "

Marjorie made no reply to that.

" Why, she's talking now," added Dolly, as voices floated along the passage. " She's talking to Babs and Mabs. That's Clara's voice."

Marjorie resumed knitting.

" You say there isn't a row, Marjorie——."

" There isn't."

" Well, it looks to me like one," said Dolly. " You don't speak to Clara, and Clara doesn't speak to you. Isn't that a row? "

Click, click, click, went the busy needles.

" We've never had rows in this study," said Dolly, dolorously. " You've always said it was silly to tiff, like Gwen and Katie do."

" So it is," said Marjorie.

" But you and Clara are tiffing."

Click, click!   The only answer came from the knitting-needles.

" Well, I'm going to speak to Clara."   Dolly slipped from the table.   " I know it's her fault——."

" It's not Clara's fault," said Marjorie, quickly.

" Well, it must be," said Dolly.   " It couldn't be yours, I suppose.   If it isn't yours, it's Clara's.   She's got her back up about something.   I'm going to tell her not to be such an idiot."

" It—it's nothing," stammered Marjorie.   " Only——."

" Only what? "

" Well, nothing.   It will be all right.   Least said soonest mended, you know.   Look here, just how did you want this to go? "

" You can't pull my leg," said Dolly.   " You know better than I do how it ought to go.   I'm going to speak to Clara, and if she doesn't come round at once, I shan't speak to her any more this term, so there."

Dolly walked out of the study: and the worried pucker in Marjorie's forehead deepened.   She half-rose, but sat down again.   Clara's new attitude distressed her deeply, and she knew that Clara was going to keep it up, until she explained about that nocturnal adventure.   But she felt no resentment: she knew that Clara's real feeling was alarm and anxiety on her account.   She could not explain —she had to keep her brother's secret.   She dared not trust even Clara with that.   It was an added trouble to the troubles that already lay heavy on her mind.   But there was nothing she could do.

Dolly, however, seemed to think that there was something she could do.   There was a determined expression on her plump, rosy face, as she went down the passage.

Clara was talking to Babs and Mabs, at the door of No. 4.   Barbara and Mabel went into their study as Dolly came along, and Clara looked round.   She gave Dolly a friendly smile.

" Coming out? " she asked.

Dolly halted, and favoured her with an accusing stare.

" That depends," she said.

" Does it? " yawned Clara.

" Yes! What are you being so beastly to Marjorie for? " demanded Dolly.

" I'm not being beastly to Marjorie. You're a little goose, Dolly. Don't bother that fluffy little thing you call a head about things you don't understand," advised Clara. " Let's go for a run, shall we? "

" No! If you're going to row with Marjorie, you can row with me as well. You're in the wrong."

" You don't know anything about it."

" I don't want to. I want you to stop being catty."

" What! " exclaimed Clara.

" Catty! " said Dolly. " I believe Marjorie's worrying about something—that precious brother of hers at Greyfriars, very likely. She was upset when he didn't come over on Wednesday, bother him. Now you go and worry her, as if you had no more sense than a boy, as a girl ought to have. Come back to the study and tell Marjorie you're sorry for being catty."

Clara drew a deep, deep breath.

" You're a dithering little duffer, Dolly," she said. " You don't know what you're talking about."

" Are you coming back to the study, now? "

" No, I'm not."

" That's that, then! " said Dolly, and she turned her plump back on Clara, and walked up the passage again.

" Dolly! " called out Clara.

Dolly neither answered nor looked round. She marched back into No. 7, and shut the door after her with a bang. Clara was left biting her lip.

" He, he, he! "

Clara glanced round, with almost a deadly look in her eyes, at the sound of that unmusical cachinnation. Bessie Bunter grinned at her.

" You're going it, ain't you? " said Bessie, agreeably.

" What are you rowing with Dolly for? **Dolly hasn't** been hiding a parcel of tuck, has she? "

" You little fat frump——."

" I'd like Miss Bellew to hear you calling me **names**," said Bessie. " She would comb your hair for you if she heard you. I wish she'd seen you shooking—I mean shaking me, this morning. I say, Gwen and Katie and Annabel laughed like anything when I told them you were stuffy with Marjorie because she kept all the tuck for herself——."

" She did not! " almost shrieked Clara.

" She jolly well did, and that's why you're stuffy, and so should I be," said Bessie. " So you needn't scream at me, Clara. Aren't you going to speak to Marjorie again, just because she wouldn't bring the tuck to the study ——Ow! Don't you shook—shick—shake me again, or I'll——yarooooooh! "

Clara had lost her temper with the fat Elizabeth once already that day. Now she lost it again. Bessie yelled, as her fat shoulders were clutched. Shaken, and even more vigorously than before, Bessie would indubitably have been, had not an icy voice interrupted.

" Clara! "

It was the voice of Stella Stone of the Sixth, senior prefect of Cliff House. It came, no doubt, from the usual vocal organs; but it sounded as if it came from the deepest, iciest depths of a refrigerator. Clara dropped her hands from Bessie's shoulders, as if those fat shoulders had suddenly become red-hot, and spun round to meet icy eyes.

" Yow-ow-ow-ow! " roared Bessie.   " I won't be shook—yow-ow-ow! "

" Be quiet, Bessie! " came from the refrigerator. " Clara! "

" I—I—I——," Clara stammered.

" Were you shaking Bessie? "

" Yes, she was! " spluttered Bessie. " She shuck— shake—I mean shooked me——."

" Be quiet, Bessie! Will you answer my question, Clara? " Even a refrigerator could not have been quite so freezing.

" Yes! " gasped Clara.

" Do you think you are a boy in a boys' school? " inquired Stella.

" Oh! No."

" Ah! " said Stella. " I thought perhaps you did! Now go down to Miss Bellew's study, Clara, with a message from me."

" Ye-e-es! What's the message? "

" Tell Miss Bellew that I have sent you to her because you were shaking another girl in your form."

" Oh! " gasped Clara.

The tall Sixth Form girl swept on. She left Clara rooted to the passage floor with dismay. Bessie Bunter —backing away to a safe distance—chuckled.

" He, he, he! "

But Clara did not heed her further. Slowly and sadly she made her way to Miss Bellew's study. She emerged from that study after five minutes of concentrated conversation from Miss Bellew, which left her in no mood for shaking anybody; but feeling considerably shaken herself. After which, Bessie Bunter was in no danger of further shakings, for the rest of that term at least.

All of which did not help to restore harmony in No. 7 Study. At tea in hall, Clara selected a seat as far as possible from Marjorie Hazeldene. Marjorie's face gave no sign; but Dolly stared down the table at Clara, and sniffed —a belligerent sniff!

The rift in the study was widening. After tea, Clara did her study work in No. 2 with Katie Smith and Annabel Hichens. Marjorie and Dolly had No. 7 to themselves, but neither of them looked as if she enjoyed it.

CHAPTER XXIII

A TOPIC IN THE FOURTH

" PACK it up! " said Barbara, hastily.

" Quiet! " murmured Mabs.

" But I say, you girls——."

" Quiet, Bessie! "

And as Bessie's capacious mouth still remained open, Gwendoline Cook tactfully trod on a large foot, which changed Bessie Bunter's intended remarks into a pained squeak.

It was quite an excited group of girls in the quad at Cliff House School on Saturday afternoon. They were all talking at once, discussing some topic that was evidently of the deepest and greatest interest.

But the discussion died out quite suddenly as Marjorie Hazeldene came along the path. Bab's injunction to " pack it up " was hardly needed; almost every girl there became dumb at the sight of Marjorie.

Some of them coloured. Some looked down, to avoid meeting Marjorie's eyes. Not one of them looked at Marjorie.

Only Bessie Bunter would have gone on talking, her big spectacles not having spotted the fact that Marjorie was in the offing; but that timely stamp on her foot had cut off the gas, as it were.

Marjorie, who was crossing to the school shop, glanced at the group. She could scarcely fail to observe how the talk had dried up as she approached; and, from that, to realise that she was the topic.

The colour wavered in her cheeks.

Every day, every hour, since she had discovered the wretched fugitive hidden in the apple-loft, she had dreaded that the story of her brother's disaster might reach Cliff House.

Sooner or later it must be known there, that Hazel was accused of theft, and that he had only saved himself from being expelled by running away from the school and remaining in hiding. Unless it came out that he was innocent, he would be believed guilty; and his name would be bandied about the school—an exciting topic, and almost an endless one. It was a terrible prospect to Marjorie; but it had to come, unless Hazel's innocence was proved before the news reached Cliff House.

Now, she could not help feeling, it had come. Whether any of the girls would turn against her, on account of what her brother had done, or was believed to have done, she hardly knew—and cared little. But for the shame, the disgrace, she cared very much indeed. The sudden silence that fell upon the chattering group of schoolgirls struck her almost like a blow.

Her face set a little, her lips tightened, and she walked on, with heightened colour. The schoolgirls exchanged uncomfortable looks. Barbara Redfern turned to Marjorie impulsively, as she passed.

" Tennis this afternoon, Marjorie," she said, with a cordiality that was almost overdone. She wanted to say something to make it clear to all concerned that the sins of the brother at Greyfriars made no difference to her friendship with the sister at Cliff House.

" Oh! Yes, if you like," answered Marjorie, and she walked on quickly before anything more could be said, and went into the school shop.

Once she was out of hearing, the talk was resumed in full force. Most of the girls had seen Hazel, at one time or another. Girls' brothers generally had some interest for other girls; but Hazel had not been liked. Hazel was good-looking, and could be agreeable when he liked—though he did not always like. But his fixed belief that girls did not amount to much, which he hardly took any trouble to conceal, was not likely to make him popular at Cliff House. A fellow who was openly amused at the idea of a girl being able to talk sense, or to do anything worth doing, was judged to be a conceited ass—indeed, Babs had been heard to allude to him as a " puppy." And now Hazel, with his ineffable superiority to the whole feminine creation, had come an awful mucker—and it was natural that few had any sympathy to waste upon him.

There was plenty of sympathy for Marjorie. Everyone knew how she would feel the shadow of shame that had fallen on her through her brother's action. Almost all the girls were anxious to let her see that it made no difference so far as she was concerned—even the acid Marcia forgot to sneer. Even Bessie Bunter, while thrilling with the excitement and thoroughly enjoying it, realised that it was hard on Marjorie.

" I suppose there's no doubt about it," said Mabs. " If there is——."

" There isn't," said Gwendoline. " I tell you I had it from my cousin, in the Fourth Form over there—I met him in Friardale, and he told me——."

" Marjorie can't know," said Mabs.

" She does," said Barbara, with a sage nod. " She's been upset lately—lots of girls have noticed it. Skewing in form, and getting into rows with the Bellew. She knows."

" Poor old Marjorie! " murmured Mabs.

" It's rotten for her," said Babs. " I'd like to smack that puppy's head."

" But I say, you girls, has he really run away from school? " exclaimed Bessie Bunter, breathlessly. " I say, I was over at Greyfriars last Wednesday, and I saw him—sulking about."

" It was after that," said Gwendoline. " After tea on Wednesday. It's really awful, you know—taking money from his form-master's study——."

" That's what he was sulking about, I suppose," said Bessie. " Hard up, you know, and then he went and helped himself.   He told me once I ought to be in a circus.''

" Ha, ha, ha! ''

" Well, you can snigger," exclaimed Bessie, indignantly.   " But I'd rather be in a circus than where he is now, wherever that is.'' '

" Where on earth can he be? " said Annabel.   " If he's been away from his school ever since Wednesday—and now it's Saturday——.''

" He hasn't gone home, or they'd know! " remarked Katie Smith.   " Must be hiding somewhere.''

" I say, he can't be hiding all this time! " said Bessie Bunter, shaking her head.   " He would have to have food, you know.''

" Trust Bessie to think of that! " chuckled Babs.

" But she's right," said Gwendoline.   " He can't be hiding in the woods, or anything like that, without food.''

" What a twerp! " said Marcia Loftus.   " He might have thought of Marjorie, and how it would disgrace her here.''

" Rot! " said Barbara, sharply.   " It's nothing against Marjorie—how could she help what her brother does? ''

" I know she couldn't! But all the same——.''

" I'm going to be nice to Marjorie," declared Bessie Bunter.   " Tain't her fault! I'm going to be nice to her. I shall jolly well go to her study to tea this afternoon! ''

" Ha, ha, ha! ''

" I mean it," said Bessie.   " Marjorie may be a cat sometimes—look at the way she wouldn't look for my brooch any more—but——.''

" Clara shook you yesterday, I've heard," said Babs.

" Yes, she did.''

" Do you want to be shaken again? ''

" Eh! No.   Wharrer you mean? ''

" Well, you will be, if you call Marjorie names.   Look here, all of you," continued Babs, glancing round over the group.   " We've all got to take jolly good care to let

9

Marjorie see that it makes no difference to any of us. It's bad enough for her already, without cats scratching her over and above." She gave Marcia a special glance. " If there's any cats present, let them hereby take warning to keep their claws well inside their paws."

" I suppose one can ask Marjorie exactly what it is that's happened," drawled Marcia.

" Yes—if one wants to be sent to Coventry by the form," said Barbara. " Not otherwise, Marcia."

" Hear, hear," said Mabs.

" I say, you girls, I shall jolly well find out exactly what's happened," squeaked Bessie. " I shall go over to Greyfriars again this afternoon and see my brother Billy. I can get it all from him."

" Much better mind your own business," said Barbara.

" Yah! " was Bessie's rejoinder to that. Gwendoline had brought in the news, but details were lacking, and Bessie was eagerly inquisitive to know any and every detail.

" What about shaking her, as Clara did? " suggested Mabs.

" Cat! " said Bessie, and she rolled away.

" Not a word to Marjorie," said Cissy Train. " She——."

" Shush! She's coming."

Marjorie reappeared from the direction of the school shop, with a little parcel in her hand. She passed the group at a distance this time, with a spot of colour in her cheeks, and her head noticeably erect. There was a dead silence until she had gone into the House.

CHAPTER **XXIV**

FRIENDS AGAIN!

" M-M-M-Marjorie! "

Clara stuttered, and almost spluttered, as she rushed into No. 7 Study.

Marjorie looked up, startled.

She was sitting alone in the study with Dolly's shape-less jumper on her knees, the knitting-needles in her hands —but her hands lay idle. Her face was clouded with painful thought.

Dolly had been in the study. She had stared dismally at Marjorie, opened her mouth several times without utter-ing a word, knocked over an inkpot with her elbow, and displayed other signs of confused thought and muddled distress, and finally drifted out of the study again. From which Marjorie would have guessed, if she had not guessed if before, that Hazel's story was known at Cliff House, and that Dolly had heard it.

It was a heavy blow to Marjorie, none the less so because she had known that it must come. She had hoped that something might come to light to clear her brother. Her hope was chiefly centred in Bob Cherry; she knew that he would keep his word, and do all he could —if anything could be done. But there had been no word from Bob—no news of any kind—and now the inevitable had happened—her brother's disgrace was a topic in the Fourth Form at Cliff House, and it seemed to her that the shame of it was almost more than she could bear.

Then there was a patter of running feet in the passage, and Clara flew into the study, stuttering in her excitement and emotion.

" M-M-M-Marjorie! Oh, I'm sorry! " panted Clara.

Marjorie gave her a startled look, and then compressed her lips. Nobody had said a word to her on the subject so far. But it was clear that Clara had just heard—and it was coming.

" You've heard? " Marjorie spoke quietly.

" Yes, yes, yes——."

" Leave it at that, then," said Marjorie. " It's not a thing I want to talk about. Don't say any more."

" I've got to talk about it." Clara slammed the study door. " I've got to, Marjorie. We're friends, aren't we? "

" Are we? " said Marjorie, with a faint smile.

" I was a fool—an idiot—a fathead—as big a chump as Bessie Bunter—you can smack my head if you like."

" What do you mean? "

" I know now, of course," said Clara. " I'm not a fool."

" You've just said that you were! "

" Oh, don't catch me up! I'm sorry, Marjorie! I've been a cat," moaned Clara, remorsefully. " But—but—but you scared me stiff, Marjorie, by going out that night ——I couldn't begin to guess what it meant——I knew you must have got mixed up in something, and I couldn't imagine what——and you wouldn't tell me——you wouldn't say a word——but of course I know, now."

" You——know? " Marjorie hardly breathed.

" Of course I do. I wondered and wondered why you should do such a mad thing. Don't you know they'd send you home if it came out? "

" I know."

" And you risked it, for that—that—that twerp! " It came out at last. Clara had always resolved that Marjorie should never hear her call her brother a twerp. But it was out now!

Marjorie's face, already pale, became paler.

" What do you mean, Clara? " she breathed.

" Think I don't know? " exclaimed Clara. " Of course it was clear at once when I heard that he had run away from school after what he had done. Think I don't know that he has landed this on you, like he does everything? Doesn't he always come whining to you if anything goes wrong——."

"Clara!"

"Well, you know he does," snapped Clara. "He can't be made to pay an account at the shop, or get a whacking from his form-master, without telling you what a wronged angel he is. And all the while he thinks that girls are just microbes or germs, while he worries and bothers a girl to get him out of his scrapes—pah!"

"You've no right to say anything of the kind. You haven't spoken to me for a day and a half. Now you can leave me alone!"

"Can I?" said Clara. "Well, I won't see? Think I don't know? Of course I know. It was on your brother's account you went out of the House after lights out. Think I don't know. He's run away because he can't face things, and you're landed with it. He's hiding somewhere, and you're looking after him. Think I don't know? Isn't that his sort all over?"

Marjorie's lips quivered.

"All the girls know that you know," went on Clara. "Well, how do you know, if you haven't seen Hazel since Wednesday. I know you've seen him. I know that that is why you went out of the House on Thursday night! Isn't it?"

Marjorie made no reply.

"You needn't tell me—I know! I wondered and wondered, but I know now. He came to see you after he ran away, and told you—landing it on your shoulders, as usual. Didn't he?"

"It was by accident—I never expected to see him——," faltered Marjorie.

"He made the accident happen—he must have been near here—and he came near here, to see you if he could—don't I know?"

Clara paused for breath. Marjorie sat silent.

" I've got it all now," went on Clara. " He's hiding somewhere—and I know now that it's somewhere near Cliff House—isn't it? "

No answer.

" You went out that night to see him—to take him something, I expect. Oh! " exclaimed Clara, a new light breaking in on her mind. " That parcel that Bessie was chattering about—I see it now. You've been taking him food."

" Don't speak so loud."

" So that's it! " said Clara. " That's your job—feeding the brute! Oh, suffering cats and crocodiles! That's it! "

" Clara! Be quiet! If anyone heard you——! " panted Marjorie.

" Well, what if they did? " demanded Clara. " You'd get into a row—but it would be all over. Your brother would have to go back and take his medicine, if he wasn't able to hide behind a girl——."

" Don't! "

" It would be all the better for you. I wondered and wondered what you could have got mixed up in—now I know you're mixed up in this—and it's pretty rotten. I've got two brothers, and I'd stick to them if they got into the soup—but not if they did what he's done! Never."

" Hazel never did." Marjorie was pale to the lips. " Clara, can't you understand there's been a mistake— an awful mistake—Hazel never did——."

" Is that what he's told you? "

" Yes! I believe him."

" You would, I suppose," said Clara.

" It's true, Clara——."

" Well, you can't know it's true, if it is true. A fellow who would pilfer would tell lies about it afterwards. You can't know——."

" I—I trust him."

" You would! " repeated Clara. " That's the sort of noodle you are, Marjorie. I wouldn't trust him an inch."

Marjorie's eyes flashed.

" Then don't speak to me again! " she said. " If that's your opinion, keep it to yourself. You've left me alone long enough—now leave me alone again. I won't stay in this study with you."

Marjorie rose hurriedly to her feet, Dolly's jumper slipping to the floor with the knitting-needles sticking in it. Clara stared at her for a moment, and then, unceremoniously gave her a push, and she sat down in her chair again quite suddenly.

" Don't be a goat! " said Clara. " Stick where you are, Marjorie. We're friends, and we're going to stay friends."

" Not if you speak of Hazel like that."

" I won't, then," said Clara, rather unexpectedly.

" Oh! " said Marjorie. The brief anger faded out of her face. " Oh, Clara, it hurts me when you say such things—I know he's got his faults, as well as you do—but I do believe him—I know he never did what they think. And—and if you saw him——overwhelmed with trouble as he is——." Her voice faltered, and the tears came very near her eyes. " You'd be sorry, Clara."

" Um! " said Clara. " Perhaps. A glorious creature so much superior to miserable females ought to be able to stand up to trouble without crumpling up, oughtn't he? Catch me running away and hiding if I was accused of anything! Poof! "

" Please, Clara——."

" Sorry, old girl! I won't do it again! Come to think of it, he's a nice boy—strong and manly, and all that, and he never did what he did——."

" I tell you he did nothing, except get misunderstood——."

" Yes, I remember he's been misunderstood, ever so often. Born to it, as the sparks fly upwards! " said Clara.

" Oh! There I go again! Look here, Marjorie, it's just mad to interfere in this—Hazel ought to go back to school, and face it—and whatever he does, he ought not to drag you into it."

" He hasn't! I've done nothing I wasn't glad to do. I must help him——he's got nobody else. And—and I told him he ought to go back——but I'm not so sure now. Nothing can be definitely settled so long as he's away and not found——and something may come out——he's got friends at his school helping——."

" Has he? I didn't know he was so jolly popular. Who are they and what are they doing? "

" Bob's doing all he can to find out who it really was, for Hazel's sake——."

" Oh, my summer sunshade! " said Clara. " I can guess exactly how much Bob is doing it for Hazel's sake! You're the limit, Marjorie! And Bob! Bob's a dear old lad, as nice as a Newfoundland dog, but fancy him setting up to solve mysteries—Mr. Sherlock Holmes of the Remove passage—ha, ha."

" He is trying to help," said Marjorie. " I—I keep on hoping that something may be found out. I—I wish there was some news."

" You'll get the latest news at tea-time," said Clara. " Bessie's going over this afternoon to see her brother Billy; and she will come back cram-jam full of it. She can't help being a Nosey Parker. It runs in the Bunter family. Look here, shall I take her round to the gardener's shed to look for that idiotic brooch again, and keep her away from Greyfriars? " Clara laughed. " I say, I'll tell her that that imaginary tramp may have dropped it in the apple-loft? "

" Wha-a-t? "

" And keep her rooting about the loft till tea-time—why, what's the matter, Marjorie? You're as white as a sheet."

Marjorie panted.

" Nothing! I—I——Oh, here's Dolly."

The study door opened, and Dolly Jobling came in. The interruption was a relief to Marjorie. Dolly gave Clara a stare, as if surprised to see her there. She crossed over to Marjorie, and continued to stare at Clara, as if she would stare her out of countenance, or out of the study.

Clara laughed.

" It's all right, Dolly," she said.

" Is it? " said Dolly. " Well, it isn't, see, unless you tell Marjorie you're sorry for having been a cat."

" I've told her that already."

" Oh! " said Dolly, taken aback. " Then I suppose it's all right. Is it all right, Marjorie? "

" Yes, dear; quite all right."

" Well, if it's all right, all right," said Dolly, after some moments' meditation. " I—I say, you haven't told Marjorie——about—about——? "

" I knew already, Dolly," said Marjorie, quietly. " And there isn't a word of truth in it. It's all a mistake, about my brother."

Dolly looked at Clara. Clara looked at Dolly. Then they both said together:

" Of course it is."

And they tried as hard as they could to believe that they meant it.

CHAPTER XXV

BEASTLY FOR BESSIE!

" JE ne comprends pas! " said Mademoiselle Lupin.

Mamselle shook a puzzled head.

There were four of them in the Staff Room: Miss Bellew, form-mistress of the Fourth; Miss Bullivant, the games-mistress; Miss Moce, who taught history; and Mademoiselle Lupin, whose arduous task it was at Cliff House to drive the beautiful language of France into unreceptive heads.

The Bull was talking games, in her deep voice. The Bull generally dominated the Staff Room, when she was present. Little Miss Moce had nothing to do but to nod assent to the Bull; she would never have dared to interrupt her. But Miss Bellew was a more decided character than little Miss Moce; and with calmness, though without emphasis, she headed the Bull off games, and got to " sets." Here Miss Moce hoped to get in a word edge-wise, as her subject, history, was taught in sets. As for Mademoiselle Lupin, she had been making remarks for some time, in alternate French and English, without anybody heeding her at all. Mamselle hovered on the edge of the conversation, like the sparrow that hovered on the window-sill.

Mamselle was not interested in games. She was not interested in history. She was not interested in " sets," outside the French set. She was thinking of something else entirely; but as nobody wanted to know what it was, probably it would never have got as far as utterance, had not Miss Bellew caught sight of a slip of paper in her hand.

What was written on that paper was so odd, so very odd, that Miss Bellew simply could not help sitting up and taking notice, as it were.

" Goodness gracious, what is that, Mademoiselle Lupin? " she asked.

All eyes turned on Mamselle—Miss Moce's with envy, for it was clear that Mademoiselle was going to get into the conversation,in which Miss Moce's part was nods and assenting murmurs.

" Je dit, je ne comprends pas," said Mademoiselle Lupin. " Zat is somezing zat I shall not understand. Je l'ai trouve—I have found him it is days since on ze table in my study, and always I understand him not. I understand ze Cherman, and ze Spanish, also ze Italian, and ze English I speak like one native—but what is written on zis paper I understand not."

Miss Bullivant stared. This seemed nonsense to her. However, she always expected nonsense from Mademoiselle Lupin, so that was nothing new. Miss Moce gave a little twitter of interest. She was at least able to make a remark.

" How very extraordinary! " said Miss Moce. " What——? "

Thus far did Miss Moce get, no farther. Miss Bellew weighed in, her calm voice obliterating Miss Moce.

" Please let me see the paper, Mademoiselle Lupin. I may be able to explain it."

Quite elated by anyone in the Staff Room showing interest in herself or in anything connected with her, Mademoiselle Lupin passed the slip of paper to the mistress of the Fourth Form.

" What is it? " asked the Bull. Miss Bullivant was anxious to get rid of " sets " and get back to games; and certainly she did not want any extraneous matter to be introduced. She did not believe in wasting time; and discussion of anything unconnected with Miss Bullivant was obviously waste of time.

Miss Bellew did not reply.

Her eyes were fixed on the paper Mamselle had handed to her. A frown gathered and deepened on her brow.

What was written on that paper was a hopeless puzzle to Mademoiselle Lupin. It was not so deep a puzzle to Miss Bellew. It ran, in elegant capitals:

MADMORSEL LOOPANG AYTOON SHAT

It was, in fact, the message Bessie Bunter had left on Mamselle's table for her to find, several days ago. Mamselle had found it, according to plan. But the rest had not gone according to plan, for she had not even begun to understand it. Bessie Bunter's French was too much for a native of France. Indeed, she wondered whether the strange message was written in a language with which she was wholly unacquainted. French was the very last one she would have thought of.

But Miss Bellew, reading it phonetically, " tumbled " to the hidden meaning. Hence the deep frown that corrugated her brow.

" Vat you zink? " asked Mademoiselle. " I puzzle and puzzle, but I understand him not! Zere is vun vord —ze first vord—but zat is two vords togezzer. ' Mad ,' zat is to say ' fou '—and ' morsel '—zat is to say ' morceau.' But ze two vords sticked togezzer—zat mean nozzing."

" Extraordinary! " said Miss Moce, peering over Miss Bellew's shoulder. " Very! What——? "

" Upon my word! " said Miss Bellew.

" Mon Dieu! Is it zat you understand? " asked Mademoiselle Lupin, in surprise. " You read him, n'est-ce-pas? To me, c'est un mystere, tout a fait."

" It is a piece of impertinence, Mademoiselle Lupin, which I beg you will leave in my hands," said Miss Bellew. " I think I can guess by whom this was written, and I shall inquire into the matter at once."

She rose to her feet.

" Mais—but——! " said Mademoiselle Lupin, still puzzled.

Miss Bellew departed from the Staff Room, with the paper in her hand. Her brow was frowning, and her lips were set. Miss Bullivant glanced after her, not wholly sorry that she was departing. There were no powers of resistance in either Miss Moce or Mademoiselle Lupin; and the Bull got back to games at once, with two heads nodding tired assent to her remarks.

Miss Bellew was looking for a member of her form, to wit, Elizabeth Bunter. She had not far to look. Bessie Bunter, with her hat on, was in the House doorway, speaking to Gwendoline Cook and Katie Smith.

" I'm off now," she said. " I'm going over to see Billy—I say, I shall have all the news when I get back——."

" Bessie! "

" Oh! Yes, Miss Bellew." Bessie turned her eyes and spectacles uneasily on her form-mistress. The voice of authority was always alarming to Bessie. She had many small sins on her fat conscience. " I—I say, I'm just going out, Miss Bellew——."

" Look at this paper, Bessie."

Bessie looked at it, and jumped. Gwendoline and Katie glanced at it, and exchanged a look. They had seen that paper before. Most of the Fourth had seen it before Bessie landed it in Mamselle's study.

" Oh, crumbs! " gasped Bessie. " I—I never wrote that, Miss Bellew! I've never seen it before! I—I don't think Mamselle is a cat, Miss Bellew."

" This is intended, I presume, to be French," said Miss Bellew. " I had little doubt that I could trace the writer by the spelling. You wrote this impertinent message, Bessie."

" Oh! No! " stuttered Bessie, in dismay. " Not at all, Miss Bellew. Besides I wrote it in capitals so that it wasn't my hand——it—it—it's not in my handwriting, Miss Bellew."

" You will follow me to the form-room, Bessie."

" But I—I'm going over to Greyfriars to see my brother
Billy, Miss Bellew.   I—I want to ask him something——.''

" I said follow me to the form-room, Bessie! ''

" Oh, lor'! ''

Bessie blinked dolorously at Gwendoline and Katie.
To her surprise, and annoyance, they were laughing.

" Cats! '' breathed Bessie.   " Now I shan't be able to
go over to Billy's school and ask him about Hazel——.''

" BESSIE! ''

" Ow! I'm coming, Miss Bellew.''

Bessie followed her form-mistress into the form-room,
in the lowest of spirits.   Several days having elapsed since
she had left that message for Mamselle, Bessie had forgotten all about it, and assuredly she did not expect it to rise
up in judgment against her, like this, after many days!
How Miss Bellew had traced it to her, was a mystery to
Bessie, but it was clear that Miss Bellew had!

" You will be given detention this afternoon, Bessie,''
said Miss Bellew, sternly.   " I shall set you a task——.''

" Oh dear! I—I was going over to Greyfriars——.''

" If you have not finished it by tea-time, you will return
to the form-room after tea, and complete it.''

" Oh, lor'! I—I was going to see Billy——.''

" If it is not finished by calling over, you will be
detained for a half-holiday next week——.''

" Oooooooogh! ''

" And if you should ever repeat this impertinence,
Bessie, you will be sent to Miss Primrose to deal with,''
said Miss Bellew, in an awful voice.

Bessie almost collapsed at her desk.   Miss Bellew,
having kindly provided her with a Latin paper to keep her
busy, left her to it.

" Cat! '' breathed Bessie, as the form-door closed after
Miss Bellew.

It was really beastly for Bessie.   She had looked forward with the happiest anticipation to visiting Greyfriars
and learning every detail of the Hazeldene affair from

Brother Billy, who was certain to know all about it—more than anyone else, probably, as Billy Bunter had all sorts of ways of acquiring information. She had looked forward to returning to Cliff House full of it—cram-jam, as Clara had expressed it—and retailing it up and down the school. And all those happy anticipations were knocked right on the head; and instead of a really enjoyable afternoon, she was going to sit in the form-room wrestling with Latin conjugations. Never had the tongue of Horace and Cicero seemed to Bessie Bunter so utterly weary, stale, flat, and unprofitable.

But there was no help for it, since that wretched message to Mamselle had turned up, and had been traced home to her. It was borne in upon Bessie Bunter's fat mind that, even if all the Staff at Cliff House School were " cats," it would be much wiser in future not to tell them so—even in capital letters.

CHAPTER XXVI

CLARA TO THE RESCUE

" Look here, Clara——."

" Br-r-r-r! " said Miss Trevlyn, expressively, if not very intelligibly.

" What's the matter? "

" Nothing."

" Then what are you scowling about? " asked Dolly Jobling.

" I'm not scowling."

" Well, it looks like it!   What about a spot of tennis? "

" Bother tennis."

" A walk on the cliffs——."

" Bother the cliffs! "

" Shall we walk down to Friardale and get something for tea at Uncle Clegg's? " suggested Dolly.   " We'll make Marjorie come."

" Marjorie doesn't want to walk down to Friardale with us."

" I don't see why not."

" The things you don't see, old thing, would make a list long enough to reach to the moon, and back again, and then some would be left over," said Clara.

Dolly frowned perplexedly.   Dolly was not much given to thinking; she was content to enjoy the passing day, and liked cheerful faces and untroubled brows.   But between her two friends, Dolly was getting quite a troubled time. Dolly could understand that Marjorie had had a severe jolt, now that she knew what was being said about Marjorie's brother, and she was not surprised that Marjorie was unusually quiet and grave, though as sweet-tempered as ever.   Dolly sympathised enormously, and wished that she knew some way of expressing her sympathy.   She was prepared to believe, as hard as she could, that Hazel was a spotlessly innocent character, if it helped Marjorie. But while it was natural that Marjorie should be rather in the doldrums, Dolly could see no reason why Clara should be.

But Clara was.

There had been a rift in the lute. But that was now happily mended. So Dolly could see no reason why Clara should be worried, and frowning, and tart—almost as tart as Marcia at her tartest.

Clara, however, had her reasons. She had causes for anxiety quite unknown to Dolly: and which she did not intend to confide to Dolly.

She was deeply anxious for Marjorie. Apart from that perfectly mad action in going out of the House at night— which Clara was determined should never be repeated, even if she had to lock the door of No. 7 to keep Marjorie in—there was the fact that Marjorie was helping, shielding, sustaining a boy who had run away from school. What would be the outcome, if it came out? And Clara felt that it must come out sooner or later.

Hazel could not carry on that skulking game unassisted, and would not somebody guess, sooner or later, who was assisting him?

It would mean an awful row. Marjorie believed in her brother, of course, but nobody else did or could. If he was innocent, he had, by his wilfulness and folly, made himself look guilty. It was unnerving for Marjorie to be mixed up in such an affair. Hazel had dragged her into it, and Clara's contempt for him was unbounded.

That only made matters worse. She was going to stick to Marjorie, through thick and thin: Marjorie needed her friends now, more than she had ever needed them before. Clara was a loyal friend, but not a patient one, and not a very tactful one. She simply could not speak of Hazel without revealing what she thought of him. That hurt

Marjorie, and she hated to hurt Marjorie; but how could it be helped?

And what was to come of it? It must end in an awful row, with Marjorie up before the Head—and goodness only knew what they would do. Clara's brow was quite dark as she thought of it.

" Not scowling, aren't you? " said Dolly, staring at her. " I'd like you to look in the looking-glass this minute."

" Bother! " said Clara.

" I say, are you stuffy because Marjorie wanted to be left alone? " asked Dolly. " I expect she feels she'd rather be alone a bit, in the circumstances."

" I thought that Bessie Bunter was the biggest idiot at Cliff House, up till now," remarked Clara.

" Well, isn't she? "

" No! You can give her fifty in a hundred, and beat her hollow."

" Look here, Clara," bleated the indignant Dolly. " If you're calling me an idiot——."

" No ' if ' about it."

" You're in a bad temper," said Dolly.

" Have you really guessed that one? " asked Clara, satirically. " Marvellous! How do you do these things, Dolly? "

" You'd better go and talk to Marcia! " said Dolly. " You can peck one another, see? She likes it—I don't! You're an unkind girl, Clara! "

" Oh, dear," said Clara. " Not really, old thing. You think that Marjorie wants to be left alone, because of that bother about the twerp, do you? "

" I suppose so. It's on her mind," said Dolly, nodding her head sagely. " You may not have noticed it as I have, Clara—but I can see it."

" Oh, my summer sunshade! " gasped Clara. " Don't make me laugh, Dolly."

" Eh! I'm not making you laugh," said Dolly, puzzled. " It's not a laughing matter—it's jolly serious. I can tell you that Marjorie's got it on her mind, whether you've noticed it or not."

" Whether I've noticed it or not! " murmured Clara, helplessly. " Oh, Dolly, you are too funny for words. What makes you so comic? "

" Well, I'd rather be comic than tragic, any day," said Dolly, " and if you're going to keep on scowling, and pecking like a chicken, you can go on scowling and pecking all by yourself, so there! "

And Dolly Jobling walked away, with a toss of the head. Clara felt remorseful for a moment; and then forgot Dolly. She was worried about Marjorie—and what Marjorie was going to do.

She knew, just as if Marjorie had told her, why Marjorie wanted her friends to leave her alone. She was aware that Marjorie had been making little purchases at the school shop that day, and she knew why. She was as sure that Marjorie was making up some inconspicuous package, to convey surreptitiously to a hidden " twerp," as if she had seen her doing it. Her only doubt was whether Marjorie was going that afternoon, as it was a half-holiday, or whether another nocturnal excursion was intended. In the latter case, Clara told herself grimly, she would stop her, if she had to hold her back by her hair! She couldn't and shouldn't do that mad thing again.

But what was she going to do—and where was she going —and where was that rat who had landed this trouble on her, and suppose she was spotted, and taken to the Head, and—and—and——Clara's suppositions and misgivings were endless, and disturbing, and alarming. It was, perhaps, no wonder that she had " pecked " a little in talking to the unsuspicious Dolly. She was, in fact, as she had admitted to Dolly, in a very bad temper!

Two or three girls called to her, as she loitered in the quad, but she answered with such Spartan brevity, that they stared, and went their ways; leaving her to her own perturbed reflections.

Finally, Marjorie came out of the House.

Clara, at a little distance, watched her, sarcastically. Marjorie's face was calm and grave, but Clara's searching eye could read uneasiness in it. She noted, too, that Marjorie's hand-bag had a stuffed look, as if it contained more than usual; and Clara could guess what was in it, and that the usual contents had been left out to make room. Carrying a parcel about might have drawn attention, and poor Marjorie, for once, had secrets to keep.

Clara came across to her, with set lips. It was her friendship and her anxiety for Marjorie that made her angry: but she was very angry indeed.

" You duffer," she said, curtly.

Marjorie looked at her.

" I know what you're at! But if you're taking food to that—that——I—I mean, to him, why not get the things at the village shop and take them to him direct, wherever he is? "

" Don't ask me questions, Clara dear."

Clara, naturally, supposed that the fugitive from Greyfriars was hidden somewhere near the school; but never dreamed that he was within the walls of Cliff House.

" Miss Primrose will be asking you questions, fast enough, if you get spotted by a pre. helping somebody who's run away from school."

" I know! " said Marjorie, in a low voice.

" Marjorie! It's not good enough," said Clara, earnestly. " You can't go on like this—it's bound to come out, and that means an awful row. Hazel ought to go back to his school, and face it—all the more if he's innocent, as you believe. If you leave him alone he'll have to go back."

" I must go now, Clara! Don't say any more, dear. I never meant you to know anything about it, and—and I wish you didn't.'"

Clara stood looking at her, worried and distressed, but more angry than either. It was useless to argue with Marjorie; gentle as her nature was, she was inflexible when her mind was made up. She believed that it was her duty to help that wretched " twerp," and she was going to do it, regardless of what might be the consequences to herself. Clara knew that she could do nothing—and the knowledge made her angrier than ever.

Marjorie's only feeling, at the moment, was anxiety for Clara to leave her. She was not, as her friend supposed, going out of gates—she was going to slip, as quietly as she could, round the school buildings, and get to the gardener's shed unnoticed. The coast was clear, at the moment, as Mr. Potts would be at his tea with Piper, but there was no time to waste. It was her only chance of getting to Hazel that day—if she failed, it meant the alternative of going out again after lights out—and apart from her own reluctance, she dreaded that Clara might intervene.

" Clara, dear——! " she murmured.

" I've a jolly good mind to stop you going out! " breathed Clara.

" I must go——."

" Mum! " said Clara, hastily. " Here comes Stella, and she's all ears—or very nearly! " And as Stella Stone of the Sixth came into the offing, Clara went on, in a casual tone, for the prefect's ears, " You'll have to do some unpicking to that jumper of Dolly's——."

" Marjorie! " Stella glanced rather curiously at Marjorie's face, in which the colour was wavering. She did not know that, just then, a Sixth Form prefect had unusual terrors for the schoolgirl with a secret.

" Yes, Stella," said Marjorie, faintly.

" Miss Bellew would like to see you in her study, about the Debate."

" Oh! Very well," stammered Marjorie.

Stella Stone passed on. Clara smiled, a sarcastic smile.

" You'd forgotten that the Debate meets on Saturdays, and that Bellew always has a chin about it first," she said. There was a note of triumph in her voice. The " twerp " could wait as long as he liked; Marjorie couldn't go to him now.

Marjorie was silent, utterly dismayed.

It was kind, and it was dutiful, on Miss Bellew's part, to take an interest in the junior debating society, but Marjorie, with so much on her mind, had forgotten both the Debate and Miss Bellew.

Now she had to go to her form-mistress's study, and goodness only knew how long Miss Bellew might keep her. The chance to see Hazel that day would be gone. And she had to go to him—she had to.

Clara eyed her, sarcastic and triumphant. Marjorie couldn't go to that twerp now, wherever he was, and so much the better. He could get on the best he could, without a girl running risks for him. And serve him right!

That was Clara's fixed opinion.

But that fixed opinion came unstuck, as it were, as she read the dismay and distress in Marjorie's face. She ceased to look, or to feel, either sarcastic or triumphant.

For a long moment, Clara hesitated.

Then she spoke, in a low voice:

" It's all right, old thing. Don't worry! Give me that bag."

" What——? "

" And tell me where to find him."

" But——."

" I'll go! " said Clara.

CHAPTER XXVII

AN UNEXPECTED VISITOR

HAZEL groaned aloud.

Seldom or never had any fellow felt so deeply and sincerely sorry for himself.

A stronger and manlier fellow than Hazel might have found it hard to bear. But a strong and manly fellow would never have been in his present situation.

Not that Hazel realised that the fault was his own. Whenever Marjorie's brother was in trouble, the fault was somebody else's.

He moved wearily about the apple-loft, too restless to keep still. His ears were intent for a sound below—if anyone came, he had to keep still and silent. But hardly anyone ever came to the gardener's shed, only Mr. Potts rummaging about every now and then.

Every time Hazel heard sounds below, he kept as still as a mouse, trembling. Yet he was almost glad when anyone came, he was so sick of solitude. Nobody came up to the loft—but he was always in dread that someone might come, and ready to dodge and hide behind the packing-cases. Yet a footstep, though terrifying, was welcome, as a sound of life in the silence and solitude.

Only at night, he ventured to leave the apple-loft, and descend into the shed, and even to take a walk—glancing fearfully about him—in the kitchen gardens. That was a great relief. There was a tap in the shed, and every night he filled a can to take up to the loft, to last him during the day. The food that Marjorie had been able to smuggle to him, though spare, was sufficient to keep him going.

Without her, he must have left his refuge, and faced up to what awaited him at his school.

Many times he thought of doing so—but always he faltered. He could not face it. He thought of home—but neither could he face that. Yet he knew that this could not go on—how could it?

He clung to one hope—perhaps they would find out who really had taken that registered letter from Quelch's study. He had done everything else, but he had not done that. Even Hazel could realise that the lie he had told his form-master fixed it upon him irrevocably—unless it came out who had actually done it. It might come out—it must come out—it had to come out—and they couldn't sack him, or hand him over to a police officer, so long as he remained in hiding!

Marjorie had brought him a couple of books, but he hardly looked at them. He was weary of the apple-loft; fed up to the back teeth, tired of his own bitter and miserable reflections, but there he was, and there he was going to stay, as long as he could, at least.

Marjorie had told him that Bob Cherry was trying to help. That fathead, that clumsy chump—what could he do? But contempt and ingratitude did not prevent him from hoping that Bob, somehow, might be able to do something. After all, someone must have shifted the rotten registered letter. They could find out who it was, if he hadn't made them believe that it was he. Bob might be able to find out—a pity the chap was such a silly idiot!

Outside, the sun was shining. Every now and then, some faint sound of a distant voice reached his ears—chattering shrieking schoolgirls, as he said savagely to himself.

Why didn't Marjorie come again? It wasn't easy, and it was risky: he knew that. Still, she might have come. Forgotten all about him, very likely, chattering in a chattering crowd of silly girls! She was a good sort—Hazel admitted that, even in his most irritable moments—still, she was only a girl, and girls had no sense! Hazel, in his present helpless situation, had not lost his happy sense of masculine superiority, for what that was worth.

Suddenly, he ceased to roam about the apple-loft like a caged animal, and stood quite still. He had heard the latch on the door below. Someone was coming into the shed.

That grunting old ass Potts again, no doubt. But as he listened with painful intentness, he heard a much lighter footstep than Potts'.

That footstep came across to the ladder in the corner of the shed, and he heard it mount.

Was it Marjorie? It seemed to him that it sounded like a girl's step. But if it was anyone else——.

On tiptoe, stealthily, he crept behind the packing-cases, and crouched low. There was a sound at the trap-door.

He dared not look, but he knew that the trap had been raised. With beating heart, he heard someone unseen step into the loft.

For a moment or two, there was silence: the newcomer apparently looking about in the dim light of the loft. Then came a voice. It was not Marjorie's.

" Anybody at home? "

Hazel trembled. He knew that voice; he had heard it often enough; Clara Trevlyn's. There was a faintly mocking tone in it, which had always rather made him dislike Clara. Somehow or other she had always made him feel like something small.

Now he felt not only small, but like a mouse with the cat at hand. If that shrew found him out, all was up. He could see her—in his mind's eye—rushing off, with a peal of laughter, to tell a mob of babbling schoolgirls that Marjorie's brother was hiding in the apple-loft. And she knew that somebody was there—what else could her words mean?

" Nobody at home? " went on Clara's voice.

Hazel remained perfectly still.

" If you're here, show up! " called out Clara.
" There's nothing to be afraid of—I'm not dangerous! I
know all about it, and I've come instead of Marjorie. So
brace up and show up."

" Oh! " gasped Hazel.

He understood now.   Slowly, he stepped out from
behind the packing-cases, eyeing Clara uneasily.

Dim as the light was in the loft, he could detect the
glimmer, half of amusement and half of mockery, in her
eyes.   He was untidy, unkempt, rumpled and crumpled,
and only too well aware of it.   Clara, neat and clean from
head to foot, made him feel that he disliked her more than
ever before.

" Oh! " he said, awkwardly.   " You! "

" Little me! " said Clara.   She tossed Marjorie's bag
on a box.   " Unpack that, will you?   I shall have to take
the bag back."

" Did Marjorie tell you——? "

" I'm a moderately intelligent girl," said Clara, " fairly
good at crosswords, and guessing puzzles.   But I couldn't
have guessed that you were here, if Marjorie hadn't told
me."

" I told her not to tell anybody——." muttered Hazel,
sulkily.   " I suppose a girl can't help talking."

Clara breathed hard.

" Marjorie couldn't come," she said, quietly.   " She's
with Miss Bellew, and can't get away.   Would you like
her to tell Miss Bellew that she had to go, because she had
to take something to a Greyfriars boy hiding in a loft? "

Hazel did not answer that.   He gave his attention to
extracting sandwiches from the bag.

" Has she told anybody else? " he asked, after a pause.

" No!   She didn't want to tell me.   Nobody else knows
you're skulking here," said Clara.

Hazel gave quite a jump. Apparently it had not occurred to him that his hiding in the apple-loft might be regarded, by others, as " skulking." His face crimsoned with mortification.

" You're safe, as far as that goes," said Clara. " I wouldn't have come on your account—I did it for Marjorie. Done with that bag? "

Hazel eyed her with furtive resentment.

" Has—has she told you anything else—besides my being here——."

" No! No need to, either—they've had the news from Greyfriars," answered Clara. " Everybody knows what you've done, and that you've bolted. Nobody knows you're here."

" So it's all over the shop," muttered Hazel. " Every silly girl in the place cackling about it, I suppose."

" Oh, we've got some other topics," said Clara, cheerfully. " Nothing so important as your affairs, of course —but little things that interest us, you know."

Hazel's only reply was a glance of intense dislike. He handed her the bag.

" Well, if you want to know, I never did anything," he snapped. " Quelch is making a silly mistake, that's all."

" So Marjorie thinks," said Clara.

" And you don't? " sneered Hazel.

" Well, running away doesn't look terribly innocent, does it? " said Clara. " Catch me running away! But then, of course, I'm only a girl! Boys know best, no doubt. Any message for Marjorie? "

" No! " grunted Hazel.

Clara turned to the trap, and descended from the loft. She was glad to go, having had quite enough of Marjorie's brother. And Hazel, little as he liked the solitude of the apple-loft, was glad to see her go: he had had quite enough of Miss Trevlyn.

" What a shrew! " he murmured, as he closed down the trap.

" What a twerp! " murmured Clara, as she descended the ladder.

Hazel was left to sandwiches and solitude—and such comfort as there was in meditating upon his wrongs and grievances.

CHAPTER XXVIII

NO LUCK!

" Oh! Get out! " said Bob Cherry.

" Oh, really, Cherry——."

" Buzz! " growled Bob.

Bob Cherry was not in the sunniest of tempers. The sight of Billy Bunter's fat face in the study doorway seemed to afford him no satisfaction whatever.

It was Monday, and during the days that had passed since he had met Marjorie Hazeldene in Friardale, Bob had not been idle. But he might as well have been, so far as results went.

Bob was the only member ot the " Famous Five " who believed that Hazel was not the guilty man. His friends hoped that he was right, for Marjorie's sake. But that was as far as they could get.

And perhaps Bob knew, at the back of his mind, that if Hazel hadn't been Marjorie's brother, he would have taken the same view that all the other fellows in the Remove had taken.

All the same, the Co. backed him up loyally. They did what they could—which was little enough. The outcome, so far as there was any outcome at all, was exactly the reverse of what Bob hoped. For inquiry and patient investigation merely established the fact that Hazel was the only Remove man who had gone to Quelch's study while Quelch was out, that disastrous Wednesday afternoon.

The result, in fact, was wholly negative. The amateur detectives had been able to trace the movements of all the Remove fellows on that particular half-holiday, chiefly because nobody had anything to hide and everybody was

quite willing to relate where he had been and what he had
been doing.

So Harry Wharton and Co. now knew, practically
beyond the shadow of a doubt, that the guilty man was not
in the Remove at all, if it was not Hazel.

That settled it for the Co. though Bob still clung to
hope. He simply longed to be able to take good news to
Marjorie, and see her face brighten when he told her that
he had made a discovery. But Wharton and Nugent,
Hurree Jamset Ram Singh and Johnny Bull, agreed unani-
mously that looking in any form but the Remove was simply
tosh.

Bob, in fact, knew it as well as they did. It was quite
obvious that no one could have known in advance that
Quelch had left that registered letter on his table, waiting
for him till he went out. Only someone who went to the
study for some reason wholly unconnected with it could
have seen it there and picked it up. And no fellow outside
Quelch's form could have any imaginable reason for going
there.

After class, on Monday, Bob was prepared to carry on
—if he could imagine how! But he couldn't! He was
quite at a loss. He came along to No. 1 Study to consult
his friends: but found that they were not there—they had
abandoned amateur detective work in favour of cricket,
and were down at the nets.

Bob could hardly blame them. Investigation had only
made it clear, so far, that there was nothing doing.

He threw himself into an armchair in the study, to think
it over—or try to think it over. Bob was a good deal
better at handling a cricket bat, or pulling an oar, than at
concentrated thinking. And there seemed no clue in the
maze. And—in spite of his determination to believe what
Marjorie believed—the troublesome thought would keep
on rising in his mind, suppose Hazel had done it, after all.
It looked as if he had—everybody thought he had—and
he had run away in a funk, just as if he had!

In that worried and troubled mood, about the last inhabitant of the globe whom Bob wanted to see, was William George Bunter. He almost glared at the fat Owl of the Remove as he rolled into the study.

But Billy Bunter did not " buzz " as requested. He gave the disgruntled junior in the armchair a cheery blink, through the big spectacles that were so like Sister Bessie's.

" I say, Bob, old chap——! " he began.

" Hook it," said Bob, impatiently.

" Well, I think you might be civil to a chap, when a chap's in a jam," said Bunter, reproachfully.

" Oh! What's the trouble, old fat frump? " asked Bob. He was always good-natured, and if the fat Owl was in a " jam," he was prepared to do anything he could, putting his own problems aside for a moment.

" It's a bit awkward," said Bunter, blinking at him. " Mrs. Mimble has got a lot of fresh sausage-rolls in, at the tuck-shop. But I've run right out of cash. I was expecting a postal-order——."

" What? " roared Bob.

" A postal-order! No need to yell at a chap! But it hasn't come," said Bunter, sorrowfully. " I can't quite make out why—it's from one of my titled relations, you know! Still it hasn't come."

Bob looked round for a missile.

" So I'm rather in a jam," continued Bunter. " Think you could lend me five bob, Cherry, and take the postal-order when it comes? "

" Hand me that cushion over there," said Bob.

" Eh! What do you want it for? "

" To chuck at your silly head."

" Beast! "

Billy Bunter did not hand over the cushion. He seemed to anticipate no pleasure in having it chucked at his silly head.

He rolled to the door. But he turned again, and once more the big spectacles were fixed on Bob.

" I say, Cherry, old chap——."

" For goodness sake, leave a fellow alone," exclaimed Bob. " I've got something to think out, so don't bother."

" He, he, he! " chuckled Bunter.

" What are you cackling at, you fat image? "

" He, he, he." Bunter seemed amused. " I know! You're making all the fellows laugh, old chap. Smithy has nicknamed you Sexton Blake! He, he, he."

Bob knitted his brows. He was not unaware that his detective work had caused some merriment in the Remove. Skinner had declared, in the rag, that Sherlock-Holmes-Cherry was in search of a delinquent who wasn't Marjorie Hazeldene's brother and that anybody whose name wasn't Hazeldene would do! Which made the Removites laugh, but did not amuse Cherry.

" Will you get out, Bunter? " growled Bob.

" The fact is, old fellow, I want to help! " said Bunter. " That's really why I came here—not because I wanted to borrow five bob, but because I'd like to help you, dear old chap."

" Oh, scat! "

" Of course, we all know Hazel did it," went on Bunter. " He wouldn't have told Quelch whoppers about not being in the study if he hadn't, would he? "

" How many whoppers have you told Quelch in your time? " hooted Bob.

" Oh, really, Cherry——."

" If a chap couldn't tell whoppers, without pilfering too, you'd have been hiked off to Borstal long ago."

" Why, you beast! " howled Bunter. " Making out I tell whoppers! Me! Insulting a chap who only came here to help you—not to borrow five bob——."

" Travel! "

" But I can overlook your bad manners," said Bunter. " After all, I don't expect much from you in that line, Cherry. What I mean to say is, we all know Hazel did it, and that's why he bolted. You want to make out that he didn't——."

" I believe he didn't, you fat chump," growled Bob, "and what I want to find out is, whether anybody else went to the study while Quelch was out. You fat villain, you ought to be able to help."

" Well, with my brains, I fancy I could," said Bunter. " Is that what you mean? "

" No, that isn't what I mean. I mean that you're a prying, inquisitive little fat twerp, always nosing about keyholes. Why couldn't you have been prying about masters' studies that afternoon? " snorted Bob.

" Why, you cheeky beast——! "

" Oh, hook it," said Bob. " Get out! Travel! Mizzle! Bunk! "

Billy Bunter breathed hard through his fat little nose. For a fellow who wanted to help, he was not getting a gratifying reception. But perhaps he still had hopes of that little loan.

" Look here, I really want to help," he urged. " And with my brains, I could. If you're right, and Hazel never did it, somebody else did, see? "

" Oh, my hat! Did you work that out all by yourself? "

" Well, I've got brains," said Bunter. " I can think things out. I fancy I should make a pretty good detective. Cool, clear intellect, you know—that's what's needed. What are you grinning at? "

" Fathead! "

" Well, you can call a fellow names, but you haven't got very far as yet, and chance it," said Bunter. " You haven't the intellect for it, old chap, if you don't mind my saying so. " You're rather dense, you know. I mean to say, everybody knows you're rather an ass, don't they? "

Bob Cherry reached out, and grasped the cushion. Billy Bunter eyed him warily.

" Look here, don't you want me to help? " he urged. " I'll tell you what—you lend me that five bob——."

" I'll lend you this cushion, if you don't roll off."

" You lend me that five bob, and I'll go over to Cliff House and see my sister Bessie——."

Bob stared at him.

" What on earth good would that do? " he asked, blankly.

" Well, I think Bessie might be able to help——! "

" You blithering owl! "

" Oh, really, Cherry——. Two heads are better than one, you know——."

" Not when there's nothing in them," said Bob. " Two Bunters have just as much sense as one Bunter, and that's none at all. Now look here, you fat ass, I've got to think this out, and I can't think with a fat Owl burbling in my ears. So hook it before I land you with this cushion."

" If you haven't got five bob——."

" Buzz, you fat bluebottle! "

" Make it half-a-crown, and I'll—yaroooooop! "

Whiz!

Bob's patience seemed to be exhausted. The cushion flew, and Billy Bunter dodged too late. It landed on the widest part of Bunter's circumference, and he sat down on the study floor, with a roar.

" The inkpot's coming next," said Bob. " If you want the inkpot——! "

Billy Bunter did not want the inkpot. He bounded up, and bounded out of No. 1 Study. Bob was left to think out his knotty problem, without any help from Billy Bunter—for what that might have been worth!

CHAPTER XXIX

BESSIE'S BRIGHT IDEA!

" MARJORIE! "

" Yes, Bessie! "

" Will you keep cave for me? "

" We're busy," said Clara.

Sniff, from Bessie.

They were really busy, in the junior common-room, after classes on Monday. Marjorie was holding a skein of wool which Clara was rolling into a ball. Dolly Jobling was busiest of the three, having hooked another skein on the back of a chair, to unwind it and roll it into a ball entirely on her own—and having involved herself and the wool in an almost inextricable tangle.

Bessie Bunter did not heed the occupation of the chums of No. 7 Study. No occupation could be of any great consequence, in comparison with Bessie's own affairs. Clara's remark only drew an irritated sniff from Bessie. Really it was quite irrelevant.

" You see, it will be safer with somebody keeping cave at the end of the passage," Bessie proceeded to explain. " Bellew has gone to see the Head, but she might come back, of course."

" My dear Bessie, what have you got in your head now? " asked Marjorie. " If you are thinking of playing tricks on Miss Bellew——."

" What is it—calling her a cat in capital letters, so that she won't know you did it? " inquired Clara, sarcastically. " She will track you out by the ' k ' in ' cat ' if you do."

" I'm going to hide her fountain-pen," chuckled Bessie. " She's left it on her table—I saw it through the window.

You know what she did," went on Bessie, with deep indignation. " Kept me in on Saturday afternoon, when I was going over to Greyfrairs to see Billy. I told her I never wrote that message to Mamselle about being a cat, and she wouldn't even listen."

" But you did write it," said Marjorie.

" She couldn't know when I did it in capitals. Just guessed! " said Bessie. " And kept me in, for nothing! Well, I'm going to give her a hunt for her fountain-pen, see? You come and keep cave for me, Marjorie, and I'll give you some of my toffee."

There was a chunk of toffee in Bessie's fat fingers. It was sticky, and the fingers were sticky, and there was a sticky smear round Bessie's mouth. She held up the chunk temptingly.

Toffee would have been an irresistible bribe to Bessie. But it did not have the same effect on Marjorie. Only Bessie, in fact, could have seen anything attractive in the moist sticky chunk sticking to her sticky fingers.

Marjorie laughed.

" Thank you, Bessie—I don't want the toffee," she said. " And I don't want you to get into another row with Miss Bellew. Do keep away from her study."

" I'll watch it," said Bessie. " Didn't she keep me in for nothing on Saturday? "

" But you did write that message to Mademoiselle Lupin——."

" Bellew didn't know, and that's just the same as if I didn't! " explained Bessie. " A girl expects justice."

" But she did know," hooted Clara. " The way you spelt it——."

" Eh? What was the matter with my spelling? " asked Bessie.

" What wasn't the matter with it, do you mean? "

" No, I don't! Perhaps you can spell French better than I can, Clara Trevlyn! " said Bessie, with a sniff of disdain.

" Ha, ha, ha! "

" My French is all right, I think," said Bessie. " Bellew just picked on me. I never get justice, as you girls know. Mamselle called me an ass, in class—you all heard her——."

" She didn't! " almost howled Clara. " She said ' assez '——."

" I know what she said! And I know that Bellew kept me in for nothing, and I know I'm going to hide her fountain-pen and make her wild! " declared Bessie. " I think you might come and keep cave for me, Marjorie. If I hadn't been kept in, I was going over to Greyfriars to find out all about your brother——."

" Dry up, you little idiot," hissed Clara, as Marjorie's cheeks burned.

" Eh! I suppose Marjorie would like to know all about it, and I was going to tell her when I came back," said Bessie. " We don't know much so far, except that Marjorie's brother pinched something from his form-master's study—Ow! Who's that treading on my foot? Wharrer you stamping on my foot for, Babs? Yoo-hooh! "

Marjorie kept her eyes on the wool she was holding for Clara. She did not look up, but her cheeks were growing crimson. Every other girl in common-room looked at Bessie expressively.

Bessie, however, dropped the subject, as she caressed a large foot on which Barbara had stepped, perhaps by accident.

" Ow! ow! ow! " wailed Bessie. " Clumsy elephant! Ow! ow! "

" I say, I'm getting into an awful tangle," said Dolly Jobling. " I don't know how this wool got tangled—but it has! "

" What are you trying to do with it? " asked Mabs. " Making a sailor's knot, or a Gordian knot? "

" Ow! ow! You keep your hoofs to yourself, Barbara! Ow! " Bessie gave Babs a glare that might almost have

cracked her spectacles, and found comfort in another bite
of toffee. " I say, Marjorie, do come and keep cave for
me, in case Bellew comes back from Primrose's study."

" Nonsense," said Marjorie. " Keep away from Miss
Bellew's study, and don't be a little donkey."

" Cat! I say, Clara, will you——."

" Not half! " said Clara.

" Look here, Babs, you come and——."

" Bow-wow! " said Barbara.

" Mabs, old dear, will you——? "

" Ask next door! " said Mabel.

" I say, Dolly, you come and keep cave for me, and I'll
help you with that wool."

" If you touch this wool with your sticky fingers——."

" Cat! I say, Gwendoline——."

" Bosh! " said Gwendoline.

" Annabel, you come——."

" Tosh! " said Annabel.

Bessie Bunter chewed toffee, and frowned. There were
quite a number of Fourth Form girls in common-room,
but not one of them, apparently, was available to keep
" cave " while Bessie carried out her masterly scheme in
Miss Bellew's study. Nobody, indeed, seemed to comprehend what a bright idea it was!

To Bessie, it seemed one of the very brightest! The
contemplation of Miss Bellew hunting all over her study
for that fountain-pen was very amusing—to Bessie. It
would serve her right, just as it had served Mr. Quelch, at
Greyfriars, right, to have to hunt all over his study for a
registered letter! It was the kind of prank that seemed
quite masterly to Bessie, whose fat brain worked in mysterious ways its wonders to perform. But she did want some
girl to keep " cave " at the end of the passage, to make
all safe.

But evidently all the girls in common-room were
" cats," and weren't going to help. Bessie gave an angry
and indignant snort.

" Well, if you won't come and keep cave, I shall chance it," she said. " It will be your fault, Marjorie, if I get copped."

" For goodness sake, Bessie——."

" Yah! " said Bessie: and she rolled out of common-room, on vengeance bent.

" Bessie! " called out Marjorie, anxiously, as she went. But Fatima of Cliff House rolled away unheeding.

" Little ass! " said Clara.

" She won't get anybody to keep cave for her," said Barbara. " Bessie's the only prize idiot in the Fourth."

" It will mean a row if she does," said Marjorie, uneasily. " Miss Bellew uses that fountain-pen for everything. If she can't find it——."

" We shall hear the thunder roll! " said Mabel. " But it's no good talking sense to Bessie."

" Though you bray a fool in a mortar, yet will not his folly depart from him—and the same applies to hers as well as hims! " said Miss Clara, oracularly. " Mind how you hold that wool, Marjorie—and never mind Bessie."

But Marjorie, though she gave attention to the wool, could not help " minding " Bessie a little, and she hoped that the fat junior might possibly have sense enough to steer clear of playing tricks in Miss Bellew's study.

That hope was quite unfounded. Five minutes later there was a fat cachinnation in the doorway, as Bessie Bunter reappeared there.

" He, he, he! "

Bessie rolled in. Her fat face was irradiated by a fat grin, so extensive that it stretched almost from one of Bessie's fat ears to the other. Her gooseberry eyes danced with merriment behind her spectacles. Bessie, evidently, was in a state of triumphant satisfaction.

" I say, you girls—he, he, he! " trilled Bessie. " I've done it! "

" You've done it! " exclaimed Marjorie.

" He, he, he! What do you think? There was nobody about so I didn't want you to keep cave after all, so yah! I say, will Bellew be wild when she can't find her fountain-pen? He, he, he! "

" There'll be a row," said Clara.

" He, he, he! Bellew won't be able to guess that it was me—how could she? He, he, he! Mind you don't give me away if she comes here! I expect she will be asking everybody if anybody's seen her fountain-pen! He, he, he! "

And Bessie Bunter chuckled and chuckled, and giggled and giggled, till tears of merriment bedewed her spectacles.

CHAPTER XXX

AWFUL!

MISS BELLEW turned the handle of her study door—and uttered a slight exclamation of annoyance. Miss Bellew's fingers were slim and spotless. But they were not quite spotless after turning that door-handle. That door-handle should have been, and ought to have been, as spotless as Miss Bellew's slim fingers. Instead of which, it was sticky to the touch, as if the last comer to the study had turned it with a hand dipped in treacle.

Miss Bellew set her lips primly. She detested stickiness, slovenliness, and all carelessness in matter of personal cleanliness. Those charming qualities were to be found, in great abundance, in one particular member of her form.

Often and often had Miss Bellew lectured Bessie Bunter on that subject. Now she made a mental note to give Bessie one more lecture, not lacking in emphasis.

As the stickiness of the door-handle left her in no doubt that Elizabeth Bunter had been to the study, she rather expected to find her within, when she opened the door. If Bessie had come there to speak to her about something, she would doubtless wait till her form-mistress came back.

But the study was vacant. If Bessie Bunter had been there, she had gone again. So that lecture on sticky fingers had to be postponed. Miss Bellew had work on hand: she was busy that day preparing the term's reports, and had no time at the moment to waste on Bessie Bunter.

She sat down at her writing-table, and stretched out her hand for the fountain-pen she had left on the blotter, when she had been interrupted, half-an-hour ago, by a message from the Principal.

Then she frowned.

The fountain-pen was not there. In annoyance and surprise, she gazed round for it. It might imaginably have rolled. But it was not to be seen on the writing-table at all.

" Goodness gracious! " ejaculated Miss Bellew, addressing space.

She was not only surprised and annoyed—she was startled. The disappearance of the fountain-pen gave her a very unpleasant shock.

It had been taken away!

She knew that she had left it there. There was no doubt about that. She remembered that she had refilled it at the inkpot, and just then the message from Miss Penelope Primrose had arrived, and she had laid it down on the blotter, and left the study. Her mind was quite clear on that. The pen should have been lying on the blotter, ready to her hand: and it was gone.

Miss Bellew's face grew grimmer, as she sat staring at the blotter.

The missing article was of value. It had cost three guineas. Certainly it was valuable enough to tempt a pilferer, if anything so repulsive could be imagined to exist within the walls of Cliff House School. And what was Miss Bellew to imagine—when the pen was gone?

Someone had entered the study during her absence and removed the pen. That was a positive fact.

With her fingers still slightly sticky from contact with the door-handle, she could have no doubt who had entered the study.

Bessie Bunter had no business there. There was no reason why she should have come to the study at all. But she had been there—and an article of value was missing!

For a long, long minute Miss Bellew sat staring at the blotter, her brows corrugated with painful thought.

Then, with her lips set in a tight line, she rose, and left the study. Term's reports had to wait: this, obviously, was a matter that had to be looked into without delay.

A minute more, and the form-mistress of the Cliff House Fourth was glancing in at the doorway of the junior common-room.

A fat giggle greeted her ears, as she arrived there. Her eyes fell upon a fat face wreathed in smiles. Bessie Bunter was giggling and grinning, apparently highly amused about something.

But the giggle died away quite suddenly, as Miss Bellew was seen in the doorway. Bessie's fat face became very serious.

All the girls rose to their feet, as Miss Bellew came in, and all faces were serious, as well as Bessie's. Everyone could guess why Miss Bellew was there—she wanted to know about the missing fountain-pen.

Bessie blinked stealthily at her through her spectacles. Miss Bellew simply couldn't guess that she was the culprit —how could she? Bessie, at least, could not possibly see how she could. Still, she did not like the glint in Miss Bellew's eye, and she could not fail to note that that eye fixed upon her particularly.

" Someone has been to my study, while I was with the Principal," said Miss Bellew, quietly. " Whoever it was, please speak."

Silence.

" I desire to know who has entered my study," said Miss Bellew, raising her voice a little. " If the girl is present, I order her to speak."

Still silence.

Nobody excepting Bessie Bunter had been to Miss Bellew's study—and Bessie was not likely to speak! Miss Bellew paused, like Brutus, for a reply. Like Brutus again, she got no reply. A pin might have been heard to drop, in the junior common-room.

Miss Bellew compressed her lips in a tighter line.

" The matter is serious," she said, very quietly. " An article of some value is missing from my study. It must be accounted for at once."

" Oh! " breathed Marjorie; and many of the girls exchanged startled looks. Miss Bellew's words put a new and quite unnerving complexion on the affair.

Everyone in the junior common-room realised that at once—with the solitary exception of Bessie Bunter. Bessie's fat brain was not quick on the uptake.

" Unless the missing article is accounted for immediately, and a satisfactory explanation given, I must place the matter before the Principal! " continued Miss Bellew. " Once more I ask the girl who has been to my study during my absence to speak."

Dead silence.

" Very well," said Miss Bellew, after another long pause for a reply, " as the girl concerned does not choose to admit visiting my study during my absence, I can only conclude that she has no explanation to offer. Bessie! "

" Oh! " gasped Bessie. " Yes, Miss Bellew."

She blinked at her form-mistress in growing uneasiness. Why did the cat address her specially? She had the whole form to choose from!

" Have you entered my study during the last half-hour, Bessie? "

" Oh, really, Miss Bellew——."

" Answer my question at once."

" I—I—I——! " stammered Bessie.

" Own up, you little idiot! " whispered Clara, into a fat ear.

" Oh, really, Clara——."

" Clara, you need not speak to Bessie! Bessie, answer my question immediately," rapped Miss Bellew. " Have you, or have you not, entered my study? "

" Oh! No! " stuttered Bessie. " Certainly not, Miss Bellew. I—I've been here all the time——I—I mean nearly all the time——I—I haven't been anywhere near your study, Miss Bellew. I—I didn't know you weren't there——."

" What? "

" I—I didn't really," gasped Bessie, more and more alarmed by the grim face and glinting eye of the form-mistress of the Fourth. " I never knew you'd gone to the Head, Miss Bellew. I certainly never saw you go, and I never told any of the girls so. Not a—a—a word. You—you can ask them, Miss Bellew——they all heard me——."

" Bessie! "

" I—I mean they didn't heard me——I mean——."

" That will do, Bessie! Now hold up your hands," said Miss Bellew.

Bessie blinked at her in astonishment. Why Miss Bellew wanted to inspect her fat hands, she had no idea. Neither, for the moment, had anyone else in the common-room.

" At once! " snapped Miss Bellew.

" Oh! Yes, Miss Bellew," stammered Bessie. And she held up a pair of sticky paws that looked very much in need of soap and hot water.

Miss Bellew scanned them.

" Your fingers are sticky, Bessie." Her voice was deep.

" Oh! Are they, Miss Bellew! Shall—shall I go and —and—and wash them at once? " stuttered Bessie. Bessie, at that moment, would have been glad to escape the glinting eye, even for the purpose of an extra wash!

" The door-handle of my study is also sticky, Bessie," said Miss Bellew, grimly.

" Oh, lor'! " gasped Bessie. She began to understand.

" Do you still deny that you visited my study during my absence, Bessie? "

" I—Oh—yes—no—I mean—no—yes—oh, crikey! " Bessie was a little incoherent.

" I shall now," said Miss Bellew, " take you to the Principal. The matter is too serious for me to deal with as your form-mistress."

" Ow! " wailed Bessie. " I—I—I don't want to go to Miss Primrose, please, Miss Bellew. Oh, dear! "

" I have no alternative," said Miss Bellew. " You will return the article you have purloined from my study, Bessie—a fountain-pen. Miss Primrose must decide what is further to be done, but I can hold out no hope that you will be permitted to remain at Cliff House."

Bessie Bunter almost fell down.

" Oh! " gasped all the girls in the junior common-room. Miss Bellew's words had rather the effect of a thunderbolt, on all of them.

But the effect was most paralysing on Bessie Bunter. Her plump jaw sagged, her eyes seemed to bulge through her spectacles, and her plump cheeks, which generally looked like ripe apples, looked like dough. She gazed at Miss Bellew in panic-stricken terror.

" Come with me," said Miss Bellew. " You heard what I said, Bessie."

" Oh, lor'! I—I—I never——."

" Come! "

" I—I never——I didn't——I—I wasn't——I—I—— oh, jiminy! It—it wasn't me——I—I mean, I didn't mean, I didn't wasn't——I wasn't never——."

Miss Bellew compressed her lips.

" Come! " she rapped. And her hand fell on a fat shoulder, to lead Bessie away to judgment: and the yell of terror that came from Elizabeth Bunter woke all the echoes of the junior common-room.

CHAPTER XXXI

NARROW ESCAPE!

MARJORIE ran forward.

"Miss Bellew——" she panted.

"You need not intervene, Marjorie. Kindly be silent. Bessie, come with me at once," said Miss Bellew, icily.

"Ow! I didn't—I wasn't—I never—I don't want to go to the Head—I wasn't never didn't——."

"Miss Bellew, you must listen to me," exclaimed Marjorie. All the other girls in the junior common-room were looking on in dumb dismay; quite horrified by the awful turn the affair had taken. Marjorie, heedless of Miss Bellew's icy stare, hurried on. "It's not as you think—Bessie did not——."

"That is for the Principal to decide, Marjorie. Be silent! Bessie, come with me at once."

"But she did not!" Marjorie almost shrieked. "It's only a silly trick, Miss Bellew—Bessie has not taken the fountain-pen. She had hidden it."

"What?"

"That is all, Miss Bellew. A silly prank."

"Nonsense."

"It's true, Miss Bellew." Clara found her voice. "We all knew—Bessie told us what she had done——."

"She told us all about it, Miss Bellew!" exclaimed Barbara. "It's still in your study—it must be——."

"It wasn't taken away, Miss Bellew," said Mabs.

A dozen voices joined in. It was quite a chorus. Miss Bellew stared from face to face, almost blankly. Certainly, she would have been very glad to believe that no pilfering had taken place. But it was not easy to believe.

"I do not understand this," she said, sharply. "Do not all speak at once, pray. Marjorie, you may speak.

There is no doubt that Bessie went to my study surreptitiously, that she has told untruths about it, and that an article of value is missing. Yet you tell me——.''

" Yes, yes, Miss Bellew,'' said Marjorie, breathlesly. " But it was only a prank—I am quite sure of that—Bessie told us all what she was going to do——. She told us she was going to your study——.''

" I didn't! '' yelled Bessie.

" Be quiet, you silly little chump! '' breathed Clara.

" Shan't! '' howled Bessie. " I ain't going to have Marjorie telling Miss Bellew I said I was going to her study——.''

" Silence! '' rapped Miss Bellew.

" But I never——.''

" You utterly stupid girl, cannot you see that Marjorie is trying to clear you of a charge on which you would be expelled from Cliff House! '' exclaimed Miss Bellew.

" Oh! Is she? '' gasped Bessie. " Still, I never——.''

" Be silent! What else have you to tell me, Marjorie? ''

" We knew all about it, Miss Bellew, and Bessie wouldn't have told the whole form, if she had been going to do what you thought——.''

" Probably not,'' said Miss Bellew. " But the article is missing——. The fountain-pen has been removed——.''

" It is hidden in your study, Miss Bellew! Bessie told us so—she never took it away—she hid it——.''

" I didn't——! '' shrieked Bessie.

" Grant me patience! '' murmured Miss Bellew. " Marjorie, it is difficult to believe that even Bessie, the stupidest girl in the school, could be so unbelievably stupid as you say. However, I will question her again. Bessie——.''

" I—I never——'' wailed Bessie. " I haven't been to your study, Miss Bellew, and I never knew you had a fountain-pen at all. I never said I was going to your study to hide it—and it was only a joke—just a joke—besides, I never said anything of the kind.''

" BE QUIET, YOU SILLY LITTLE CHUMP! " BREATHED CLARA

" Oh, my summer sunshade! " murmured Clara.

" Bessie——! " urged Marjorie.

" Cat! " gasped Bessie. " Telling Miss Bellew what I told you—giving a girl away! Not that I told you, either——."

" Bessie, listen to me," said Miss Bellew. " If you have played a foolish prank in my study, you will certainly be punished——."

" I didn't—I never——."

" But if it was not a prank," said Miss Bellew, in an awful voice, " it was pilfering, and you will be taken to the Principal, and sent away from the school. Now tell me the truth "

" Oh, crikey! "

" The truth—at once! " rapped Miss Bellew. " Did you take the fountain-pen from my study, or did you not? "

" Ow! No! I never——."

" Did you hide it in my study, as Marjorie says? "

" She's a cat! I never——."

" Very well," said Miss Bellew. " If the fountain-pen is not hidden in my study, as Marjorie supposes, it has been purloined, and you are guilty——."

" Oh! I—I—I mean I did hid it——I mean I hided it——I—I—I——it's in the waste-paper basket! " yelled Bessie. Apparently her fat brain was beginning to comprehend at last.

" In the waste-paper basket! " repeated Miss Bellew.

" Ow! Yes! I never performed it——I mean purlonged it——I—I hid it in the waste-paper bub-bub-basket under your tut-tut-table."

" Upon my word! " said Miss Bellew. She gazed at Bessie Bunter. She had had a good deal of experience of of the impenetrable obtuseness of that bright member of her form, but this was the limit. " Upon my word! " she repeated. " Bessie, are you so obtuse, so incredibly stupid, so wholly lacking in commonsense, as to conceal an article of value, at the risk of being suspected of having purloined it? Upon my word.''

" I—I—I didn't——I—I mean, I—I did——! " babbled Bessie.

" I can scarcely believe it," said Miss Bellew. " However, we shall see. Marjorie, please go to my study at once, and look in the waste-paper basket. If the fountain-pen is there, bring it to me here.''

" Yes, Miss Bellew.''

Marjorie hurried from the room. She almost flew to Miss Bellew's study. There was a dead silence while she was gone. Miss Bellew stood like a statue of grim wrath. Bessie Bunter blinked at her with terrified blinks, quite overwhelmed by the unexpected outcome of her masterly scheme.

In hardly more than a minute, Marjorie was back again —with a fountain-pen in her hand.

" Here it is, Miss Bellew," she panted.

Miss Bellew took it from her, and examined it, as if a doubt still lingered in her mind. But the initials " E.B. " in gold letters were on it, and it was assuredly and unmistakeably the missing article.

" You found this in the waste-paper basket in my study, Marjorie? ''

" Yes, Miss Bellew.''

" It is undoubtedly my fountain-pen," said Miss Bellew. " Bessie, it appears that your almost incredible statement is correct. You have played a foolish and disrespectful trick on your form-mistress——.''

" I—I—I haven't——.''

" But I am thankful, deeply thankful, that the matter is no worse. It is a great relief to my mind to know that nothing has happened but an act of almost unbelievable stupidity. I shall report your conduct to the Principal, Bessie, and you must expect a severe punishment——.''

" Oh, lor'! ''

" And if anything of the kind should occur again——! "
Miss Bellew paused, and, leaving the rest to Bessie's
imagination, turned and walked, or rather stalked, out
of the junior common-room.

Bessie gasped with relief, when she was gone.

" Oh, crikey! " said Bessie. " I say, you girls, fancy
Bellew thinking that her fountain-pen had been
pinched——."

" What else was she to think, when it was gone, you
blithering little fat ditherer? " asked Clara.

" Cat! Now I've got to go up to the Head, and it's
all Marjorie's fault—telling Bellew what I said——."

" Oh, dear! " said Marjorie.

" Giving a girl away! " said Bessie. " Not the sort
of thing I would do! Now I've got to go up to the
Primrose——."

" You'd have had to go up to be sacked, if Marjorie
hadn't spoken up for you, you dithering image! " shrieked
Clara.

" Well, I wouldn't give a girl away," said Bessie,
shaking her head. " Mean, I call it."

And Bessie rolled out of the common-room, with a
sniff, leaving most of the girls there laughing. But one
thing was fairly certain—Bessie Bunter was not likely to
play a prank of that kind again. She had absolutely no
further use for such bright ideas!

CHAPTER XXXII

STARTLING!

" HAD a good time? "

Bob Cherry spoke sarcastically.

It was not often that Bob was sarcastic. But he had a disgruntled feeling that afternoon. Sitting in the armchair in No. 1 Study, thinking over the problem that worried him, had produced nothing but a slight headache. He was no nearer a solution—indeed, he could not help doubting whether there was a solution at all. His ruddy face was clouded when his friends came in, fresh and cheery from the cricket, and ready for tea.

" Quite! " said Harry Wharton, with a smile. " Why didn't you come down to the nets, Bob? "

" Something else to do! " grunted Bob.

" Such as sitting in an armchair? " asked Johnny Bull. " Must have kept you frightfully busy."

Snort, from Bob.

" Don't be an ass, if you can help it," he suggested.

" Hem! " murmured Frank Nugent. " What about tea? "

" Blow tea! "

" Shirty about something? " inquired Johnny Bull, staring.

" Oh, no," answered Bob, sarcastic again. " I've got a stinker of a worry on my mind, and I fancied that my pals were going to help. But naturally you can't think about anything but cricket. Don't mind me."

" Well, you don't think about much else as a rule," remarked Johnny.

" Br-r-r-r! " said Bob.

" My dear chap," said Harry Wharton.   " We'll

chuck that, or anything else, if we can help, but I don't quite see what we can do."

" The seefulness is not terrific, my esteemed Bob," remarked Hurree Jamset Ram Singh.

" Have you been thinking it over here? " said Nugent.

" Yes," grunted Bob.   " I have."

" Well, what's the result? "

" Nothing."

" Might as well be at the nets, as thinking it over and getting nowhere," remarked Johnny Bull.

" The helpfulness of our absurd selves will be terrific, if you can tell us anything we can do," murmured Hurree Jamset Ram Singh.   " We are all preposterously keen to restore the idiotic equanimity of the beauteous Marjorie."

" It's rotten," growled Bob.   " Did you see Hazel's pater when he came down yesterday? He looked pretty sick. That ass hasn't been home—he can't be found—goodness knows where he is, or what's become of him. And—and I feel sure that Marjorie's got it right—he never did it."

" Who did, then? " asked Johnny Bull.

" What's the good of asking me that, fathead? We ought to be able to find out somehow. But I can't do anything, and you fellows can't—especially as you're so busy with cricket——."

" Draw it mild, old chap!   We'd do anything we could," said Nugent.

" And nobody else wants to help! " growled Bob. " Excepting Bunter! " he added, with a snort.

" Bunter! " repeated Harry Wharton.   " Has Bunter offered to help? "

" Oh, yes!   He offered to go over to Cliff House and get his sister Bessie to help, too! " snorted Bob.   " Two heads fatter than one—I suppose that's the idea."

" How on earth could Bessie help? "

" She couldn't, of course."

" What did Bunter mean, then? "

" He meant to stick me for five bob, on a postal-order he's expecting," snorted Bob. " I chucked a cushion at him."

" Bessie can't know anything about it. I remember she was coming over that day, to go to a circus with Bunter—I don't know whether she came——."

" Oh, she came," grunted Bob. " I took her into the Rag, where the fat ass was frowsting. I didn't see her again after that."

" They couldn't have gone to the circus—Bunter was gated," said Nugent.

" Oh, blow Bunter, and—and—and bless Bessie! " grunted Bob Cherry. " May as well have tea, I suppose. I——"

" I say, you fellows——."

" Hallo, hallo, hallo! Here he is again. Hand me that cushion, Franky."

" Oh, really, Cherry——."

" Hold on, Bob," said Harry Wharton. " May as well get out of the fat ass what he meant, if he meant anything. Trickle in, Bunter."

Billy Bunter blinked into the study, warily, through his big spectacles. His eyes and his spectacles lingered on a parcel Nugent had dropped on the study table. Then they fixed on Bob Cherry's clouded face. Perhaps Bunter knew that there were sausage-rolls in the parcel. But he was uneasy about the cushion.

" I say, you fellows, if that beast is going to chuck things at a chap——! " began Bunter.

" Oh, roll in, barrel! " growled Bob.

Bunter rolled in.

" Well, if you're going to be civil, all right," he said. " Chucking things at a chap, when he offered to help——. Ungrateful, I call it. It's like what Spokeshave said—I mean Shakespeare—how sharper than a thankless child it is to have a serpent's tooth——."

" Ha, ha, ha! "

" Well, you can cackle," snorted Bunter. " But a fellow might be grateful. I say, I'll unpack that parcel, if you like."

Without waiting to ascertain whether the juniors liked, Bunter proceeded to unpack the parcel, revealing sausage-rolls. His little round eyes glistened at them behind his big round spectacles. Bunter had had only tea in hall so far, and he was quite ready for sausage-rolls.

" And how were you going to help? " asked Harry Wharton. " Do you know whether any fellows beside Hazel went to Quelch's study last Wednesday afternoon while Quelch was out? "

" We've asked the fat ass that before, and he doesn't," growled Bob Cherry. " He can't help—except to get rid of the sausage-rolls."

" Let him speak, anyhow," said Harry. " Look here, Bunter, do you know anything about what happened last Wednesday in Quelch's study? "

" Eh! Of course I don't," answered Bunter. " How could I? I say, mind if I begin on these sausage-rolls? They look good."

" You don't know anything about it? "

" Not a thing, old chap." Bunter started on a sausage-roll. " I never knew anything about it till I heard that Hazel was up for pinching. Of course, he did it. We all know that. Still, somebody else might have gone to the study."

" That's what we want to find out, ass. Were you anywhere near Quelch's study? "

" No fear."

" Then you couldn't have seen anybody——."

" Of course I couldn't! But Bessie might have," explained Bunter, his voice a little muffled through a barrage of sausage-roll. " Not that I believe anybody but Hazel went there, you know. Still, if anybody did, Bessie might have seen him."

" How on earth could Bessie have seen him? "

" I mean, when she went to the study, you know——."

" WHAT? "

Five fellows spoke, or rather, shouted, that word, all at once, staring blankly at William George Bunter. Bunter, startled, jumped. A considerable segment of sausage-roll went down the wrong way, and Bunter choked.

" Oooogh! " gurgled Bunter.

Bob Cherry almost bounded across the study. He grasped the Owl of the Remove by the shoulder, and shook him, in his excitement.

" Did you say Bessie went to the study? " he panted.

" Groooooogh! "

" Answer me, you fat chump."

" Wooooooooogh! "

" You fat villain! If you don't answer——."

" Urrgh! Gurrggh! " Bunter cleared his fat neck at last. " Ooogh! Yes! You see, Bessie went to Quelch's study to ask him to let me off gating—ooogh—leave off shick-shuck-shaking me, you beast—grooogh."

" Oh! " gasped Bob.

And the chums of the Remove looked at one another, with startled eyes, while Billy Bunter, after a few more gurgles and guggles, re-started on the sausage-rolls.

CHAPTER XXXIII

DANGER!

" MARJORIE! "

" Oh, run away and play, Bessie! " said Clara, before Marjorie could speak.

" Cat! " said Bessie.

And she did not run away and play!

Bessie, at that moment, was superfluous—as Bessie often was. Marjorie and Clara, after tea, were in consultation in a corner of the quad. Dolly Jobling was in No. 7 Study, and so the consultation had to be elsewhere, as Dolly was not in the secret.

Clara, though with much suppressed feeling on the subject, was playing up, like a loyal pal, since she had learned how matters stood. Her own sincere wish was that Hazel might be discovered in his hiding-place, and marched back to his school, to take that for which he had asked. But with great self-control she contrived not to tell Marjorie so.

Her help was a great relief to Marjorie. Food and other necessities had to be conveyed, somehow, to the hidden refugee in the apple-loft. Marjorie had to help him—and Clara, as a pal, had to help Marjorie. So she suppressed her own feelings and helped. Now the two girls were consulting on the subject—when Bessie Bunter happened. Never had the plump Bessie been so superfluous. Clara, whose temper was not quite so equable as Marjorie's, looked at her as if she could have smacked her.

Which was a trifle light as air to Bessie Bunter. What the two girls might be discussing Bessie did not know, and did not care.

" What is it, Bessie? " asked Marjorie, patiently.

" Want somebody to keep cave again? " sniffed Clara.
" Are you going to the Head's study to hide her inkpot? "

" Don't you keep on talking, Clara. You're always
talking. I say, Marjorie, I want you to come and
help——"

" But what——? " asked Marjorie.

" My brooch——! " began Bessie. She got no further.
She was interrupted by almost a howl from Clara Trevlyn.

Marjorie and Clara had quite forgotten about that lost
brooch. Bessie, it seemed, hadn't! Bessie believed that
missing brooch to be an article of considerable value, if
nobody else did. Like Rachel of old, she mourned for
that which was lost, and could not be comforted.

But everyone else was quite fed up with that brooch.
Even Marjorie looked impatient, while Clara uttered a
sound that could only be described as a howl, not unworthy
of a Red Indian.

" That brooch again! "

" I haven't found it yet——," explained Bessie.

" Bother the brooch! Bother you! Oh, suffering
cats and crocodiles! Go away," hooted Clara. " I've
told you I'll give you the next one I get out of a cracker!
It will be much more valuable. Now go away."

Bessie Bunter passed that by like the idle wind which
she regarded not. Her eyes and spectacles fixed on
Marjorie.

" Come and help, Marjorie, will you? If we don't
find it, it will be hidden by all that straw——."

" What straw? " asked Marjorie.

" Potts is taking straw into the shed. He's spilling it
all over the shop. Lot of good looking for the brooch
with straw all over the shop. You know Potts," sniffed
Bessie. " He will spill as much about the shed, as he
takes up into the loft."

Marjorie's heart stood still.

Clara caught her breath.

Both of them stood looking blankly at Bessie Bunter. She had interested them now—there was no doubt about that! It was a moment or two before Marjorie found her voice.

" Is Potts taking straw up into the apple-loft? " she asked, faintly.

" He's bringing it into the shed, ready," explained Bessie. " I told him my brooch was lost somewhere in the shed, and he took no notice. He's stacking it by the ladder ready to take up.   He doesn't care if my brooch is buried under it—brute! "

" Oh! " breathed Marjorie.   " Are—are you sure he is going to take it up into the loft, Bessie? "

" Well, he said so," answered Bessie.   " He's going to get the loft ready for the apples, he said—I believe they stack apples in straw, or something.   But he's careless— he's spilling it everywhere——.'

" I'll come," said Marjorie, abruptly.

Her face was quite pale.   To her—and to Hazel—the apple-loft had seemed quite a secure hide-out, as it was as yet nowhere near the time for packing apples.   Evidently it was not so safe as it had seemed!

" Come on, then," said Bessie, happily: and she trotted away, followed by Marjorie and Clara.   It was, Bessie thought, the last chance of recovering that precious brooch, now that Potts was spilling straw " all over the shop." Marjorie and Clara were not thinking of the lost brooch!

Clara pressed her friend's arm, as they followed Bessie.

" Brace up, old girl! " she whispered.   " You're look-ing as white as a ghost."

" If—if—if Potts goes up into the loft——! " breathed Marjorie.   " Clara!   If—if—if he finds him there—Oh! "

Clara, in her heart of hearts, regarded that as the best thing that could happen.   She was angrily resentful of the trouble that had been brought on her pal by a wayward scapegrace. But she forgot that now, in her sympathy for Marjorie's fear and distress.

" He mayn't find him," she whispered. " Hazel will keep doggo if he can, and—and it's pretty dim up in that loft. Very likely Potts will just chuck the straw in, without even looking round. Brace up! "

" Oh, here you are! " Dolly Jobling came up at a run. " I've been looking for you. Aren't you coming up to the study? "

" Not now, Dolly," stammered Marjorie. " We—we——we're going——."

" We're going after that brooch of Bessie's." Clara came to the rescue. " We're never going to hear the end of that brooch."

" Stuff and nonsense," said Dolly.

" Quite! " agreed Clara.

" I say, you girls." Bessie Bunter blinked round through her spectacles. " I say, come on. Potts will be smothering the whole place——."

" I'll come, if you're going," said Dolly. " But it's all nonsense. I don't suppose the silly thing was lost in that shed at all."

" Do come on! " squeaked Bessie.

" We're coming, Bessie."

Bessie Bunter trotted on again, with the three girls in her wake. They arrived at the gardener's shed. Potts, the gardener, was carrying in a bundle of straw, as they arrived.

They looked in after him. Six or seven bundles of straw were stacked at the foot of the ladder leading up to the loft. Potts added his bundle to the stack. Then he fanned himself with his hat, after his exertions, and stared across the shed at the schoolgirls in the doorway. His rather crusty face relaxed a little as he saw Marjorie in the group.

" Do you mind if we come into the shed, Mr. Potts? " asked Marjorie, politely.

"Bessie thinks she lost a brooch here," explained Clara.

"I don't think—I know!" interjected Bessie, "and I'm going to look for it before you smother everything with straw, Potts."

"A man can do what he likes in 'is own shed, I spose!" said Potts.

"Of course," said Marjorie. "But if you wouldn't mind——."

"You come in if you like, miss," said Potts.

"Thank you," said Marjorie.

"I shouldn't wonder if it's right under that heap of straw," squeaked Bessie. "I know it's here somewhere."

"Well, I'm jest going to move that there straw," grunted Potts. "I ain't put it there to stay there."

"Aren't you going to fetch some more?" asked Marjorie, her heart beating hard. She had a vague hope that, if Potts went for another bundle, Hazel might contrive somehow to dodge away while he was gone. But Potts shook his head.

"That there's the last bundle, miss. I'm taking them up into the loft, to get ready for the apples."

"Just pitching them into the loft?" asked Clara.

"Well, I ain't spreading out the straw, till the apples is ready, miss," answered Potts. "Jest keeping it dry in the loft, ready like."

Marjorie had a gleam of hope. Hazel, above, could hear what was said in the shed below, and there was no doubt that he would pack into what cover he could. Potts might only stand on the ladder and pitch the bundles in. There was still a chance for the wretched fugitive.

Potts mounted the ladder, and pushed up the trap, lodging it wide open. Then he descended, picked up the top bundle, and re-ascended. Marjorie watched him with bated breath. As she had hoped, he stood on the ladder, and threw the bundle into the loft. She breathed again.

" I say, you're not looking for my brooch," squeaked Bessie. " I say, you didn't come here just to stare at Potts, did you? "

" Wait till the straw's taken up," said Clara. Marjorie didn't speak—she did not even hear Bessie.

" Well, you might as well be looking," grumbled Bessie. She sat on a box, and gave Marjorie and Co. a reproachful blink. " Not much good standing about and doing nothing. Lazy! "

" Oh, dry up," snapped Clara.

" Cat! " said Bessie.

Potts came down the ladder again, slowly. All Potts' movements were leisurely. He saw no reason for haste; and certainly had no idea of the intense interest his proceedings had for two of the onlookers. Slowly and methodically, Potts carried up bundle after bundle, and pitched them one after another into the loft. Marjorie felt that her heart would cease to beat, when Potts pitched the last bundle in, and stood on the ladder mopping his brow with a red handkerchief. If he would close the trap and come down——.

But Mr. Potts, having finished mopping his perspiring brow, did not close the trap. He did not intend to leave the bundles of straw lying just where they had dropped when he pitched them in. Potts was a slow, but a methodical worker. Those bundles had to be packed in the right place in an orderly manner. And Potts, restoring the red handkerchief to his trousers' pocket, heaved himself up from the ladder, and disappeared into the apple-loft.

CHAPTER XXXIV

CAUGHT!

HAZEL, suppressing his breathing, crouched low behind the packing-cases in the loft. The perspiration stood out in clots on his forehead.

Every word uttered below had reached him, and he knew that the Cliff House gardener was coming up; and when the trap was lifted, and Potts' head and shoulders rose above the level of the floor, the wretched fugitive could hardly doubt that his game was up. But, like Marjorie below, he still hoped that the man might be content with pitching in the bundles of straw—till the creak of the plank floor, under the gardener's boots, warned him that Potts had stepped up into the loft.

Like a mouse with the cat at hand, he remained perfectly still, in the dusky corner where he crouched hidden.

There was a chance yet—if a faint one—that Potts might not discover him, in the dim twilight of the loft. The danger of discovery, of being taken back to Greyfriars to face his headmaster, perhaps to face an officer of the law, made his head swim.

In sheer terror, he crouched and listened.

Potts was moving about in the loft. If he did not look behind the packing-cases—was there still a chance? There were three long wooden packing-cases, piled one above another—an ample screen, if——.''

The wretched boy could scarcely suppress a cry, as he felt them stir. Potts had grasped the top one: why, Hazel did not for a moment comprehend. The man had not seen him yet, and did not dream that anyone was in the loft. Then it flashed into his mind that Potts intended to pack the straw into the packing-cases—probably that was what they were there for.

Hazel did not stir. But his heart was beating to suffocation. Potts lifted off the top packing-case, and dumped it down. Then, as he turned to lift the second, he could hardly fail to see the crouching figure behind. In a desperate hope that the dimness of the loft might save him, Hazel remained perfectly still. He could see Potts now—would Potts see him?

For a moment or two, it seemed that the unsuspecting gardener might notice nothing. He had half-lifted the second case—and then, suddenly, he let it drop again, and stared over it. He had seen the crouching schoolboy.

His eyes grew wide with astonishment, as he peered at the crouching figure in the dimness.

" Cor! " ejaculated Potts, blankly. " Who's that? Wot you doing here, you young raskil? Who are you, and what you doing 'ere? "

He stood staring at Hazel, over the packing-cases. A face white as chalk stared back at him.

Astonishment gave place to wrath, in Mr. Potts' gnarled countenance. He did not recognise Hazel, or guess for the moment that he was the runaway schoolboy for whom a search was going on all over the vicinity. There had sometimes been pilfering from the kitchen gardens, of Mr. Potts' vegetables; and his impression was that he had caught one of the pilferers.

" Come out of that, you young raskil! " exclaimed Mr. Potts. " Caught you, 'ave I? Wot you been pinching, you young rip? Arter my spuds and cabbages, in broad daylight! My eye! Come out of that, I tell you."

There was a startled squeak from below.

" I say, you girls, there's somebody in the loft! I say, perhaps it's that tramp again, and he's got my brooch."

" Potts has found somebody in the loft," said Dolly Jobling, in wonder.

Marjorie did not speak. She leaned on the wall of the shed, feeling helpless and weak. Clara pressed her arm.

" Brace up, old thing," she whispered. " It can't be helped, now. You've done all you could—it can't be helped."

But there was little comfort in that for Marjorie.

Over their heads, the voice of Potts was rising in angry excitement.

" You coming out of that, you young rapscallion? You're going straight to Mr. Tozer, you are—I'm 'anding you over to the police, I am—I know who's had my spuds, I do! Come out of it."

And, as Hazel did not move, Potts reached out a horny hand, and grasped him, and hooked him out bodily into the middle of the loft.

Hazel did not resist. There was no resistance in him. He sagged in Mr. Potts' grasp, as if he would have fallen if not held.

Mr. Potts scanned him with an angry and resentful eye. Scanning him close at hand, Mr. Potts realised that he was not a village urchin who was there for a daylight raid on " spuds." Recognition came into his face. He had seen Hazel more than once, when the Greyfriars junior had come over to Cliff House, and he could see that he was a schoolboy. Slowly Mr. Potts comprehended.

" Blow my buttons! " said Mr. Potts. " You, is it? You wot they've been looking for all week, what run away from school? Whoy, I been asked myself if I seen anything of you, and you 'iding in my loft all the time, blow my buttons. You're young 'Azeldene, that's who you are."

Hazel tried to speak.

" Let me go." His voice came husky. " I've done no harm here——let me go——I—I'll go away at once ——only let me go——."

" Not 'arf! " said Mr. Potts, shaking his head, and tightening his grip on Hazel's arm. " You got to go back to your school, you 'ave. Running away from school and 'iding in my loft—whoy, they might think that I had a 'and in it! You been 'ere all the time? "

" Yes, yes! Let me go——."

" I'll let you go when I've 'anded you over to Miss Primrose," said Mr. Potts. " She'll look arter you till you can be fetched. My eye! 'Iding in my loft, and giving a man a start a-seeing of you sudden! You come along."

Hazel tottered towards the trap, with Mr. Potts' grip like iron on his arm. The gardener lifted him to the ladder, and, still holding him fast, stepped on the ladder after him. They descended into the shed, where four pairs of eyes and a pair of spectacles fastened on them.

" Ooooooh! " squeaked Bessie Bunter. " It's the tramp! "

Dolly gave almost a shriek.

" It's your brother, Marjorie! "

" Oh, crikey! " ejaculated Bessie, her eyes almost popping through her spectacles. " So it is! Marjorie's brother! Oh, scissors! "

Hazel's eyes turned on Marjorie. Perhaps even at that moment, he hoped that his sister might be able to help him somehow.

Marjorie stepped in the way, as Mr. Potts was leading his captive towards the door.

" Mr. Potts! " she said, faintly. " It's my brother—do please let him go: he came here only for shelter——."

" Sorry, miss," said Mr. Potts, with a shake of the head, and a sharp look at the girl's pale troubled face. " Praps you knowed he was 'ere—I ain't saying nothing about that, and you better not neither—but I got to take him to the 'Ead, and I'll thank you to step out of the way, miss."

And Mr. Potts, gripping Hazel's arm harder than ever, marched him out of the shed, and marched him away. Bessie Bunter, her eyes gleaming with excitement behind her spectacles, followed on, almost bursting with the startling news that was to cause a sensation in Cliff House School. Dolly Jobling, almost equally excited, followed

Bessie.   Marjorie sank down on a bench, covering her face
with her hands.

"Don't blub, old girl!" muttered Clara, miserably.
"It can't be helped now.   And—and he ought to go back,
you know.   It's best."

Marjorie did not answer.   The tears were running
through her fingers.   There was no hope now: the fugitive
was caught, and had to go back and face what was coming
to him; and what was that?   She sat crying silently, and
Clara stood by her, silent and dismal, unable to say anything that could comfort her in her distress.

Meanwhile, Mr. Potts was marching his prisoner to the
House.   Bessie Bunter rolled ahead, almost shrieking the
news.   There were many girls in the quad, and a myriad
of astonished eyes were turned on Hazel.   With crimson
downcast face, he walked beside Mr. Potts to the doorway
of the House, while Cliff House girls gathered from far
and near, to look at him in wonder, and to buzz with
excitement.

"He was hiding in the apple-loft!" Bessie Bunter
shrieked over and over again.   "Potts found him hiding
in the apple-loft!   It's Marjorie's brother, who ran away
from school—and Potts found him hiding in the apple-
loft."

"Marjorie's brother!" exclaimed Mabs.

"Poor old Marjorie!" murmured Barbara.

"Hiding in the apple-loft, and Potts——" spluttered
Bessie.

Miss Bullivant bore down on Potts and his prisoner.
The Bull's face was astonished, and very grim.   She knew
Marjorie's brother by sight, and did not need Bessie's
excited shriek to tell her who he was.

"Where did you find him, Potts?" asked the Bull.

"Up in my loft, miss," said Potts.   "'Ow long he's
been there I dunno, nor 'ow long he might 'ave stayed, if
I hadn't been taking up the straw for the apples——."

"I will take him to Miss Primrose," said the games-mistress. "He will be detained here until he can be sent for from Greyfriars." Potts released Hazel's right arm, as a much more powerful grip closed on Hazel's left. "Boy! Come with me."

Hazel gave her a bitter look, but did not speak. He went into the House with Miss Bullivant, and disappeared from the sight of the excited crowd in the quadrangle. Girls of all forms were left breathlessly discussing the startling discovery of the runaway schoolboy of Greyfriars within the walls of Cliff House—and Bessie Bunter, for once, was in request, to relate particulars of the discovery: even Stella Stone of the Sixth condescending from her lofty altitude to listen!

CHAPTER XXXV

LIGHT AT LAST!

" THAT's Bob," said Clara Trevlyn.

Marjorie did not look up.

" Is it? " she said, almost indifferently.

It was a bright sunny afternoon, with fleecy clouds sailing in a blue sky, and the sea rolling and shining in the distance beyond the cliffs. But to Marjorie Hazeldene the sunshine seemed to have been blotted out.

The two girls had remained in the gardener's shed till Potts came back. Then they went out: but they did not go back to the House. Only too well Marjorie knew the excitement that would be caused in Cliff House by the discovery of the fugitive from Greyfriars. The whole school would be in a buzz—Hazel's name, and her name, on every lip: and she felt that she could not face the sea of curious eyes. The echo of excited voices reached her from the quadrangle, as she left the shed with Clara. They did not go towards the quad, but left the kitchen gardens by the back gate, and walked into Pegg Lane.

It was yet more than an hour to lock-up, and they were free till the bell rang for Piper to shut the gates. Then she would have to face the crowd at the school: but it was at least a respite.

Marjorie's face was pale and clouded, and she did not speak. Clara walked silent by her side, in the leafy lane. She could do nothing and say nothing to help, but she would not leave her chum. Marjorie hardly noticed whether she was there or not. Her thoughts were with her brother—detained at Cliff House until someone, a master or a prefect, could be sent over, to take him back to his own school. What was to happen then?

Innocent or guilty, he had been judged guilty by his own fault. If he had stayed to face it, if he had even gone back of his own accord, there might have been some hope. What hope was there now? He would be expelled—sent home in disgrace—even if nothing worse happened, as he dreaded. Perhaps he had been right to remain in hiding and postpone the evil hour, in the hope that the truth might be discovered. Bob had said that he would help all he could—and she did not doubt that he had done his best—but nothing had come of it. It was all over now, at all events: there was no more flight, no more hiding, for Hazel—he had to face his sentence, whatever it might be. She could picture him, sullen, scared, resentful, sitting in Miss Primrose's study, waiting—and her heart ached for him. And there was nothing she could do.

Clara broke her silence at last, as she looked along the road, and caught sight of a cyclist far in the distance. Distant as he was, she recognised the ruddy cheeks and the mop of flaxen hair. It was Bob Cherry, coming from the direction of Greyfriars, as fast as his sinewy legs could drive the pedals. Whether he was coming to Cliff House, or riding for the cliffs, Clara did not know; but if he came on, he would pass the two girls in the road, and in those dismal moments, she was rather glad to see a friendly cheery face.

But Marjorie did not even glance towards him. She had hoped something from Bob, but the days had passed, and she had had no word from him, and the faint hope had died. And much as she liked Bob, she was in no mood for his company, or anyone else's, now. If the Greyfriars junior had passed them on his bike, merely with a wave of the hand, she would have been rather pleased than otherwise.

But Bob Cherry did not pass them.

He came up with a terrific rush as he saw them, and jammed on his brakes so suddenly that the bicycle rocked.

His face, always ruddy, was almost crimson—he had ridden hard and fast from Greyfriars.

" Marjorie! " he exclaimed, as his bike whirled against a tree by the roadside, and he dragged the cap from his unruly head. " I'm glad I've met you—I was coming over to Cliff House to speak to you——." Then, as he scanned Marjorie's face, his own fell. " What's up? Anything happened? "

" Yes," said Marjorie, in a low voice. " They—they——." She faltered.

" They've found him," said Clara, finishing the sentence for her.

" Oh! " exclaimed Bob. " Hazel? "

" Yes."

" We've heard nothing at Greyfriars," said Bob. " He hasn't come back——."

" It wasn't half an hour ago."

" Where is he now, then? " asked Bob.

" Waiting at Cliff House, to be taken back to Greyfriars," faltered Marjorie. " I—I suppose Miss Primrose will telephone to your headmaster, and—and——." She broke off.

" You see, he was found at Cliff House," explained Clara. " He's been camping in a loft over the gardener's shed for a week nearly. He was found this afternoon, and they're keeping him till called for."

" Oh! " said Bob. " I understand. Everybody wondered where he could be, and how he was able to stick it out, wherever he was—I understand."

" Marjorie had to help him," said Clara. " He's such a good brother, never worrying or bothering anybody—— such a dear boy in every way.——Oh, sorry, Marjorie—— I—I didn't mean——." Clara stammered.

" It's all over now, anyway," said Marjorie, quietly. "Nothing can be found out now till it's too late." She smiled faintly. " I know you did anything you could,

Bob—but there was nothing you could do, I know that now—it was good and kind of you, all the same.''

'' But there is something,'' exclaimed Bob. '' That's why I was rushing over to Cliff House to see you, Marjorie. I can tell you I've made the fur fly since I pushed out my jigger.''

Marjorie looked at him, startled.

'' You don't mean——! '' she exclaimed, breathlessly. In her eagerness, she caught his arm. '' Bob, you don't mean—you haven't found out who did it——.''

'' No! No! Not that! But we've found out something and it may help——.''

The eagerness died out of Marjorie's face. For a moment, she had hoped that the impossible had happened.

'' What have you found out? '' asked Clara. '' Marjorie's convinced that Hazel never did it——.''

'' I know he did not, Clara.''

'' Well, then, somebody ought to be able to find out something. Carry on, Bob.''

'' Perhaps it isn't much,'' said Bob. '' But it's something. You see, we've been trying all this time to find out whether some other fellow went to Quelch's study that afternoon, and I can tell you we've rooted it out pretty thoroughly, but—but all we found out is that no Greyfriars man went there while Quelch was out excepting Hazel——.''

'' That will do Hazel a lot of good! '' said Clara.

'' But that's not all,'' pursued Bob, eagerly. '' It did look like clamping it tighter on Hazel, but—only this afternoon—that fat idiot Bunter let out something he never thought of mentioning before, like the howling idiot he is—you know what a chump he is——.''

'' Oh, quite! '' said Clara. '' We've got one like him at Cliff House. But what on earth did Billy Bunter let out? It wasn't Bunter, was it? ''

'' No! No! But you may have known that his sister

Bessie came over to Greyfriars that afternoon, to go to a circus with Bunter——.''

" Yes: she got out of detention to do it," said Clara.

" Well, they couldn't go, as Bunter was gated. But that fat frump said this afternoon that Bessie went to Quelch to beg him off if she could——.''

Marjorie started.

" Bessie! She went to Mr. Quelch's study? ''

" Yes, and that was after Quelch had gone out and left his registered letter on the table, and before Hazel was sent to the study," said Bob. " From what I can make out, Bunter told her to go to Quelch's study, as he supposed that Quelch was there—but the old bean had taken his Form papers out into the quad, to nurse them under a shady tree. So, you see, when Bessie went to the study, Quelch wasn't there——.''

" Oh! '' breathed Marjorie.

Clara pursed her lips and whistled, a boyish way she had.

" So, you see, we've got on to something," went on Bob. " It seemed to be as clear as daylight that nobody but Hazel was on the spot—and now it comes out that Bessie Bunter was."

" But—but——you don't think it was Bessie——that's impossible! '' exclaimed Marjorie. " You wouldn't think——.''

" No! No! No! How could I think a girl did such a thing! '' gasped Bob. " I don't mean that—that never entered my head at all. But, you see, Bessie was on the spot, and we've been trying all out to find somebody who was about the place at that time, and who may have seen somebody nosing about—don't you see? It couldn't have been Bessie, of course, but she may know something, as she was there——.''

" It's a hope," said Clara.

" She was there before Hazel went to the study? '' said Marjorie.

" Yes, a little while before."

" Hazel has told me that he never saw any registered
letter on Mr. Quelch's table, and that he feels sure he
would have noticed it if it had been there.   He thought
that Mr. Quelch might have put it somewhere else, and
forgotten.   Oh, Bob, it was gone before Hazel was sent to
the study at all," panted Marjorie.

" If that's right, Bessie very likely knows something,"
said Bob.   " She may have seen the very man hanging
about——."

" Oh! " exclaimed Marjorie, suddenly.

She gave a sudden, violent start. A thought had flashed
into her mind, that made her almost giddy for the moment.

" Bessie! " she gasped.

Bob looked at her.

" You don't think——? " he began.

" Yes—no—yes——."   Marjorie pressed her hand to
her forehead. It was as if a sudden light had dazzled her.
Back into her mind came the recollection of Bessie Bunter's
egregious trick in Miss Bellew's study.   " Bessie—that
silly, silly girl—it's possible—Oh, can it be possible that
the registered letter was never taken at all, but—but——."

" Well, it was gone," said Bob.   " Quelch isn't the
man to make mistakes of that kind, Marjorie.   It was gone
all right."

" Yes, yes, yes, but—tell me."   She caught Bob's arm
again.   " Tell me—Bessie asked Mr. Quelch to let her
brother off to go to the circus, and he refused—is that it? "

" Yes, from what Billy says."

" Then the silly little donkey may have been annoyed
with him, just as she was with Miss Bellew, and may have
done a silly thing just as she did here——."

" Eh!   What——? "

" Oh, if it should be that! " panted Marjorie.   " Clara,
Clara, you know what Bessie did this very afternoon in
Miss Bellew's study——suppose—suppose——."

" Oh, my summer sunshade! " ejaculated Clara. She gave quite a jump. " Would even Bessie be idiot enough —but then, isn't she idiot enough for anything? "

" I must see her—ask her—I must go back at once—— good-bye, Bob." Marjorie stayed for no more: she almost flew up the lane towards Cliff House School, leaving Bob Cherry standing like a statue of astonishment.

" What—what—what——? " stuttered Bob.

Clara chuckled.

" Congratulations, Mr. Sherlock Holmes of Greyfriars," she said.

Bob blinked at her.

" What do you mean? "

" I mean that ten to one what you've just told Marjorie has solved the jolly old mystery. Just that! " said Clara. " Can't stop to talk now—but if you remain spotted around the landscape, one of us will cut out and tell you the news —if any."

" But what——? " stuttered Bob.

But there was no answer from Clara—she was running like a deer after Marjorie. Bob Cherry stood in the road, staring after them till they disappeared, lost in astonishment and wonder. He could only decide to remain spotted around the landscape, as Clara suggested, in the hope that someone would " cut out " and tell him the news—if any!

CHAPTER XXXVI

BESSIE ALL OVER!

" BESSIE! "

" Oooogh! " spluttered Bessie.

Barbara and Mabel stared.

The door of No. 4 Study burst open as suddenly as if a cannon-ball had struck it. A breathless girl hurtled into the room.

On the table in No. 4 was a jug of lemonade. Bessie Bunter had filled a tumbler with that refreshing fluid, and lifted it to a capacious mouth, just as the door flew open and Marjorie Hazeldene hurtled in.

Babs and Mabs stared in astonishment. It was so utterly unusual for Marjorie to be seen in a state of breathless excitement, that they could only stare. Bessie was much more disconcerted than Babs or Mabs. She jumped, and the stream of refreshing lemonade went down the wrong way. Bessie spluttered and choked and gurgled.

" Bessie——! " panted Marjorie.

" Urrrggh! " gurgled Bessie. " Wurrggh! Oooo-er! Woooogh! "

" What on earth——? " began Barbara.

" I must speak to Bessie! Bessie, listen to me——."

" Oooooooch! "

" Is the little idiot here? " Clara Trevlyn appeared in the doorway. " Oh, here she is! What are you putting in those musical effects for, Bessie? "

" Woooogh! I'm chook—chock—chack—choking! Grooogh! Wharrer you make me jump for like that, Marjorie? Ooooogh! Rushing into a study like a wild Indian—wooooogh! Look at my tunic—all splashed! Ooooogh! "

BESSIE SPLUTTERED AND CHOKED AND GURGLED

" But what's the trouble, Marjorie? " asked Mabs.
" What has our prize idiot been doing now? "

" C-c-cat! Oooogh! I haven't been doing nothing—
I mean I've done anything—I mean—urrrrggh! "

Marjorie was fairly trembling with impatience. But
Bessie had to be given time to recover her breath.

" Bessie knows something about what happened at
Greyfriars last week," Clara explained. " At least, it
looks as if she does."

" About Hazel——? " began Barbara—and stopped
suddenly.

" Yes—about Marjorie's brother. Know where he is
now? "

" Waiting in Miss Primrose's study," answered Mabs.
" We're all awfully sorry about it, Marjorie——."

" I think it may be cleared up," said Marjorie, trying
to calm herself. " I—I think Bessie knows something
that may clear it up. Bessie dear, I'm not angry with you
——I know you can't help doing silly things——but you
must tell me——."

" I should think not," hooted Bessie. " Angry with
me—after rushing in, making me spill lemonade all over
the shop, and choking and suffocating me. Is there any
more in the jug, Babs? "

" Never mind that now, Bessie——" urged Marjorie.

" I do mind," said Bessie. She clutched the jug and
blinked into it. " Lucky there's some left! If you girls
don't want any more, I'll finish it, shall I? "

Babs and Mabs were not given time to state whether
they wanted any more, before Bessie finished it.

" Now, Bessie," said Marjorie. " I want you to tell
me what happened when you were over at Greyfriars last
Wednesday afternoon."

" Eh! Nothing special," answered Bessie, in surprise.
" That was the afternoon your brother pinched something
from his form-master's study, wasn't it? Has he told you
what it was he pinched? "

Marjorie winced.

" You must tell me what you did there, Bessie——."

" Eh! I don't mind," answered Bessie. " I went over to go to the circus with my brother Billy, as I told you. I saw your brother loafing about looking sulky and ill-tempered as usual——."

" Never mind that! Tell me——."

" I asked him where Billy was, and then Bob Cherry took me to the room they call the Rag, and Billy was there. He told me he was gated. We never went to the circus after all. I smacked his head."

" Wha-a-t? "

" Well, what would you have done? " demanded Bessie, warmly. " We couldn't go to the circus, as he was gated, and old Quelch wouldn't let him off when I asked him, the awful old hunks, and then Billy told me he'd swopped the circus tickets for a packet of toffee, and eaten all the toffee. Suppose your brother——."

" You went to Mr. Quelch's study to ask him to let your brother off? " asked Marjorie, her voice trembling with eagerness.

" Yes—Billy told me to. But he wasn't there, and I had to go and look for him, and that nice Australian boy told me where he was, and I went to him where he was sitting under a tree, looking like a gaygoyle——."

" Like a what? " ejaculated Clara.

" Like a gaygoyle——."

" Oh! A gargoyle——."

" I said a gaygoyle, and I mean a gaygoyle," answered Bessie. " One of those ugly thingumbobs they stick up on a what-do-you-call-it——."

" Never mind what Mr. Quelch looked like," interrupted Marjorie. " He refused to let Billy off? "

" Yes, like an old grumpy bear——."

" And I suppose that put your silly back up? " said Clara.

" Well, I wanted to go to the circus with Billy, didn't I? " demanded Bessie. " I asked him very nicely and prettily, and what more did he want? He has awful manners—speaking to a pretty girl just as he would to some inky kid in his own school——."

" When you were in Mr. Quelch's study, did you see a registered letter lying on his table? " asked Marjorie, breathlessly.

Bessie Bunter jumped.

She had, by that time, utterly and completely forgotten the trick she had played in the Remove master's study at Greyfriars, in retaliation for his refusal to let Billy off, to go to the circus. She was quite startled when she was reminded of it.

" Eh! How do you know there was a registered letter on his table? " she exclaimed. " You weren't there."

" Then you did see it! " panted Marjorie.

" Well, I may have seen it, and I may not," said Bessie, cautiously. " If there's been any fuss about it, I don't know anything about it at all. I'm not going to have that grumpy old bear complaining to Miss Primrose, and getting me into a row. I've had enough of Miss Primrose, I can tell you—why, she jawed me for at least half-an-hour over Bellew making out that I hid her fountain-pen, and I've got detentions for two half-holidays, and——."

" Never mind Miss Primrose now——."

" She makes us mind her," said Bessie. " You have to mind the Head! When she jawed me about Bellew's fountain-pen, she looked just like a gaygoyle, like old Quelch——."

" Did you touch the registered letter? "

" Why should I? " answered Bessie. " That was before I saw old Quelch, as he was out in the quad. I wasn't stuffy with him then—of course I thought even a grumpy old schoolmaster would let a boy off to go to the circus when his pretty sister asked him——." Bessie frowned. " But he refused—actually refused—snapping just as if he had been speaking to some sulky boy like your brother——.''

" Did you go back to the study? "

" Perhaps I did, and perhaps I didn't! " answered Bessie, with renewed caution. " That's telling! "

" You must tell me, Bessie——.''

" I shall please myself about that," said Bessie, independently. " If that grumpy old Quelch hasn't found his registered letter yet, and there's a fuss about it, I'm not going to be dragged into it, I can tell you. I've had enough jaw from Miss Primrose. The fact is, I believe she doesn't like me——.''

" You did go back to Mr. Quelch's study? "

" That's telling! The fact is, I'd rather not tell you," said Bessie. " Look how you gave me away to Miss Bellew this afternoon——.''

" You must tell me! That registered letter is missing! " panted Marjorie.

" He, he, he! " chuckled Bessie Bunter.

" Bessie thinks that funny! " said Clara. " Bessie all over! "

" Well, isn't it funny? " giggled Bessie. " Fancy that grumpy old bear hunting all over his study for his registered letter—he, he, he! But he must have found it by this time, if he's looked for it."

Marjorie and Clara exchanged a glance. They knew, now. What had only been a possibility was now a certainty.

Babs and Mabs listened in wonder.

" Mean to say he hasn't found it yet? " went on Bessie, blinking at Marjorie. " He can't have looked for it, then. Men haven't much sense—especially schoolmasters. Has there been a fuss about it? "

" You hid it, the same as you did Miss Bellew's fountain-pen——.''

" Not if there's a fuss about it," said Bessie, promptly.

" I tell you I'm not going to be reported to Miss Primrose again and jawed——.''

" Where did you hide it? "

" I'd rather not tell you anything about it, Marjorie. Least said, soonest mended,'' said Bessie, sagely, and she rose from her chair. " I'm going down now—I don't want to miss it when they take your brother away——.''

Clara shut the study door, and put her back to it—a proceeding that made Elizabeth Bunter blink at her in wrathful astonishment.

" Look here——! '' squeaked Bessie.

" You're not going yet, Fatima,'' said Clara. " Where did you hide Mr. Quelch's registered letter last Wednesday? ''

" Find out! '' retorted Bessie.

" What's all this about a registered letter? '' asked Barbara. " Has it anything to do with your brother, Marjorie? ''

" Oh, don't you see? '' panted Marjorie. " It was a registered letter that was missed, and that my brother was believed to have taken. Nothing else—only a registered letter that was missing——.''

" Oh! '' gasped Barbara and Mabel together.

Bessie Bunter jumped.

" Oh, crikey! '' she ejaculated.

" Now, Bessie——,'' said Marjorie.

" Cough it up! '' said Clara, encouragingly.

Bessie blinked at them, through her spectacles, like a startled owl.

" But—but——that—that registered letter wasn't pinched at all,'' she gasped. " It's in the grumpy old bear's study all the time. He would have found it if he'd searched the study for it. Why didn't he look for it? ''

" You indescribable idiot,'' said Clara. " How could Quelch guess that a dangerous lunatic had been in his study playing potty tricks? Of course he thought it had been taken away, when it wasn't there.''

" Well, he might have looked in the bookcase first,''
said Bessie. '' Schoolmasters haven't much gumption, I
know, but he might have looked in the bookcase before
he fancied that his silly registered letter had been
pinched——.''

" In the bookcase! '' repeated Marjorie.   Her face
glowed. '' Then you did hide the letter, and you hid it
in Mr. Quelch's bookcase? ''

'' I—I—I say, you're not going to tell him? '' exclaimed
Bessie, in alarm.   '' I—I say, I should get into a row with
Miss Primrose——.''

'' That's awfully important,'' remarked Clara, sarcastically.   '' Never mind if your brother is bunked from his
school, Marjorie, so long as Bessie doesn't get into a row
with Miss Primrose.''

'' Yes, you see that, Marjorie, don't you? '' gasped
Bessie, blind and deaf to sarcasm.   '' You can't get me
into a row with Primrose, after the way she jawed me
to-day about Bellew's fountain-pen——.''

'' Bessie, dear, come with me and tell Miss Primrose
yourself,'' said Marjorie.   '' It must come out now——.''

Yell, from Bessie.

'' I ain't going to get into a row with Miss Primrose!   I
tell you she glared at me like a gaygoyle, and jawed
me——.''

'' Don't you see that it must—it must—come out now?
My brother——.''

'' I don't like your brother!   He said I ought to go into
a circus!   Your brother isn't nice at all, like Bob Cherry
—Bob wouldn't say that a girl ought to go into a circus,
because she's got a figure, and isn't skinny like you——.''

'' But you must——'' urged Marjorie.

'' Well, I won't——.''

'' Dear Bessie, it can't be helped now.   You must——.''

'' Shan't! '' roared Bessie.

Marjorie said no more. Perhaps, in the fullness of time,
it might have dawned upon Bessie Bunter's solid brain

that there was no help for it now. But Marjorie could not wait for the fullness of time! She turned to the door, and Clara opened it.

" I say," howled Bessie, as Marjorie disappeared into the corridor. " I say, don't you go and tell Primrose—I say, I never hid old Quelch's registered letter, and it ain't in his bookcase at all—I never put it behind the books in the bottom shelf, and it ain't there now! I never went to his study that day—I never went to Greyfriars at all— I was somewhere else all the time while I was at Greyfriars, and I don't know anything about it—Cat! "

Marjorie was gone.

CHAPTER XXXVII

ALL CLEAR!

" HALLO, hallo, hallo! "

Bob Cherry jumped off the stile in Pegg Lane. He had been sitting there, waiting, his eyes on Cliff House in the distance. From the direction of Cliff House School, a bicycle came whizzing. Bob had expected to see Marjorie again, but he had hardly expected to see her on her bicycle, riding as if in a race.

She came up almost in a flash but did not stop. She released one hand and gave him a wave in passing, that was all. Then the bicycle was past, whizzing on up the lane, leaving Bob staring.

He stared for only a moment, however. Then he jumped on his own machine, and pedalled after Marjorie.

Marjorie was going all out, and covering the ground swiftly, but it did not take Bob more than a minute to draw alongside.

" I say, hold on, what's up? " he gasped.

Marjorie did not hold on for a moment. But she gave him a quick bright glance and a smile. He could see that her face was full of eager hope. It was as if years of trouble had fallen away.

" Got something from Bessie? " exclaimed Bob.

" Yes! I think it's all right now—thanks to you, Bob! I've got to get to your school as fast as I can, and see Mr. Quelch."

" What I told you—was it any use——? "

" Its done everything, I think. Thanks, and thanks again, for all you've done, Bob."

" Oh, good," said Bob. " I don't quite make it out, but good—jolly good. I say, if you're in a hurry, let's take the footpath through Friardale Wood—it will save a lot of time. I'll get your bike over the stile.''

Not a moment was lost on the way, but during that swift rush on the bicycles Marjorie, in a few breathless sentences, explained what had been learned from Bessie Bunter. Bob Cherry heard it with amazement, but great satisfaction. As they came out of the woodland footpath into Friardale Lane, and headed for Greyfriars School, two stalwart figures came in sight from the direction of Greyfriars—two prefects of the Sixth Form, who turned into the footpath. Both Bob and Marjorie could guess easily enough where they were going—to Cliff House for Hazel.

But that mattered little now.

'' O.K.,'' said Bob. '' They've gone for your brother, Marjorie—but we'll have good news for Hazel when they bring him back, what? ''

'' Yes, yes, I am sure of that, now,'' breathed Marjorie. '' But oh, Bob, if you hadn't helped——.'' Her voice faltered.

'' Jolly glad I barged in,'' said Bob. '' But who'd have thought——! Hallo, hallo, hallo, here we are, and here they are waiting for me.''

Harry Wharton and Frank Nugent, Johnny Bull and Hurree Jamset Ram Singh, were standing in the gateway, as the two riders came up with a rush, and jumped off their machines. They were looking for Bob, but why he had brought Marjorie back with him was a mystery to them.

'' What——? '' began Harry Wharton.

'' My esteemed Bob——! '' said Hurree Jamset Ram Singh.

'' No time to chin now,'' said Bob, hurriedly. '' Look after the jiggers, will you—I've got to take Marjorie to Quelch at once.''

'' But what——? '' exclaimed Nugent.

'' It's good news,'' said Marjorie, breathlessly. '' What

Bob did has set everything right—at least I hope so—I think so.''

And leaving four astonished juniors with the bicycles, Marjorie hurried in with Bob Cherry.

They crossed the quad to the House, a good many glances falling on Marjorie as they went. She did not heed them—in fact was unconscious of them. Billy Bunter rolled up as Bob and Marjorie came into the House.

'' I say, they've got him,'' said Bunter, full of news. '' I say, Wingate and Gwynne have gone to fetch him back —I heard Wingate say to Gwynne—wow! ow! Wharrer you shoving me for, you beast? ''

Bunter tottered out of the way, and Bob led Marjorie on, leaving the Owl of the Remove blinking.

'' Oh! Here's Quelch! '' whispered Bob.

Mr. Quelch was standing in his open study doorway. He was in conversation with Mr. Prout and Mr. Capper, in the corridor.

All three masters glanced round, at the sight of a breathless schoolboy and a breathless schoolgirl hurrying up the passage.

Mr. Quelch frowned. He was acquainted with Hazeldene's sister at Cliff House, and he had a high opinion of that young lady, but he was very far from pleased to see her now.

The news that the runaway schoolboy had been caught. and that it only remained to fetch him back to Greyfriars and deal with him, had been a relief to Mr. Quelch. A troublesome and extremely disagreeable affair was coming to an end at last—a most distasteful affair, with which Mr. Quelch would be very glad to have done. He was quite anxious to see Hazel—but not at all anxious to see Hazel's sister. No plea for the wretched delinquent could avail—and he could only suppose that that was Marjorie's object.

His frown, fixed on Bob Cherry, was quite thunderous.

Mr. Prout and Mr. Capper exchanged a glance, and faded away up the passage.

" If you please, sir——! " panted Bob.

" Cherry! What does this mean? You should not have brought Miss Hazeldene here—above all in the present circumstances. What——."

" Please let me speak to you, sir," said Marjorie, breathlessly. " I have something to tell you——."

" I am sorry," said Mr. Quelch, sincerely enough. He had a kind heart under his crusty exterior. " I am sorry —very sorry indeed—but——."

" My brother, sir——."

" That is a matter I cannot possibly discuss with you. Cherry, I shall speak to you very severely about this——."

" But, sir——! " stammered Bob.

" You need say no more. I shall——."

" But I must speak to you, sir," panted Marjorie. " My brother——."

" I repeat that I cannot discuss that matter with you, Miss Hazeldene. I am sorry—very sorry indeed—but please go away at once."

Mr. Quelch stepped back into his study, and put his hand on the door. He supposed that that was the end. But that was quite an error. Marjorie, taking her courage in both hands, so to speak, stepped into the doorway after him.

" Mr. Quelch." Her voice was firm. " You must hear me. I know and can tell you what happened here last Wednesday. I can tell you where to find the registered letter that is missing."

" Oh! " said Mr. Quelch. " In that case, I must hear you. Please step in, Miss Hazeldene. Is that why you brought this young lady here, Cherry? "

" Yes, sir! " gasped Bob.

" In that case I shall excuse you! You may go away."

Mr. Quelch shut the study door, almost on Bob's nose. Then he turned his gimlet-eyes on Marjorie's flushed face, his crusty countenance relaxing into as kindly an expression as his severe features permitted.

" Please proceed, Miss Hazeldene," he said.

" I have come here to tell you, sir. It was all a mistake—I know that my brother was very much to blame, but he did not do what you supposed——."

Mr. Quelch raised his hand.

" Please do not touch upon that," he said. " If you have anything definite to tell me——."

" The registered letter was not taken away at all, sir! "

" Really, Miss Hazeldene——! " Quelch breathed hard through his thin long nose. " I can understand your distress, and sympathise with it, but if you have come here to make such wild statements——."

" It is still in this study, sir."

" WHAT! "

Mr. Quelch almost jumped.

" It was not taken away at all, sir—it was a silly trick —a prank—it was hidden in this study! " stammered Marjorie.

" Impossible! "

" I assure you, sir——."

" Absurd! " exclaimed Mr. Quelch. " If your brother had played so foolish, so obtuse, so fantastic a trick, he would certainly have told me so, when he was charged with purloining the letter——."

" It was not my brother, sir," panted Marjorie. " It was someone else who came to the study while you were absent——."

" Nonsense."

" But I can tell you where to find the letter, sir! " exclaimed Marjorie. " It is still in this room, and I can tell you where."

" Upon my word! " said Mr. Quelch. He was impressed at last. " If that is possible—if you can do as you say——."

" I can do so at once, sir. But——" faltered Marjorie. " I have found out who it was, and I must tell you to save my brother, but—but——."

" But what? " rapped Mr. Quelch.

" Oh, sir, I know it is a great deal to ask, but—but will you pardon the silly girl who played that silly trick and caused so much trouble? "

" A girl? " repeated Mr. Quelch, quite blankly. " Are you dreaming? There are no girls in this school—you are surely aware that Greyfriars is not a co-educational establishment——."

" A Cliff House girl, sir. I will tell you her name. But will you be so kind, so good, as to forgive her, or else she will be punished by Miss Primrose, and it will be because of me? " said Marjorie, almost with tears in her eyes.

Mr. Quelch gazed at her. His look was grim, but it slowly relaxed. There was a silence.

" I understand," said Mr. Quelch, at last, in a very kindly voice. " If what you tell me is correct, Miss Hazeldene, you are in a very distressing position, and I shall certainly do all I can to make it less so. Indeed, if it prove that no theft has been committed, and that the whole affair is nothing worse than a foolish prank, it will be an immense relief to my mind. Any lesser consideration is a matter of little moment. You may speak quite frankly, Miss Hazeldene, and I shall certainly lay no complaint at Cliff House on the subject."

Marjorie's face brightened.

" Oh, thank you, Mr. Quelch," she exclaimed. " Now I can tell you—it was Bessie——."

" Bessie! " repeated Mr. Quelch, at a loss. Apparently he had forgotten the existence of the plump Elizabeth.

" Bessie Bunter, sir——."

" Oh! " Mr. Quelch recalled an episode of the previous week, and frowned. " I remember—the sister, I think, of a boy named Bunter in my form——."

" Yes, sir. She came to your study, and you were not here, and—and——she is a very silly girl, sir, and even now does not understand how serious it was——but I found it out from her——and came over as fast as I could to tell you——."

" You say that the registered letter is still in this study? "

" Yes, sir—Bessie hid it in the bookcase——."

" Upon my word! "

" Behind the books on the bottom shelf, sir."

Mr. Quelch gazed at the bookcase. On the bottom shelf was a row of somewhat ponderous volumes, containing the historical works of Josephus. The historical works of Josephus were rated at a proper value by Mr. Quelch, but he seldom perused them! Probably not one of those massive volumes had been perused that term—and quite probably wouldn't the next term, and perhaps not the term after! Really, no securer hiding-place could have been found than in the narrow space behind the valuable works of Josephus.

Having gazed at the bookcase, Mr. Quelch gazed at Marjorie; he gazed at the bookcase again. Then he got into motion, crossed to the bookcase, and groped behind the works of Josephus. His hand came out a little dusty, but with a registered envelope grasped in it.

Marjorie caught her breath. She had been sure—quite sure—there was no doubt: but the relief of seeing the actual registered letter, which her brother was accused of purloining, actually in Mr. Quelch's hands, made her almost giddy.

Mr. Quelch, in deep silence, laid the registered envelope on the table, and slit it with a paper-knife. There it was, addressed and sealed, just as he had seen it last, but Quelch was a methodical man, and he was going to examine the contents. Examination of the contents only made assurance doubly sure—there was his letter within, and folded in the letter, the three pound notes. Mr. Quelch drew a deep, deep breath of relief.

He gave Marjorie a very kindly look.

"Thank you for coming here, Miss Hazeldene," he said. "I am more glad than I can say."

"And—and my brother, sir——!" faltered Marjorie.

Mr. Quelch frowned for a moment.

"Your brother brought suspicion upon himself by his own actions, Miss Hazeldene, and I can feel but little sympathy for him. But he is, of course, quite cleared now, and I have little doubt that his headmaster will pardon his folly in running away from school, in view of what I shall now explain to him. You need have no uneasiness about your brother."

"Oh, thank you, sir," murmured Marjorie.

Mr. Quelch, with quite a genial smile, shook hands with her, and she left the study, feeling as if she were walking upon air.

CHAPTER XXXVIII

AT LAST!

" I say, you girls! "

Bessie Bunter was beaming.

What Bessie had to beam about, nobody knew; and, as it happened, nobody particularly wanted to know! There were five girls in No. 7 Study, all looking merry and bright, and not one of them was interested. Indeed, Clara Trevlyn waved a hand at the fat figure in the doorway, and said succinctly:

" Blow away, Bessie."

And the talk in No. 7 ran on, just as if Bessie wasn't there, blinking into the study through her spectacles.

" Gratters, Marjorie," Barbara was saying. " So it was all right when your brother got back to his school? "

" We saw the two Greyfriars prefects come in," said Mabs. " Your brother didn't look very happy when he went with them. But——."

" But it was all right," said Marjorie. " Right as rain! He came in just as I was leaving, and—and I was so glad to be able to tell him that the trouble had blown over. It was not his fault——."

" Wasn't it? " asked Clara.

" Well, of course he was to blame a little——."

" Only a little? "

" Dry up, Clara," said Dolly Jobling. " We're all jolly glad how it's turned out, and you as much as anyone."

" Oh, quite! " agreed Clara. " In fact the gladfulness is terrific, as that nice Indian boy says. But——."

" The conjunction ' but ' may here be deleted! " said Babs, in a delightful parody of Miss Bellew's instructive manner, which made the whole study laugh.

" I say you girls! " squeaked Bessie, in the doorway. But again the voice of Elizabeth Bunter was like unto a voice crying in the wilderness. Five girls seemed quite deaf to it.

" And it was really Bob Cherry who worked the oracle," said Mabs. " If he hadn't helped Marjorie——."

" Thank goodness he did! " said Marjorie, with a deep breath.

" Sherlock Holmes of the Remove! " said Clara, with a chuckle. " Dick Barton hasn't a thing on him! "

" And it was all that little idiot Bessie——! " said Babs.

" Cat! " came a squeak from the doorway.

" That little ditherer Bessie," said Clara.

" Minx! " came another squeak.

" And you had the nerve to go to Greyfriars, and beard the lion in his den, the Douglas in his hall! " said Babs.

Marjorie smiled.

" Mr. Quelch is a very kind man, really," she said. " He was very kind indeed, when I had to tell him about Bessie hiding the letter in his bookcase——."

Yell, from the doorway.

" You've told old Quelch! "

Clara looked round.

" Didn't I say blow away, Bessie? " she inquired.

" Cat! Look here, Marjorie, if you've told old Quelch that it was me, it wasn't!" spluttered Bessie. " I'm not going up to Primrose for another row? I've had enough of her glaring at me like a gaygoyle——."

" There isn't going to be a row, Bessie. Mr. Quelch said that he would say nothing about it here——."

" Oh! " said Bessie. " That's all right, then! If there isn't going to be a row, I did hide the silly thing in his dusty old bookcase, and serve him right, too, after speaking to a pretty girl just as if he was speaking to a boy in his form. But I say, you girls," went on Bessie, dismissing the matter as an unimportant trifle. " I say, I came here to tell you I found it——."

" You found it! " ejaculated Marjorie.

" Yes, I found it——."

" Mr. Quelch found it——."

" Eh! Old Quelch hasn't been here——."

" He found it in his bookcase——."

" It wasn't in his bookcase. How could it have been? I found it in my study, in the jam-jar in the cupboard——."

" What? "

Five girls stared at Bessie Bunter. It seemed to them that Fatima of Cliff House was wandering in her mind— such as it was.

" You see, I had the last of the jam," explained Bessie. " It must have fallen off while I was scraping out the jar—the pin was rather loose—and I never noticed it——."

" What are you talking about? " shrieked Clara.

" Eh! My brooch, of course."

" Your brooch? " gasped Marjorie.

" What did you think I was talking about? I came here to tell you that I found it, only a few minutes ago— I thought there might be just a spot of jam left in that jar, and looked into it, and there was my brooch——."

" Ha, ha, ha! "

" It never fell off in Potts' shed after all. It fell off into that jam-jar—and I found it——."

" Ha, ha, ha! "

" Well, I don't see anything to cackle about, in a girl's valuable brooch falling off into a jam-jar," said Bessie. " It's all sticky, and I shall have to wash it——."

" Ha, ha, ha! "

Bessie Bunter, having imparted the great news, rolled away, doubtless to wash the stickiness off that valuable brooch—leaving the girls in No. 7 Study still laughing.

THE END.